Harper Monogram

D0348610

Nothing Else Matters

⊶ SUSAN SIZEMORE ⊷

HarperPaperbacks
A Division of HarperCollins*Publishers*

HarperPaperbacks   *A Division of* HarperCollins*Publishers*
                    10 East 53rd Street, New York, N.Y. 10022

Copyright © 1995 by Susan Sizemore
All rights reserved. No part of this book may be used or
reproduced in any manner whatsoever without written
permission of the publisher, except in the case of brief
quotations embodied in critical articles and reviews. For
information address HarperCollins*Publishers,*
10 East 53rd Street, New York, N.Y. 10022.

Cover photograph by Herman Estevez

First printing: July 1995

Printed in the United States of America

HarperPaperbacks, HarperMonogram, and colophon are
trademarks of HarperCollins*Publishers*

❖ 10 9 8 7 6 5 4 3 2 1

"I'M SORRY YOU WERE MADE TO MARRY A STRANGER," ELEANOR SAID QUIETLY.

Tentatively, she reached up to run her fingers along Stian's face. "Earlier today, I thought you were an angel. Then, when you were with the wolf, I thought you surely must be a demon."

"In time, I will be," he replied. "I doubt even the priest's best prayers will save me."

"You are a barbarian."

"I'm a man," Stian said and kissed her to prove it. Eagerness kindled in her as his mouth took possession of hers. Eleanor heard herself moan, and strained against him as his lips moved to her throat. His touch, the heat of his mouth, the tang of his skin, the sweet memory of his words, combined into a longing for him that would not be denied. She suddenly wanted all she could get of Stian. She hungered for everything that could join them.

Books by Susan Sizemore

Wings of the Storm
My First Duchess
My Own True Love
In My Dreams
Nothing Else Matters

Available from HarperPaperbacks

This book is for Winifred Frances Halsey
and Julie Watkins, baronesses both.

Nothing Else Matters

1

In the Year of Our Lord 1175

    "The Queen's at Salisbury, and so's my wife."
Roger of Harelby was not surprised at Hugo FitzWalter's words, but he wasn't sure how he should respond to them. So he nodded sympathetically and took another sip of Hugo's fine French wine.

"She's been a good wife," Hugo went on without any urging from Roger. "It was a love match," Hugo continued. "But she also brought me fine lands as dowry. It worked out well for us. Her Queen Eleanor married Count Henry and then Henry became our King."

"Henry and Eleanor have been fine rulers," Roger said, not wanting to give any opinion on his friend's marriage or the current tense situation between the King and Queen of England.

Hugo gestured around the high-ceilinged expanse of his great hall. "A good marriage I've had. But Jeanne was born in Poitou and her first loyalty has always gone to Eleanor." Hugo downed another cup of wine and mumbled into the empty vessel, "The meddlesome shrew!" Hugo banged a fist down loudly on the table before them. Cups and trenchers clattered in the aftermath of his frustrated gesture. "I hope the King keeps the Queen locked up in Salisbury for the rest of her life!"

"But that's the rub, isn't it?" Roger questioned. "While Queen Eleanor remains King Henry's prisoner your lady wife won't leave her side."

"Precisely. Exactly." Hugo looked around as if seeking something he could take his frustration out on. There were no servants on the dais at present, so he contented himself with throwing a cup against the wall. As crockery shattered, Hugo went on speaking to his guest. "It's a damn nuisance when royalty's quarrels interfere with our lives."

Royal family quarrels got other people killed, as Roger well knew, never mind a bit of connubial inconvenience. He nodded at his friend's complaint. "This particular quarrel has made the Scots think Henry's rule in England is weakening."

"You fought them off up north," Hugo said, giving Roger a jovial pat on the shoulder.

Roger nodded. There was no need to point out that the Scots were never going to be fought off for long. "The Scots are a nuisance," he said agreeably, then chuckled. He held out his cup for a refill. While a servant came forward with the wine jug and Hugo gave him a puzzled look, he explained, "I'm about half Scots myself, so that makes me a bloody nuisance about half the time. So, what will you do about your wife?" Roger asked, getting back to Hugo's problem.

Hugo rubbed distractedly at his graying beard. "Wait for her," he admitted. "Can't really fault the woman for her loyalty to Eleanor. The Queen's been good to Jeanne. Like a mother. She helped her find wives and places for our younger sons. Stood godmother to our youngest girl. My Eleanor is named after her godmother. Jeanne wants me to send our girls to her, but I've said no. Though I don't know what to do with them now that I have them back from that wicked court of Eleanor's."

Hugo gestured toward the sunlit corner beneath the high windows. It was the spot where Roger's glance had been constantly straying anyway. A pair of young women sat in the corner. The rich colors of their clothing shone like jewels in the light. Their fingers were busy with embroidery, and their eyes were modestly downcast. The pair looked the perfect picture of demure young womanhood. Roger found more than their industriousness to admire as he gazed at them. Hugo's daughters, Edythe and Eleanor, were quite an attractive pair of young women. Edythe reminded Roger of an autumn willow, slender, gold, fair, and pliable. She was about the most beautiful woman he had ever beheld. Eleanor, with whom he'd shared a trencher and cup during last night's meal, had proved to have a quick mind, a gleam in her dark eyes, and a lovely smile once he'd coaxed her into conversation. His acquaintance was brief, having arrived only the night before, but he thought he liked both girls very much.

"What am I going to do about the girls?" Hugo asked, cutting into Roger's wandering thoughts.

"Hmmm?"

"They should have been wed or in convents long since," Hugo pointed out. "But Jeanne let them linger at that devilish court in Poitiers looking for husbands who could spout poetry on command instead of proper knights. That place spoiled the girls for real men. And they've some notion that they can't be separated." Hugo spat. "They're like two peas in a pod, those two."

More like beads, Roger thought as he looked over the pair, *one of gold and one a black pearl.* "I don't think it's possible to find one husband for two daughters," he told his friend.

"Be a waste of their dowries," Hugo said, totally unaware that Roger was joking. "Jeanne wants them, but sending them to Salisbury would be like condemning them to prison. Besides, I don't want the King to suspect I'm taking his wife's side in their quarrel."

"I can see your problem," Roger acknowledged sympathetically. "I spoke with your Eleanor last night," Roger said. "A most intelligent girl."

"I know. More's the pity. I've thought of beating it out of her, but she's too old to change her ways now. And I've no taste for beating women," he confessed. "But if her words bother you, tell me and I'll have the seneschal give her a thrashing she won't forget."

"No, no." Roger waved his friend's offer away. "I found no offense in the girl." *None at all,* he thought to himself. "She'll make her husband's life interesting, I'll wager."

Hugo banged on the table again. He glared at his daughters, as if their court upbringing were their fault. "It's finding the husband that's the problem.

I'm determined to see them wed—to men loyal to King Henry. I need strong alliances to counteract my wife's behavior. Marrying the girls to Henry's men would do me good. But what proper Englishman would want such delicate flowers, I'd like to know?"

Roger brightened considerably at the question. Here was a subject he didn't mind turning his attention to. He ran his hand over the bald spot spreading through his once thick brown hair. He smiled toward the oblivious sisters while Hugo spluttered on at his side. "As to your daughters finding husbands," he said. "I might have a few ideas."

"I have a son, you know," Lord Roger told Eleanor as they sat down to dinner.

Their father had retired early to sleep off an excess of wine, so she and Edythe were heading the high table, with Father's guest seated in a place of honor between them.

"A son?" Edythe said from Lord Roger's right.

The handsome older man turned toward her sister. Eleanor decided that her duties for the evening were already over, as Edythe was ever so much better at dinner conversation than she was. Edythe was as beautiful as a sunset, vividly, heartbreakingly lovely. Eleanor knew that she was not. She sometimes joked that there were times when Edythe's perfection made sisterly devotion very difficult. Fortunately, Edythe was also sweet natured, gentle, and a joy to be with. Edythe was easy to love, and knew Eleanor's tartness meant nothing. There were only eighteen months between their births. They had never been parted and never wanted to be.

Eleanor could not claim to be sweet natured. She knew she was temperish and sharp-tongued enough for a mother abbess and tried hard to control these unmaidenly qualities. Edythe cozened her and gentled her tempers, while she protected and spoiled Edythe to the best of her abilities.

Edythe was content with being beautiful. Eleanor couldn't keep her busy mind still no matter how hard she tried. In Poitiers her sharpness had been considered witty. In Poitiers her love of books was shared by many another court lady. Wit and learning were not appreciated by her father. Or the members of his English mesne. Here, all she and Edythe had were each other.

"A fine son," Lord Roger went on while Eleanor crumbled the edges of her flat-bread trencher in homesick misery. "About your age, Lady Edythe, or a little older. Near twenty, I think. Recently knighted."

"A gentle and God-fearing knight, I trust?" Edythe asked. Eleanor smiled at Edythe's easy compliment of the unknown knight.

Lord Roger laughed. The sound was so boisterous and merry, Eleanor couldn't help but be drawn out of her brooding over the lost, warm days in sunny Poitiers. Eleanor liked her father's friend. She knew the two men were of an age, but Father seemed ever so much older than the northern lord. She knew most of Roger of Harelby's lands were on the wild Marches of Scotland, but the man was no more savagely barbaric than any other Englishman. He was actually more kindly disposed toward her and Edythe than any of the knights in her father's rowdy household.

"Stian's a good lad," Lord Roger assured Edythe. "And gentle in his way." He spared a glance for

Eleanor. She noted the humor in his eyes as their gazes met. "He found a wolf pup last year and tried to raise it like a dog. Once it was grown he set it free."

"He must be brave, to deal with a wolf," Edythe said.

"Very," Lord Roger answered, still looking at Eleanor.

It seemed he wanted some comment from her on his son. She didn't understand why anyone would bother to raise a wolf in the first place.

"Why did he release it?" she asked.

"Because he loved it," Roger answered.

"How could anyone love a wolf?" Eleanor asked, completely confused by the man's statement.

"It's the sort of man he is."

"I see," Edythe spoke up. "Gentle and loving."

Eleanor didn't think gentle men would take much interest in dangerous wild animals, but she didn't want to insult Lord Roger's son by pointing this out.

"Sir Stian sounds . . . interesting," she told his father.

His smile widened, showing strong white teeth. "Very interesting. You'd like him." He turned to Edythe. "Both of you would like him. He can sing. I'm told singing was all the fashion in the Queen's court."

"It was," Eleanor agreed. She tried not to sigh for what was past.

Music did not ring out in their father's halls. He had even forbidden them from practicing their lutes outside the ladies' chamber.

"Not only sings, but reads."

"Your son?" Edythe asked, reminding Eleanor of the conversation. "Sir Stian reads?"

What was there to read, Eleanor wondered, in a

land that had no troubadours? "Ovid?" she asked with little hope.

Lord Roger shrugged his broad shoulders. "Whatever it is, it is in Latin. We have the one book. My late wife brought it with her from Denmark."

"Your—late wife?" Edythe questioned. Her blue eyes shone with sudden sympathy—and sudden interest in their distinguished-looking guest, Eleanor noticed, not without amusement. She and her sister shared a quizzical look.

Lord Roger lowered his gaze for a moment. "For nine long years, I'm afraid." He smiled up through long lashes at them. "And northern nights can be cold, dear ladies."

Eleanor doubted anyone with such a rascally glint to his eye ever went to bed without a warming companion, but she was charmed by his statement just the same.

She had to admit her interest in Lord Roger was stirred by the knowledge he was not presently wed. It was merely nostalgia, she thought. Queen Eleanor's lively court had been the center of the continental marriage market. Every parent who could manage it had sent their lads and maidens to Poitiers to add the gloss of chivalry and sophistication to their prospects. Talk of marriage and romance had been on every tongue; assessing looks had always been in everyone's eyes. Even now that she was in England, Eleanor couldn't help but react to the knowledge that she was in the presence of an unmarried man. Her urge was to find the man a wife.

"No wife," Edythe said before Eleanor could. "We must see to finding an heiress for you."

"It's the least we can do for a guest," Eleanor agreed.

Lord Roger laughed. He had a deep, hearty laugh. "And a wife for Stian while you're at it," he said. "It's high time the lad was wed. Have I told you about Harelby?" he went on. "Such a lovely place in the spring. I can hardly wait to get home."

The rest of the meal was spent listening to descriptions of the Cheviot Hills, of the fishing in streams he called burns, and of the sight of flowers blooming along a ruined wall said to have been built by the Romans. Lord Roger also recounted tales of his and his son's encounters with their wily Scottish neighbors. The man was a fine storyteller, almost as gifted as a troubadour. By the end of dinner Eleanor was entranced. When he asked her to play the lute for him, she was enthralled.

"What do you think of Lord Roger?"

Edythe's question caused Eleanor a moment's pause as she brushed her sister's thick blonde hair. They were in the chamber their father grudgingly gave over to the gentlewomen of his household. They had retired early while most of their roommates remained among the menfolk in the hall.

"I think he's . . . interesting," Eleanor answered, glad they were not completely surrounded by the other women. Her hand stilled.

"So do I." Edythe looked at her reflection in their silver hand mirror. "I had no idea England would have interesting men."

"He's interesting for an Englishman," Eleanor clarified. She had no intention of letting her loyalties get confused. "He can't be compared favorably with the men of Aquitaine or Poitou."

"Or even France," Edythe hastened to agree. "But tell me, little sister, what do you know about him?"

"He's better spoken than I thought an Englishman would be."

"High praise, from you." Eleanor could see merriment in the blue eyes she saw reflected in the polished silver of the mirror. "Have you found someone you might want to aspire to your affections at last?" Edythe questioned teasingly.

Eleanor laughed. It disturbed her that the sound lacked conviction. She doubted Lord Roger of Harelby had taken notice of her as a woman. "He is merely pleasant to talk to."

"Yes," Edythe agreed. "Very. He seemed to enjoy our playing as well. Pity Father came into the hall and made us stop."

Eleanor sighed. "Yes." She began to braid Edythe's waist-long hair.

"I wonder why Lord Roger wanted to talk with Father? As drunk as Father is, Lord Roger can't hope to get any sense out of him."

"Perhaps he was just tired of female conversation," Eleanor suggested.

"Perhaps. I've noticed very few English knights enjoy conversation with ladies. Why is Lord Roger here?"

Edythe never paid attention to anything going on outside the ladies' bower. When she wanted news she relied on Eleanor's curiosity to ferret out anything she might want to know. Eleanor couldn't help but smile at Edythe's certainty that she would know about Lord Roger. Edythe was certain because, of course, she was right.

Eleanor took a seat on the bench while Edythe got up and began to brush her hair for her. Eleanor carefully put the mirror face down on the seat beside her. She closed her eyes and luxuriated in the feel of the brush sliding through her hair.

"Well?" Edythe asked.

"Ah," Eleanor said contentedly. She yawned. "All I know is that he's a Marcher lord on the Scottish border."

"So he said. Where is that?"

"I'm not quite sure," Eleanor admitted. "Far north of here, I gather."

"It must be very unpleasant despite his tales of flowers. Northern places are cold. He said the nights are, I recall."

Eleanor, used to the sun-warmed castles of Aquitaine and Poitou, shivered. "Colder than Sussex? I doubt it. I wish Father hadn't brought us to England." Eleanor opened her eyes and concentrated on the flame from the hour candle on the table in front of her. She pretended the tiny flame was the southern sun.

"England is cold and damp and disagreeable," Edythe agreed. "But why is Lord Roger visiting Father?"

"He's on *chevauchée* to inspect his southern holdings."

"Is he rich, then?"

"Oh, yes. And something of a hero as well." Edythe's hand paused briefly, then she began to brush Eleanor's hair again as Eleanor explained, "Apparently there was a war with the Scots recently, and their King was captured."

"Lord Roger of Harelby captured a King?" Edythe sounded ready to be impressed.

"He was involved in the capture," Eleanor clarified. "The ransom will go to the King, I'm sure."

"I see. What a fascinating man," Edythe replied.

Eleanor thought Lord Roger fascinating too. Before she could say so, there was a knock on the door. Their waiting woman answered it. A moment later she hastened over to them.

"Lady Edythe," she said, "your father will see you in his chamber. Immediately, his man said."

Eleanor exchanged a puzzled glance with her sister. Edythe said, "I'd better hurry."

Edythe left and Eleanor waited, worried and nervous, while the other household women trickled in from the hall to prepare for bed. What was the matter? Had word come from Mother? Was she unwell? Was the Queen? It must be grave news indeed for Hugo FitzWalter to bother informing his daughters at all. It must be the gravest possible news for him to send for Edythe straight away instead of letting it wait for morning.

She'd worked herself into a state of barely controlled terror by the time Edythe came running back into their chamber.

"What?" Eleanor questioned.

Edythe grabbed her hands. Eleanor marked the wide smile on her sister's face as she was whirled around the room. Rushes flew beneath their feet and the shadows whirled past. They tripped over the pallets of the other gentlewomen, while the women themselves crowded around to hear the news.

"Oh, my dear," Edythe declared happily when she'd spun Eleanor one last time. "We're to be married!"

2

"Jesu, where am I?"

A ripe aroma of pig permeated Stian's nostrils. He woke up with a fierce headache and a fiercer need to urinate. As his senses returned, he became vaguely aware that he must be in Hulda the swineherd's hut.

Hubert came into the hut. Stian looked at his thin, curly-haired friend in dazed annoyance. "Wha—?"

Behind him, Hulda groaned, and Lars snored on in her arms. Stian had a horrible suspicion that there was no ale left in the jug they'd brought with them last night. And Hubert had a look on his face that said he wanted something. If the Scots were attacking, they'd better have strong drink with them, because Stian wasn't going to have anything to do with anyone who couldn't hand him a full winecup.

"Dame Beatrice says for you to come to the hall," Hubert said.

Hall. There'd be wine at the hall. Stian snorted and

looked around for his clothes. Hulda scrambled across her dark, cramped hut and gathered up his braccos and tunic for him while Lars's bare, pale ass shone like a full moon in the middle of the room. Stian vaguely remembered losing his boots in a dice game, though he couldn't recall to whom, or when.

If he asked Hubert, he'd tell him how long he'd been drunk, but he didn't want to know. He wanted the headache to go away or to get drunk again, whichever came first. He began to dress, fingers clumsy, feeling as thick as his tongue. It seemed too complicated a task to pull the tunic on over his head. He threw it on the dirt floor.

"Dame Beatrice says—" Hubert tried again.

"Hall. Going." Hulda handed him his belt. He strapped it on as he followed Hubert out of the swine-herd's hut.

Sunlight hit him in the eyes with screaming force. Hubert gave him a push and he stumbled his way from the village, moving slowly up the rising ground toward the hall. He noted an increase in activity in the inner bailey as he walked through, but only because he'd been trained to notice anything that might affect the security of the castle whether he was drunk, sober, or in-between. Right now he was at that in-between state; sober enough for his head to hurt, still drunk enough to be moody and reckless.

Dame Beatrice was standing on the wooden steps leading up to the castle's entrance. The shortsighted woman squinted at him as he came up to her. She shook her head and tucked her hands in her wide sleeves. She frowned at Hubert.

"You might have mentioned to him that his father is home."

"I was lucky to find him." Hubert ducked his head under her glare. "I'll be in the chapel."

Hubert hurried away as Dame Beatrice shook her head at Stian. "You'll have to do as is. Come along."

Dame Beatrice still treated him like a stripling youth—which sometimes had its advantages. But Stian was in no mood for being treated like a child right now. His footsteps dragged into the hall after the woman. At the entrance, he ducked his head into the water basin set into the wall. He came up feeling more clearheaded and shook himself like a dog. He pulled wet hair out of his face and stepped through the screen doorway into his father's fine, wide hall.

He didn't see his father at first as he looked toward the dais at the rear of the room. It was the golden-haired, willow-slender girl dressed in pale blue who immediately caught his attention. And took his breath away.

Stian stopped in his tracks, bare feet buried in thick rush matting. His mouth hung slightly ajar; his headache and thirst were forgotten. He thought, *I'll have her*, as lust lanced through him. It settled as a driving ache in his groin.

As he took a step toward the dais, a heavy hand landed on his shoulder. He turned at once, right hand automatically closing around his sword hilt. He relaxed instantly as he saw his father's smiling face. Stian gave his father a hurried embrace and a kiss of welcome.

"Who's the—"

"Rejoice, lad," his father cut him off. He gestured toward the girl standing by the high table. "I've brought you home a wife."

Stian needed to hear no more. He sprang onto the dais. Taking the golden vision into his arms, he gave her a lusty kiss. When he'd grown heated from the taste of her, he remembered courtesy enough to hold her out at arm's length and say, "What do I call you, maiden?"

His eyes were fixed on the wide blue ones of the gold vision, but his sharp ears caught the rustle of cloth. An unfamiliar, acerbic voice spoke up beside him. "You call her 'Mother.'"

He looked away from the blonde beauty's flushed face and found himself looking into the disapproving dark eyes of a girl he hadn't noticed before. She was a little thing, brown skinned and black eyed, dressed from veil to hem in pale gray.

"What's this?" he questioned. "A talking mouse?"

His father came up and eased the golden vision away from him. Lord Roger's arm went around the willow woman's shoulder. Possessively. Stian could barely suppress a jealous snarl.

His father gestured toward the dark girl. "This is Eleanor FitzWalter," he told Stian. "Your betrothed." He pulled the beauty closer and gave her a fond smile. Which she returned. Stian gaped at the pair. "This is Eleanor's sister, Edythe, whom *I* have taken to be my wife."

In the next few moments several facts permeated Stian's fogged brain. The gold prize he ached to claim was already the possession of his father. He was betrothed to the mouse-sized leftover sister of the most beautiful woman he'd ever seen. People were laughing at him. The hall rang from floor to rafters with merriment at his mistake. The laughter was worse than the loss. His ever-quick temper flared at the sound.

Stian cast a quick glare at his father and the rare beauty he held. Then he turned the same look on the talking mouse-girl and, smiling like a cat, he lunged.

"I'm not marrying her!"

"You certainly are!"

Stian bellowed, "The bitch bit me!" It was a wonder he could shout at all, for the pain throbbing through his tongue. "And she clawed me!" He pointed to the scratch marks on his bare chest.

"You shouldn't have grabbed her like that," Roger bellowed back. "She's gently reared. You frightened her."

"All I did was kiss her."

"Half ravishing a maiden on the top of a table is more than a kiss."

"I wasn't ravishing her. I lost my balance when she kicked me. We tripped onto the table."

His father struck him on the shoulder. Roger of Harelby had always had a hard hand, though he often added a loving word or two after a beating. Stian had learned never to flinch, and always to stand up for himself.

"You frightened the girl," his father said, as though this Eleanor's emotions mattered to him.

"Mice frighten easily," Stian replied. She'd fought him like a hellcat, in truth. Stian had been surprised by her spirited response.

"Mice don't generally inflict wounds," his father pointed out and laughed. Stian growled at the sound. Roger called for more wine and handed him a cup when it came. "Calm down," he ordered. "Let us talk."

Stian was suspicious of too much talking, but his

father was fond of it. He perched himself on the edge of the table and drank down his wine. "What?" he mumbled when he was done. "I'm not marrying her," he added, just in case his father hadn't heard him the first time.

"It's time you married," Roger declared. "I've chosen Eleanor for you. You'll wed her tonight."

"No."

"You'll do as you're told."

"Why?" Stian began to pace across the dais.

"To give me grandchildren."

Stian gestured at the large crowd of servants gathered in the hall who gaped openly at them instead of going about their business. "I must have sired some of the brats down there."

"You've probably sired half the brats in the shire," his father said. "It's heirs I want out of you. Babes born in wedlock to inherit our lands. A grandson to hold in my arms."

Stian drank more wine and scratched his bare stomach. His chest bore several bloody lines, raked through his reddish chest hair by the mouse's claws. "Nicolaa Brasey," he said after looking at the scratches for a while. "I'll wed the Brasey widow."

"You'll do no such thing. You'll marry Eleanor FitzWalter! And," Roger added, shaking a fist at Stian, "you'll treat her with respect."

"She's a mewling, mousy virgin!"

"She's no mouse."

Stian recalled his aching tongue. "More like a cornered rat," he acknowledged. "Damn!" He threw himself into the room's one high-backed chair. It was his father's place, but he paid no attention to that formality. Neither did Roger.

"I don't mind the thought of marrying," he said. "One bitch is as good as another for breeding on. But this girl . . ." He didn't quite remember what she looked like, though he had an impression of soft breasts crushed against his chest when they fell. He had her round bottom under his hands the instant before that. "Why can't I have the pretty one?" he complained.

His father's eyes narrowed dangerously. "Eleanor is pretty."

"The other one's prettier."

"Edythe is my wife." The cold, firm tone warned Stian away from arguing. And away from Roger's property.

Oh, aye, take the best for yourself and leave me with the scrapings, Stian thought resentfully. Then he felt immediately guilty at his own surly jealousy. It was his father's right to marry whom he chose. It was also his right to order his son to marry.

"Damn," he said, but the word was spoken more in acquiescence than in protest.

"You'll like her," Roger said, as though he needed to temper a simple command with persuasion. Stian had never understood his father's need to talk things out after he'd already made up his mind. Still, he was fond enough of the man to listen when he felt the need to talk. Stian grunted to let Roger know he had his attention.

"The girl has the wit you lack," Roger said. "There's plenty of sense in young Eleanor, though I don't think she knows it herself yet. She'll keep your bed warm and get your brain working. What more could you want?"

Stian didn't answer for a time. He'd never lacked

for a warm bed. As for a working brain, he didn't have much use for one anymore. He didn't see what use a woman would have for one, either. Or why his father wanted a thinking woman in his household. It was all more than he was going to try to puzzle out.

"I don't want anything," he said at last.

"I know," Roger acknowledged. "The more fool you. You'll marry her," he added, voice edged with iron.

Stian growled angrily, the sound of a caged animal, but he nodded. He well knew when to cease arguing with his father.

"I'm not marrying him!"

Eleanor stepped back from the comforting hands as Edythe reached toward her. She shook her head and had to grab at the veil covering her braids to keep it from falling to the floor. The barbarian had left not only her emotions, but her clothing, in complete disarray.

"I won't marry him," she repeated. She glared fiercely at Edythe. "I won't."

To forestall conversation, she turned her back on her sister and the disapproving chatelaine of Harelby, who'd hustled them up the stairs to the bower a few minutes before.

Feeling trapped by the thick stone wall in front of her, she stumbled a few steps to where windows let some light into the small room. The bower windows were small, more like arrowslits than openings intended to let in light for the gentle pursuits of ladies. The glass in them was ill made and hard to see through.

Her lips ached, and her body still felt the imprint of the monster's rough hands. She remembered bloodshot eyes boring into her as he swooped down on her. The fur on his chest had been bright red, and there had been a great deal of it. His heavy mustache and bristly jaw had scraped her cheeks practically raw. At least she thought that was why her face burned so, from bruising as well as from shame.

"He smelled of pig." Eleanor sniffed distastefully, recalling the stench of him. Not just pig, but sour ale and male sweat permeated her clothing.

"He was with Hulda, then," the chatelaine said, as though a question of only mild interest had been answered. "I thought as much."

"Who?" she heard Edythe ask. Eleanor did not want to know.

"Never you mind," the woman answered sharply.

Eleanor remembered that the chatelaine had been introduced as Dame Beatrice, widow of Lord Roger's brother. She was fine looking and proud and not at all happy to have two new women in her household. Eleanor didn't care if Dame Beatrice disapproved of her, or of her refusal to marry Lord Roger's lout of a son.

"I won't," she whispered fiercely. "I won't. I won't." She looked out the window, and, with some effort, saw the deeply forested hills beyond the castle walls. This was no civilized land. She did not belong here. She also was aware of how foolish her words were. The situation was quite hopeless, and she knew it.

She heard the rustle of cloth as someone came up behind her. A hand touched her shoulder. "You will marry Stian." The voice belonged to Dame Beatrice.

Eleanor turned her head to look into the other woman's stern face. "I cannot be forced to wed. The Church does not permit forced marriages."

"What nonsense," the woman answered.

"It's Church law," Eleanor insisted. "I have heard a bishop say so to the Queen herself. I cannot be forced to marry." She doubted Church law meant anything in this place, but her knowledge of it gave her a glimmering of a plan. "I will write to Mother. *And what will you do in the weeks it would take to receive a reply?* a grimly hopeless voice in the back of her mind asked.

"I care not what Queen and bishops say," Dame Beatrice replied. "If Roger of Harelby brought you here to marry his son, then you will marry his son."

Edythe came to her and took her hands in her own. To Eleanor's surprise, it was her sister's hands that were cold. Her expression was full of worry. "You must marry Sir Stian," she said, her voice a desperate whisper. "For if you go away, what will I do without you?"

Eleanor ducked her head rather than look into her sister's sad eyes. She knew she could refuse Edythe nothing when she looked at her like that. She understood her sister's fears, for she certainly shared them. They'd been forced from their happy life in Poitiers to their father's dark castle in Sussex, knowing no one but each other. Then, it seemed like they had traveled endless days to reach this northern land.

The way had been very hard. Her sense of isolation had grown with each mile they traveled beneath the cloudy English sky. Edythe had spent much of the time with her husband. Eleanor had ridden pillion behind one of Lord Roger's men and bedded down in caves and castles and forest firesides alone, but she and Edythe had still been together. Close as they already were, the journey had made them closer.

"Lord Roger is kind to me," Edythe said, "but I have no one but you I can confide in. You must stay."

Eleanor twisted her hands together. "How can I?"

She was calm now. She would not cry, but thinking about her prospective bridegroom sent a shudder through her. She had grown more anxious about meeting her husband with each day of the journey. She had been nervous, but she had had Lord Roger's stories of his son to allay her fears. She did not say it out loud, not to Edythe, who was content with her husband, but she was well aware that Lord Roger of Harelby had lied to her.

"He is no chivalrous knight." She didn't know if she meant the father or the son when she spoke the words.

Behind them, Dame Beatice snorted loudly. "There are hungry men downstairs and I have a meal to see to. Calm yourself, girl," she directed Eleanor, "and come get married. Stian's no worse than any other man," she advised before she left. "Better than most," Eleanor heard her add before closing the bower door behind her.

Better than most? Eleanor didn't know whether to laugh or cry at Dame Beatrice's claim. She did know that she had no choice in the matter. She was at Harelby, and Sir Stian of Harelby was the husband her father and Lord Roger had chosen for her. She could not fight those two formidable men now. Perhaps someone as strong-willed as her mother could fight them, but she could not. She would do what she could when the time came.

She sighed and stepped away from the window. She looked at her old, travel-stained clothing. It was a sturdy but ugly garment, made over twice since her grandmother had first owned it. It had been good enough for traveling in, but she couldn't help but feel lumpy and ugly in the old gray wool. Now it smelled intimately of Stian of Harelby, and Eleanor would very much like to have it burned.

Instead, she said, trying to be brave in the face of tragedy and disaster, "I think we should make ourselves presentable for dinner."

"You married her?"

Roger turned, shocked by the stern disapproval in Beatrice's voice. In all the years he'd known his brother's widow he had never heard her use that tone of voice. Not on him, at least. He was tired from the journey, and the confrontation with Stian had been about all the tension he'd be willing to face before dinner and a good night's rest.

Servants were setting up tables in the hall for dinner. Roger drew his sister-in-law to the central hearth where they could share the fire's warmth while keeping out of the way. A look from him sent several loitering men-at-arms on their way.

"You married her," Beatrice repeated when they were alone by the fire.

A disapproving frown marred her fine features. She was still beautiful, he noticed, despite having nearly as many years as himself. He should have arranged another marriage for her long ago, he knew, but her presence at Harelby had grown familiar and comfortable.

He gave her a conspiratorial smile. "It was a bargain, you see," he told her. "I saw a chance to get two for the price of one, and so, I took it."

She tucked her hands in her sleeves. "Oh, you've the Scots' eye for a bargain, Roger of Harelby. But what's thrift to do with marrying that girl?"

Roger leaned closer to Beatrice. "It's like this," he told her, eager to share his cleverness with someone. "The dowry was higher if I took the set."

Dame Beatrice did something Roger had never known her to do: she tapped her foot. The rushes were soft and deep, but he heard the sound of her impatiently rapping out an annoyed rhythm just the same.

"A bargain," she said. "I see. You risked Stian's anger and—" She bit her tongue on what else she was going to say, and took a deep breath.

While she was composing herself, Roger said, "Stian has nothing to be angry about."

"Really? Perhaps you didn't witness his greeting of your wife."

Roger waved her concern away. "A simple misunderstanding."

"Stian won't see it that way. He'll think you've cheated him."

"We've discussed it already." He didn't want to talk about his marriage with Dame Beatrice. "Let it go, my dear. All is well."

She shook her head, clearly not believing him. "Is a pretty girl in your bed worth the trouble it could bring? You know the boy's temper."

Roger chuckled, and not just at the memory of Edythe filling his nights. "I'm not worried about Stian."

"I can see you're not." She shook her head and looked past him to the activity in the hall. "Well, I have servants to see to." As his sister-in-law walked away he heard her say, "I almost pity the girl you brought to wed that mountain cat you sired."

Roger thought about his son and about his other sister-in-law, Eleanor, who was also about to become his daughter-in-law. Now, there was a complicated relationship for the heralds and priests to wrangle about. "Should I call her sister or daughter?" he wondered and chuckled again, because it wasn't Eleanor he pitied.

3

"*No, no, no,*" *Edythe declared* as she tugged Eleanor's hands down. "No braids for you tonight." While she wielded the silver mirror in one hand, she shook a finger under Eleanor's nose. "No veils or wimples, either. Tonight you must let your hair flow free."

Eleanor had just started to arrange her freshly washed hair in the usual braids when Edythe stopped her. Her sister did not have to add that this was her last chance to show her unbound hair in public. Eleanor well knew that old custom forbade a married woman the loose, flower-bound tresses of a maid. The old customs would no doubt prevail in this backward, back-of-beyond northern land.

"Lord Roger is very firm about some things," Edythe told her, then giggled. Then she became serious. "From the time of the wedding your hair, and the rest of you as well, are objects for your husband's pleasure. This is not Poitiers, my dear. We must strive to please our men, and not they us."

"But—"

"So you will make the most of your beauty tonight. And of your marriage bed," she added with a sly smile.

Eleanor stood rooted to the floor, staring wildly at her sister. Words would not come, but the realization that tonight the red-furred brute would cover her body with his and she would be a maiden no more sent a shudder through her. She remembered that his hands were very large, his lips firm and forceful. He stank to high heaven, but his body had the lean-muscled strength of a warrior.

"Oh, my God," she whispered, and thought for a moment that she might faint.

Eleanor took a hasty step back as Edythe picked up the ivory comb. Edythe pointed to the wooden chest at the end of the bed. Eleanor sat.

"I—" she began as Edythe combed out her hair. She couldn't get out any other words for a while.

Edythe hummed as she worked. Eventually, she said, "Don't act the martyr so. Your Sir Stian will be easy enough to deal with."

Eleanor turned her head sharply, painfully tugging hair out of Edythe's hands as she croaked, "What? Deal with? How?"

Edythe was smiling a very knowing smile. She put down the comb and sat down beside Eleanor on the chest. She put her arm around her shoulder. "Don't you remember anything Lady Constance told us?"

Lady Constance? The very mention of the woman brought a smile to Eleanor's lips. The name conjured sunny days and spicy, warm nights, bright, sophisticated conversation, and wildly amorous tales that educated as they entertained the Queen's court.

"There is no one like Lady Constance," Eleanor

recalled fondly, though she felt her cheeks grow warm at the memory of one of the lady's more ribald tales. "I wonder if she truly did escape from a paynim's harem wearing nothing but jeweled bells and a breadbasket?"

Edythe waved Eleanor's question away. "That matters not right now. What matters are the things she taught us."

Eleanor blinked. "Things?"

"By all the holy saints, your mind's rattled!" Edythe sighed in exasperation. "I thought you were the quick wit of the pair of us."

Eleanor looked at her lap rather than at her sister. Edythe was right; she should be using what few wits God had seen fit to give her. "I feel dull and fearful," she admitted. "It gets in the way of thought."

"Silly child, you've not a thing to fear."

Eleanor understood Edythe's confidence—Edythe was not being foisted off on a very large lout. Eleanor gave herself an angry mental shake at the unkind thought. Despite the terror that made her bitter, she knew her sister would not say something she did not mean.

"And why," Eleanor asked, "do I have nothing to fear?"

"Because of Lady Constance."

It all seemed self-evident to Edythe, so Eleanor made herself think, to remember. After a while she smiled, though she was blushing hotly. She touched her fingertips to her warm cheeks. Edythe was giving her a triumphant smile.

"Oh, yes," Eleanor admitted to her sister, voice cracking somewhat. She cleared her throat. "I see what you mean."

Edythe nodded. She patted Eleanor's shoulder. "All will be well," she promised. "Believe me. I know."

Which explained, Eleanor supposed, why Lord Roger spent so much time alone with his lady wife and smiled so much to himself the rest of the time.

"You, there, fill my winecup. It'll numb my tongue."

Stian had let a servant shave his cheeks and trim his hair. In fact, he'd nearly blistered his skin in a washtub full of hot water before his father was satisfied he was clean enough to share a meal with his soon-to-be wife.

"Wife," he grumbled now as he stood in the hall wearing his best tunic and an ugly expression. "I don't see why we have to wait for the women. I'm hungry," he complained to his cousin and best friend, Lars the Dane, as they stood together by the hearthfire.

It was often remarked that Stian and Lars looked alike. The Dane was shorter than Stian, compact where Stian was rangy, his hair gold where Stian's was red, but they both had blue eyes and fair complexions. They were of an age, and closer than brothers, having shared bread, board, battles, many a cask of wine, and women from stripling youth to manhood. Stian could not imagine life without his lively, troublemaking cousin, though Lars frequently claimed he'd soon be heading home to his father's lands across the sea.

Lars clamped a hand on Stian's arm. He held up the goblet full of Lord Roger's best wine. "This is a rare treat. The later the meal, the more time we have to sup it."

The wine was well watered, but it was strong just the same. Stian was on his second goblet, though Dame Beatrice had frowned when the steward had poured the wine out for him. Well, the devil could take Dame Beatrice's worries for his sobriety.

"I think I'll drink the whole barrel before this night's done," he told his friend glumly, then took a deep drink from the goblet.

Lars spat into the smoking fire, making it hiss and crackle briefly. "Why so dour? She's a woman. Bed her, then go about your business."

"Aye," Stian agreed with Lars's advice. But he didn't smile at the thought of bedding the girl. He didn't know why, for thoughts of rutting generally brought a smile to his face.

"Your groin's not burning at the thought of the bitch, is it?" Lars asked as Stian took another drink. "What's she like, then?"

"She's a gray and ugly little mouse," Stian admitted. "No, a biting rat." His tongue ached, and his chest stung from where she'd marked him. His pride stung even more. He added bitterly, "While my father has a sleek mare to ride, I'm given a rodent for my bed."

Lars shrugged unconcernedly. "Fathers are unfair; that's the way of the world. If a bitch bites, muzzle it."

"Rat," Stian corrected.

He wanted to say that Roger wasn't like most fathers, but today's events were proof that Lars was right. It hurt to know that his father would be so unkind. *She's an ugly little mousy rat*, he thought to himself as he took another drink. What had he done to deserve such a wife?

It didn't help that his humiliation was going to be public. Word had spread quickly that Lord Roger was

home with a new wife and that Stian was to marry.
Harelby's great hall was crowded close to its smoke-
draped rafters with liegemen and neighbors come to
gawk and gossip and judge as they celebrated the family's good fortune. Deep in his soul Stian was a shy
and private person. He hated living his life in public,
though he knew he certainly wasn't fit for a cloister.

Soon his father's beautiful wife would be coming
down the stairs from the upper floor. Her mousy little
sister would trail in her wake and all eyes would turn
to the pair of them. There would be calls of congratulations and envious looks for Lord Roger. And for
him there would be sympathy, and snickers and jests
that would make him want to draw his sword. Oh, he
could see it clearly before it even happened. He'd be
mocked, but his father would scowl and shake his
head and tell him to hold his temper. There'd be more
laughter at his expense then.

And it would all be the mouse's fault.

He hated her. And he couldn't even remember her
name.

There was a stirring and murmuring in the crowd
around him. Lars turned from the fire, and so did the
squires who'd come to stand beside them. Stian came
out of his angry reverie as his father stepped to the
foot of the stairs. Roger, dressed in a finely embroidered surcote, had a bright smile on his face. Stian
would have preferred not to look, but his gaze was
drawn to the women as they appeared around the
turn of the steps.

He didn't recognize the girl who walked ahead of
his father's wife. Her shining, unbound hair was black
as night. It framed her face and fell straight and thick
to below her narrow waist. She was small, delicately

made, dressed in black embroidered in thick bands of
silver needlework. A hint of a garnet red underdress
showed above the deeply cut neck of the black dress.
It wasn't the red underdress Stian noticed so much as
the outline of the girl's rounded bosom and the neat
line of collarbone the color showed off. Her chin was
small and pointed, her eyes large and dark. Her
mouth—

He'd kissed that mouth, hadn't he? And not even
noticed how full and rich and ripe it was. What had
happened to his mouse?

He stood rooted in place, unable to turn his gaze
from her, feeling more the fool now than he had a
moment ago.

People were turning his way, offering hearty congratulations, pushing him toward his bride. All he
could manage as he walked stiffly forward was to
bare his teeth in the semblance of a smile. All he
could think was that his father had played an elabo-
rate joke on him and that the girl, the attractive,
graceful, poised foreign girl, had been a part of the
hoax all along.

His hands twitched into fists at his sides. His
father was practically immune from his anger, so he
merely gave the man a curt nod in passing. His gri-
mace turned into a real smile, a feral one, as he came
up to the tiny woman who was to be his bride.

Eleanor did not like the look in her betrothed's
eyes. She wanted to turn and run, but pride, and the
fact that Edythe was right behind her, kept her from
bolting back up the narrow stairs. His eyes, full of hot
anger, were blue. When they'd met before, she'd
noticed only that they were bloodshot.

As he came to loom over her she backed up a step,

for he was very tall and hard to look at from her normal height. His hair was at least combed, and his hard-muscled chest was decently covered. He seemed clean; at least he didn't smell of pig. There was wine on his breath, but that was normal enough. He reached out his hand toward her. It was large and callused.

His size and the menace in his movements frightened her, but since she could not run she lifted her chin and forced herself to look into his eyes. She could only hope that her trembling wasn't too evident as he took her hand in his and tugged her forward. She stumbled on the last step and lost her balance. She fell hard onto Sir Stian's massive, immovable chest. His arms came around her, and the next thing she knew he was holding her tightly against him. She was aware of the heat of his body through all the layers of clothing between them. Their gazes locked, and for the first time in her life she knew what it was like to feel like prey.

She was the only one who heard the low growl that rumbled from his throat, for the sound was masked by a roomful of ribald laughter. Eleanor got so lost in the fierce aura of the man that she forgot to breathe until Lord Roger stepped up to his son and broke the spell.

"Wait for the wedding, you two," she heard Lord Roger say.

Stian's soul twisted as the laughter rang in his ears. His face blazed with embarrassment, and he cursed the fair skin that showed his every emotion. He forced himself to look at his father, to see his confident smile and the teasing turn of his head. He envied the man his self-assurance more than he did his lovely wife. The knowledge that he could never be like his father rankled more than the laughter, and burned away the hard need that had sprung up when the girl's body had been pressed tightly to his.

He loosened his hold, and the girl slipped out of his grasp. She seemed eager to escape his touch. He stepped aside with a grim nod, letting his father take both women by the hand.

They stood on either side of the Lord of Harelby, fair and dark, dressed in court finery, their small, soft hands resting in Lord Roger's. Lady Edythe looked demure and gentle, content to bask in the admiration of those around her. Stian's bride's features were still and proud, only small spots of color on each cheek betraying any agitation she might be feeling.

Stian followed in Roger's wake as he escorted the ladies to the high table. His gaze raked the girl's swaying hips as she walked ahead of him.

"That is the finest rump I've ever seen," Lars confided, his lips close to Stian's ear as they reached the dais. Stian turned on his cousin, only to have his anger dashed as Lars added, "And hair gold as ripe barley. Those braids are as thick as my fists." Lars elbowed him in the ribs. "You've been cheated, my friend."

Stian ignored his cousin's comments about Lady Edythe. He might not be reconciled to having lost the more beautiful sister, but his attention was more closely occupied with ways to deal with the wife he had.

4

Eleanor sat on the hard bench next to Sir Stian and tried very hard to recall some of the things Lady Constance had said about men. Sir Stian sat stiffly beside her, his eyes facing forward, one hand wrapped around the goblet they were supposed to share. Eleanor didn't know what could be so fascinating in the hall to hold his attention so closely.

Perhaps he just didn't want to look at her. Somehow, the notion that the brute was uninterested in her stung her already-sensitive emotions. Well, why should she want him to look at her? she thought, trying to hide her fear for the future in pride. She reminded herself, as sternly as she could, that marriage had nothing to do with emotional entanglements. She would be foolish to think otherwise—or that even Sir Stian, the lout of Harelby, would be interested in dalliance with her.

When she looked down from her seat at the high

table she saw nothing more than three trestle tables full of noisy strangers grouped around the smoky fire, with dogs and servants in about equal numbers moving among them. Two tall candles graced the high table, but otherwise the place was dark but for the fire and a few rushlights around the walls. There wasn't a jongleur or troubadour or minstrel or jester in sight.

She and Edythe had dressed for a feast, one in black, the other in white. The contrast would have been remarked upon and complimented in Poitiers. Here, she felt overdressed and out of place with Lord Roger's guests, who were dressed only a little better than the peasants in their fields.

Or perhaps the people crowded together at the trestles were the peasants in out of the fields. She had no idea of what the backward society of this land was like. She decided that she had best start finding out. This was her land now, and she was ever curious to know what was going on around her.

Lord Roger had spoken much of his lands on their journey, but now she saw that his observations were colored with his love of the place. His tongue had the storyteller's craft for exaggeration. Or, she thought unkindly with a sideways look at the son he'd praised so highly, Roger of Harelby was simply an outright liar.

She wondered if the man beside her was capable of conversing in more than grunts and curses, for she had heard not a word from him since they had come down to dinner. Perhaps she should be grateful for his silence, and his indifference. She hoped she would be content enough with her lot if the man left her to herself. As long as she was with Edythe and had her few books to keep her company, her life would not be unbearably lonely. Still, for now she was hungry despite her nerves, and curious despite the strangeness of her situation. She hoped a bit of civilized dinner conversation from her betrothed might be obtained along with a few bites of the meal.

She and Sir Stian had a single trencher of food before them. A mixture of meat and vegetables had been ladled onto the thick round of bread which served as a plate. Ignoring custom, the red-haired lout had yet to offer her a bite of the meal. She'd waited in self-effacing silence for Sir Stian to gallantly offer her a tasty morsel. She was beginning to realize that she could starve waiting for the man to behave properly.

Patience, she told herself. *Be patient, be gentle, be dutiful. For you are his to command from this day forward.* She reminded herself once more of Lady Constance's lessons and moved a bit closer to Stian.

"My lord?"

She wondered if he was as aware as she was of her thigh pressing against his as he answered, "What?"

She had spoken meekly, politely. His tone showed no signs that he noticed. So she found herself saying, "You might think to offer me a small sup of wine."

"Oh," he said and thrust the goblet toward her.

All her efforts toward meek acceptance couldn't keep her indignation at bay. Her temper flared merely at the sound of his voice. Eleanor did not know why the man made her angry by his mere existence, but it took a mighty effort not to snatch the goblet from his hand and toss the liquid in his face.

Perhaps if he had not dared to kiss her sister in such an unseemly fashion, or treated her with such lewd contempt, dealing with him would not rankle so. Whatever it was that caused her incautious emotions,

Eleanor curbed the desire to deal violently with the brute and forced a smile.

She saw him looking at her as if he'd just noticed her presence and made her lips form a smile. She wanted to shout at him. She had her duty to perform, and Lady Constance's lessons as a weapon. Somehow, she had to make the man see her as desirable. She could not manage to look Sir Stian in the eye, but she did deliberately turn the cup so that her lips touched the same spot his had. Then she took a small sip of Lord Roger's very bad wine.

Stian was used to sharing his meal with Lars, not a mouse with pretty manners. She smelled good, and her body felt good sitting snugly next to him on the bench. He wanted to reach down and touch her, to run his hand up and down the soft inside of her thigh. He almost laughed thinking how the mouse would react to such a touch. He wondered if she'd bite, or scream, or kick.

Then she smiled and drank from the goblet in a deliberate way that made him think that perhaps her closeness was no accident. Her action left him more confused than ever.

"What do you want?" he demanded.

The girl flinched at the sound of his voice, but she pointed at the trencher. Her eyes flashed up at him as she answered, "Some supper."

"Oh."

He shoved the trencher closer to her. He hadn't realized he'd been keeping the meal to himself. He'd been trying not to think at all. And instead he'd been thinking and feeling far too much.

He'd been trying to cope with the fact that another woman was seated in the place that had been empty since his mother's long-ago death. He hadn't known how much he still missed her until his father graciously put Lady Edythe by his side at the high table. Stian's life had changed drastically since his mother's death. The pain of it was throbbing anew inside him as he tried to accept that his father had a new wife.

There had been music and fine stories at Harelby before his mother died. There had been laughter and love and kindness between his parents and him and his two little sisters. Then Mother and the girls died of a fever and the world went dark. His father had fled his grief, gone to court and to wars. He'd been anywhere but at Harelby. For years Stian had known nothing but the pain of being abandoned. He'd learned to drown the pain and keep himself entertained.

When his father had come home nearly two years before, they had made peace and reaffirmed that they loved one another. It was damned hard to remember how much he cared for the man as he watched his father proudly gazing at the woman in his mother's place. Stian didn't know where to look, what to say, what to do.

He'd been trying not to give in to the urge to touch the mouse. Until now, he'd never had to talk to a woman before lifting her skirts, and he didn't know how to do it. He listened to his father's easy way with words and Lady Edythe's easy answers, knowing he could never entertain a court-bred woman in such a way. Roger had been able to teach him how to fight, but there hadn't been much of his easy polish that his father had been able to pass on to him.

He'd been casting sidelong glances at Lars, seated farther down the table, and at the men-at-arms eating at the trestle tables below. He kept telling himself that their laughter and lewd gestures were well meant, but he hated being the butt of even friendly jokes.

And, most importantly, he'd been trying very hard to get drunk enough not to care about any of it. It seemed to him that he was being remarkably unsuccessful at getting drunk.

He might have apologized to the girl for keeping her from her meal, but she slapped the goblet back into his hand just as the server appeared with the wine pitcher. Stian let the moment pass and took another glass of wine.

"Well, my dear, how do you like Harelby so far?"

Eleanor didn't know what to say as Lord Roger led her toward the chapel. Stian had disappeared with a group of young men the moment the meal had ended. She'd had a moment of relief to be out of his presence. Then Lord Roger had announced it was time for the wedding. He'd had her on the way to the chapel before she'd had any chance to flee. Her mind was racing, alternating schemes of escape with a litany of all the marital advice she'd ever heard. Now Lord Roger wanted her actually to answer a question. She could do no more than look up at him and blink.

He responded with a fond smile and a pat on the head. His reassurance helped to steady her nerves. She tried not to think about the swift pace Lord Roger was setting across the courtyard, or about the crowd of merrymaking strangers around them. She tried not to think about the fact that she was going to her doom. She tried to think about Lord Roger's question, and look around her at Harelby.

The night was clear, but it was the dark of the moon. There were servants carrying torches, giving illuminated glimpses of structures she barely remembered seeing by daylight. There was light spilling out through the chapel door. She found herself concentrating on the arched entrance of the small building as they hurriedly approached it. In the depths of her mind she saw the doorway as the mouth of a fearsome dragon, fiery maw opened to engulf her. Or perhaps it was the very gates of hell.

She was shocked out of her panic by her blasphemous thought. She said a swift prayer under her breath, not only for forgiveness, but for strength. And for inspiration, for surely there was some way out of this tangle.

Then it struck her as Lord Roger swept her through the door that perhaps the priest could help her. If she protested to the priest that this was not a willing union, perhaps he would take her plea up with the bishop.

"Where is the nearest bishop, my lord?" she heard herself asking Lord Roger even as the plan formed in her mind.

She gasped at her own words. Though she and Edythe were of no great rank, they had been raised in a queen's court, where every word and gesture must be carefully considered before being made. When had she forgotten caution? What was it about this wild northland that made her abandon sense? It seemed as if she'd been nothing but a bundle of reckless emotion since Stian had forced his brutal kiss on her.

Lord Roger gave her an odd look, but answered, "York. The bishop is in York."

Of course she had no idea where York might be.

They had passed through no town large enough to be a bishop's seat on the long journey. She hoped the distance to this York was not too far. Perhaps she could write a letter to the bishop there and prevail upon Harelby's priest to deliver it for her.

"And here, my dear," said Lord Roger as they neared the altar, "is Father Hubert."

Eleanor came to a dazed halt. "You are the priest?" she asked as she looked dubiously at the thin young man before her.

Hubert had masses of thick, dark hair and a scraggly, barely there mustache. He was dressed like all the other young men, in braccos and tunic, without the slightest hint of a tonsure. She had seen him in the hall and assumed him to be one of the squires.

His face was narrow, his smile was not. His eyes lit with pride as he answered. "Oh, aye. Like my father before me and his father before him and his father before him and his, and his mother before him. No matter the religion we've always been priests in my family."

Eleanor did not understand. "What sort of pagan, barbaric place is this?"

"Well," the young man said pleasantly just as Stian came staggering up, his arm around another of the castle's supply of rowdies, "it gets pretty cold in winter, but you'll learn to like it."

Eleanor ignored Stian as she stared in shock at the priest. Father Hubert was obviously not the one she could plead her case with. Still, she asked, "Do you know where York is? Do you know there's a bishop there?"

Hubert scratched his chin. "Aye. And I pray the bishop stays right where he is."

Before Eleanor could respond, Dame Beatrice pushed forward and said, "Get on with it, Hubert. It grows late."

Late. *Oh, indeed, it grows very late*, Eleanor thought as she closed her eyes. People bustled around her at the chatelaine's command. She could feel Stian's large presence as he moved closer, swaying slightly before he drew to a halt. She breathed in a hint of flowery scent as Edythe touched her shoulder then was gone. The members of Lord Roger's household took their places, leaving her and Stian with the priest before the altar.

Eleanor opened her eyes. She couldn't bring herself to look at Stian. She concentrated on the young priest. If she was going to do something to save herself it had to be now. She knew she must go on with the marriage ceremony, but there was a way she might be able to break the vows later.

She took a deep breath, though her voice came out as only a whisper when she spoke. A whisper that carried no farther than to the priest, and the man looming like a stone wall beside her. "I consent to this wedding because I am forced to. I do not make this marriage of my own free will," she said to Hubert. Her voice barely shook, but she was trembling all over, inside and out.

The priest gave a sympathetic look to her and Stian. "Oh," was all he said.

Stian, however, was quivering in rage. Though she kept her gaze firmly fixed straight ahead, she could feel her groom's evil glare.

When he spoke, his voice was as quiet as hers had been, but cold and deadly with it. "I'd sooner marry a plow ox than this mouse, Hubert."

"Oh," the priest said again. He didn't seem at all perturbed by their declarations. He crossed himself, smiled his bright smile, and said, "May the Lord Christ bless this union."

Eleanor could find no more brave words of protest. In fact, as the ceremony went on she could find no more words at all. She could only nod when the priest asked her to acknowledge the wedding vows. Stian merely grunted when Hubert asked the questions of him. She supposed that it didn't matter that she had no voice and that the bridegroom didn't bother to speak, not with all the witnesses to swear that the marriage was true.

Like it or not, they were wed.

5

"Your horse is outside," Lars whispered in
his ear as Stian dragged his bride toward the chapel
door.

Stian felt a moment of confusion, then he remembered the plan. He gave his cousin a curt nod. The
idea had been Lars's, but Stian liked it just fine.
Privacy was what he wanted. He did not want every
person in the castle to oversee his bedding of the
woman. In the forest would be silence, freedom. He
could hardly wait to get away.

He held the mouse firmly by the arm as he hustled
her toward the chapel door. Several people clapped
him on the back as he pushed past. He saw his father
smiling, with one arm around Edythe, his other hand
on Dame Beatrice's shoulder. Beatrice was squinting
and scowling, her hands tucked into her sleeves, suf-
fering the situation and his father's touch with no
great grace. Lars followed hard on Stian's heels,

laughing loudly. Everyone was making for the door to form the procession to the bedchamber. Bodies surged around him, but he was the biggest, strongest man in the crowd, and they had to make way for him.

The night was cool. As he stepped outside he saw that a groom held a cape as well as his horse for him. Stian swung his bride up in his arms as they stepped across the threshold. Ignoring her small cry, he made it to his horse in two swift strides. He threw the cloak over the girl's head as she began to struggle. A couple of quick twists and the material of the cloak bound her near as tight as a rope.

"Be still," he ordered and tightened his grip as he felt her shudder of fear. He ignored the muffled whimper she made in response.

With the groom to hold the stirrup then hand him the reins, he had himself and his prize settled onto the big animal almost before anyone else in the crowd knew what he was about. He gave the horse a kick in the ribs, while Lars hurried forward to slap it on the rump. The horse broke into a run as a surprised roar went up from behind. Stian laughed as he rode away.

Lars and the groom had done their work well; the night guards had the gates to the inner and outer bailey open for him. Their lewd calls followed him out into the night.

Soon he had all the silence and darkness he could wish for as he entered the forest close by Harelby's gates. It was just him and the woman he held close against his chest. He ran his hand up and down her back, then pulled the cloak aside. When her head came up to look at him, he caught her mouth in a forceful kiss. He looked forward to reaching their destination. Once there he'd have her quickly on her back.

*   *   *

"Roger, what does that boy think he's about?" Beatrice demanded as she tugged hard on his sleeve. "Where is he going?"

Edythe chimed in anxiously, "What will happen to Eleanor?"

Roger ignored both women while his son rode away. The courtyard was full of questioning, confused people. Roger ignored them as well. He did spare one annoyed look for his nephew, who leaned against the chapel wall pointing toward the gate and laughing drunkenly. Lars was ever an annoyance.

Finally, Roger rubbed the back of his neck and said to the anxiously watching women, "Bride stealing is an old custom."

"Aye," Beatrice agreed. "But men don't generally steal their own brides." She pointed toward the keep. "There's a bed waiting for them in the tower, with a fine new mattress."

Roger understood his chatelaine's irritable reaction. She worked hard to see that life at Harelby ran smoothly. He waved away her complaint. "It's best to have the boy out of the way for a few days, Beatrice. We've the shire court to prepare for, you and I."

He looked sternly at Beatrice until she finally lowered her eyes. After getting a grim nod from his chatelaine acknowledging his mastery, he turned his attention to his anxious wife.

"Eleanor will be safe," he assured her.

"But where did he take her? Why?"

Roger put his arm around his wife's shoulder and began to guide her back toward the hall. He knew exactly where his son had gone, but he gave a kinder description of the place than it deserved for Edythe's peace of mind. "He keeps a secret bower deep in the forest. It is a dry, fragrant place next to a serene pool." He ignored Beatrice's sarcastic chuckle as he went on. "They'll make love on a soft bed of furs with only the stars to keep silent watch."

Edythe was looking up at him with a soft, intent expression, hanging admiringly on his words. She leaned against him as they walked along, making him well aware of her supple young body. Need for the golden beauty kindled inside him. It was to his own bed he wanted to retire, never mind the arrangements his son made for himself.

"Come, my dear," he told his wife. He ran the back of his hand across her soft cheek. "Let us lie down together in our own big bed."

She answered him with a mischievous smile. "We will lie down, my lord, but not to sleep, I trust."

"No," he agreed. "Not to sleep."

From nearby he heard Dame Beatrice mutter, "Randy old fool."

Roger ignored her comment as he took Edythe into the hall. What others thought of his behavior had never meant anything to him. Nor should it. It was one lesson he had never been able to teach his son. Roger knew very well why Stian had run off with the girl. Well, he wished him well on his wedding night, then dismissed all but thoughts of Edythe from his mind.

Though it had been tempting, it hadn't seemed proper to bite her husband. So Eleanor suffered the intrusion of his tongue into her mouth. At first the sensation nauseated her. Gradually, an odd warmth began to radiate from the spot where their mouths touched. Eleanor did not understand it, but she welcomed any heat as the cold air rushed by. The tangling cloak wasn't enough, the heat radiating from the big body holding her so tightly wasn't enough, but the kiss, the kiss heated her from the inside. Nothing had ever done that before.

She had started the ride terrified, and nearly stifled by the heavy wool of the cloak covering her. She'd been too tangled to move, and too frightened to try. The darkness hadn't brightened any when her captor freed her head. She hadn't had time to look around. He'd kissed her before she had time to draw breath for a scream. The kiss tasted darkly of wine, and, like the wine she'd drunk at Lord Roger's table, it was unpleasant, but intoxicating.

The kiss didn't go on forever, though it seemed to. Eventually, Stian set his attention on guiding the horse along the track. He still held her close against his chest. Eleanor didn't try to struggle for fear of falling from the big animal. She didn't want to be trampled under its feet or lost in the black forest. So she held herself still in Stian's iron grip, all her senses alert while her mind was practically numb.

She was afraid. Of where they were going. Of what would happen when they got there. She hated being afraid. Mostly because fear also made her recklessly angry. Recklessness was the last thing she needed to deal with the unpredictable, bad-tempered man who had abducted her.

Stian knew from the kiss that the wine had conquered him. It had been sweet to delve into the heat of her mouth, but no arousal had been sparked by his action. Nothing. A fire should have been growing in his loins.

Instead, he was becoming dizzy, listless with drink. He'd been trying to get drunk all night; now he realized just how well he'd succeeded. Sleep wasn't far off as he struggled to keep his eyes open, his grip on his prisoner, and his mind on the horse. Fortunately, the mare knew the way and the girl had sense enough to keep still.

"Not far," he mumbled as the horse moved downhill. Stian could hear the rush of water nearby. The trees narrowed and the slope became steeper. The way was tricky. They were whipped by branches, and a startled owl hurtled past, brushing Stian's cheek with its wing, but they made it into the clearing no worse for wear. The place had a haunted feel to it. The small pool spread out as a deeper patch of dark on this moonless night. The cave looked like the humped back of a giant sleeping bear.

The horse stopped of its own accord before the entrance of the cave. Stian swayed in the tall saddle, tilted slowly sideways, and eventually fell off, taking the girl with him. He had just enough sense to do his best to cushion her fall as much as he could. They landed in a tangle of arms and legs, the cloak bunched up around them. The horse snorted and backed away. Stian lay looking up at the stars for a few moments. He smiled as they seemed to whirl through the night, just out of his reach.

"Fine wine," he murmured. "Very fine wine."

The girl lay stiff and still beside him. Eventually, he recalled her presence. He brought her with him when he sat up. He couldn't have done otherwise the way the cloak was now wrapped around both of them. It was the mouse who pushed and pulled and got them untangled from the cloth. Stian was pleased, for he couldn't have managed it on his own.

Once out of the cloak, Eleanor sprang to her feet. When Stian got up and staggered into the cave, she followed. She could see little; she could only tell that the cave was dry, and big enough for Stian to stand upright.

Now that she was on solid ground again, anger was overcoming her fear. "Where are we?" she asked. "Why have you brought me here?"

Stian's hands landed heavily on her shoulders, then slid down her arms and away. "Going to take you," he said. He pointed to the ground. "Right here." He laughed, a low sound, but it echoed off the stone walls surrounding them. "Going to—have—you."

Eleanor drew herself up to her full, inconsiderable, height. "I won't be ravished on my wedding night!"

"Fine," Stian answered, the word slow and slurred. He sounded annoyingly cheerful. "I'll ravish you in the morning." He slid to the ground.

Eleanor waited for long minutes without moving, staring down at the unmoving lump she'd married. Finally, she stepped forward and prodded him with her toe. "Sir Stian?" He didn't move. "My lord?" Nothing. He was asleep. "Damn!"

Eleanor didn't know what to do about this incredible turn of events. She'd been resigned to a proper bedding, to the pain of doing her wifely duty amid proper ceremony. There should have been a bed, and jokes and advice from those who helped them undress. They should have sat stiffly side by side, naked under the covers, while Lord Roger made a speech and offered toasts to the newlyweds. Edythe should have been there with advice and an encouraging goodnight kiss. There should have been sly winks and open laughter, encouragement and congratulations. It should have been done properly.

She had been prepared for doing it properly.
Then she would have felt married. She wouldn't
have minded so much when they were left alone and
Stian bade her open her legs for him. She would
have felt like a martyr, but she would also have felt
like a wife.

This was all wrong. It was mad. And here she was
alone in a cave the holy saints knew where, with a
man too drunk to do anything but sleep. She didn't
know what she was going to do. She couldn't just
run back to Harelby and pound on the gate until
someone let her in. She had no idea where she was or
how she'd gotten there. There were probably wolves
or bears or wildcats in the forest. She was just going
to have to wait for him to wake, wasn't she? She
didn't know what she was going to do until then.

She did, however, take momentary satisfaction in
kicking Stian in the rump as hard as she could. She
ended up with aching toes, and he just turned over
and began snoring. Eleanor wanted to kick him
again, and to swear at him as well.

"I do not wish to be in your company," she informed
him. "Sleeping or awake. Drunk or sober," she added.
"Not that I'll probably ever have to worry about seeing you sober."

She turned around and spent a good while standing in the cave mouth breathing in the cold night air.
Eventually, she picked the cloak up off the ground
and stood holding it, knowing how useful it would be
as a blanket. It wasn't that she minded sleeping on
the ground. She had slept on the ground many nights
on the journey from Poitiers, and on the way to
Harelby. She was used to sleeping with Edythe by her
side, or very nearby. Now Edythe slept beside Lord

Roger at Harelby, and Eleanor had never felt more alone in her life.

It wasn't just for tonight. She had her whole life before her to spend alone with this man. She had to decide what to do.

All she could do, she supposed, was live with him. If he wanted to spend his wedding night in a cave, who was she to gainsay him? If he wanted to rape her in the morning, well, she would have something to say about that. She, and the teachings of Lady Constance.

Eleanor ran a hand down the front of her over-dress. She looked back at the dark lump that was Stian and fought down the shudder that was part fear and part anticipation. Then, thoughtfully, deliberately, she began to unlace her dress.

6

Stian was used to waking up on the ground with a pounding pain in his head. It wasn't all that uncommon to wake up to the feel of a soft female breast under his cheek, as he did now. It wasn't uncommon for him not to remember what he'd done, where he was, or how he'd gotten there. What was uncommon was that he woke up with the nagging feeling that this time it was important he remember all these things.

He also needed to remember someone's name.

But first he needed to throw up.

Once he'd crawled outside and accomplished that, he felt a bit better. It was dawn, and the waking birds were making an ungodly racket. Stian didn't quite have the energy to shake his fist at them, but the noise did cause him to look around. He saw the hillside, the ancient trees, the trickle of water that bubbled out of the rock face and flowed down into the small pool next to the cave. The cave. How had he gotten to the cave?

As he struggled to his feet he saw his horse calmly cropping spring grass. As he walked toward it the mare raised its head to give him a questioning nicker. At least the animal's presence answered how he'd gotten to the cave. He still couldn't recall the why. What he did know was that no matter how his head hurt and his stomach heaved, the horse needed to be cared for. Fortunately, it didn't look to have been ridden hard. He got the saddle off and found a bag full of provisions in the process.

He was glad someone had thought to provide him with food and ale. Perhaps he would even want them eventually. First, though, he pulled off his clothes and plunged into the pool. He rinsed the sour taste out of his mouth, then splashed around the waist-deep water to loosen cramped muscles as much as to get himself clean. The icy water helped to clear his head. Once his head was clear he remembered the naked girl.

When he stood up, he saw her standing in the mouth of the cave. Only she wasn't naked; she had his saffron yellow cape wrapped tightly around her body. Her silky hair spread like a black mantle across the rich color of the cloak. Her lips were slightly parted; her cheeks were tinged with spots of color. She stared at him with wide, dark eyes. Stian stared back. He thought it might be important for him to remember who she was.

Then, after several minutes had passed and the girl had gone from blushing to pale to blushing again, she took two steps out of the cave mouth and spread her arms. The cloak fell down around her feet like a shower of gold. A dark fall of hair obscured her face as she modestly turned her head away, but the rest of her was clear to Stian's view.

Stian forgot all about the chill water of the pool as the sight of her warmed him. All his questions vanished; stiff muscles and the pain in his head were forgotten as well. The pleasant, heavy ache in his groin was all that mattered as he stepped from the water. He didn't know who the girl was, but if she was going to offer herself to him so blatantly, he certainly wasn't going to turn away the gift.

Eleanor hadn't known what to do when Stian woke and immediately moved away from her. She missed him as soon as he was gone. His hands had touched her sometimes during the night, then his head had found its way to pillow on her breast. His body had warmed her and his touch had not been unpleasant. With the warrior beside her she had even felt safe enough to sleep in the cave. She had not felt so alone even though he'd been oblivious of her presence.

At first she had been mortified at the rejection when he left. Then she'd heard him puking into the bracken and every bit of annoyance she'd felt at him the day before was rekindled.

"Drunken lout," she'd muttered as she pulled the cloak around her and followed him outside intending to berate the fool for his behavior. She'd ended up hesitating at the entrance of the cave, stiff with anger, but holding her tongue. She'd put a hard rein on her temper and made herself think. She remembered her intentions of the night before to entice Sir Stian of Harelby with loving eagerness. She remembered her wedding vows. They may have been spoken under

duress, but they were binding on her, for now, just
the same.

It was her duty to give Stian of Harelby her body.
The problem was, how did she go about getting his
attention long enough to accomplish the deed? Only
one thought came to mind as he stood up and looked
about him, naked as the day he was born. Then the
thought fled momentarily as she got a good look at
just what the priest had enjoined her to submit to the
night before.

The curling hairs on his broad chest were redder
than the gold-red of the hair on his head. Her gaze
traveled down past his hard belly and narrow hips to
find that the hair at his groin was the reddest of all,
almost wine dark. She knew what men and women
did together, and had speculated wildly about what
the act truly would be like. Knowledge was all very
well and good, but practical experience was lacking,
and she knew not how to begin. After all, Stian was
more wild than tame; perhaps he would not recognize
any efforts at gentle seduction. She feared her marriage bed would be a rough and turbulent place.

Now, seeing him as God had made him, she found
herself more fascinated than fearful at the sight. It
seemed the most natural thing in the world to show
herself to him, to be as naked as he was in this
primeval place. She let the cloak fall away, playing
Eve to his Adam.

It was not shameful to be naked in front of one's
husband, but Eleanor still could not bear the hot
scrutiny of his gaze. She looked away, hiding her face
behind a wall of hair, not daring to look at Stian of
Harelby. She waited, hardly able to breathe as she
heard him approach.

When he touched her she knew not how to react, for the sensation was both cold and hot and the hand that splayed across her hip did so with gentle pressure. His other hand brushed her hair aside, then his fingers traced across her cheek. He drew her closer, and she turned her head to look at him at last. He was smiling.

It was the first time he had looked at her without anger, without resentment, without a threatening glare. Oh, there was heat in his glance, but heat that had nothing to do with anger. There was nothing mild about his regard, but neither was it threatening. She even found herself smiling a little in response.

He pulled her closer, making her aware of his need. Far from being disturbed, a ripple of pleasure went through her. What he needed she could give; if not gladly, it would at least be without fear or grudging acquiescence.

She tried to recall the things Lady Constance had said about pleasuring a man's body, but there was so much of Stian she didn't know where to begin. Just looking at him was a daunting experience. So she took him in a bit at a time, and where her gaze touched, she let her fingers follow.

Stian felt a burst of warmth at the spots where she touched him, like sparks stirred up from a fire. His flesh had been cool, still damp from the water, but now it felt warm enough to raise steam. She moved her hands with easy friction along the wet skin of his chest, up and down his arms, along his collarbone. She took her time, and, to his surprise, he let her. He liked the feel of her soft little hands as they ran over him.

He'd been hot to have her when he'd first come

out of the water; he was growing hotter still. But, somehow, the waiting made the wanting sharper, better. When he bent his head to kiss her, her mouth touched his first. Her tongue teased his lips open, delved, and explored. His breath was coming in ragged gasps by the time she was done kissing him. He quickly pushed away the vague memory of sharp teeth and a bitten tongue.

Her hands moved down his ribs to his hips, then around to his buttocks. She pulled him closer. Without thought, Stian lifted the girl. The soft roundness of her buttocks fit his hands perfectly. He forgot everything else as he carried her into the cave.

He kept a pile of furs and wool blankets in the back of the cave for his visits. He took the girl to them, kissing her as he lowered them both to the ground. He ignored the faint musty smell from the furs as they lay down together. His hands found her breasts, rolling the tight peaks between his fingers. His mouth soon followed his hands. He drew a straining nipple into his mouth and suckled while the girl continued to caress his shoulders and back. He breathed in the scent of her skin, ran his cheek along the softness of her belly.

When sharp claws bit into his shoulder he took a light nip at the side of the girl's breast. She moaned and he laughed and whispered, "Open for me."

After a moment of teasing hesitation the girl did as he commanded. He moved to quickly settle himself between her spread thighs. She gave a sharp cry as he entered her. He was aware of the tight pressure surrounding him, of hot slickness, then he was lost to all but the building need. His hips pumped and ground against her, hard and fast, seeking sweet release.

Eleanor had been so intent on trying to remember just what she was supposed to do she hadn't realized she was actually enjoying herself until the pleasure abruptly stopped. She wanted to scream when he entered her, she wanted to push him away as he kept on penetrating her burning insides, but this was what the marriage bed was all about. This was woman's punishment for Eve's sin. Never mind the pleasures promised by Lady Constance; she knew that the best she could do was endure the experience.

Still, she recalled her lessons. She clutched hard at Stian's back, closed her eyes, and lifted her hips to meet his pummelling thrusts. Oddly enough, the pain lessened with her participation in the event. While the pain didn't disappear entirely, Eleanor was beginning to recapture some of the earlier eager aching by the time Stian was done with the act. When he pulled out of her she almost wished he hadn't. She thought that if it had gone on a bit longer she might have gotten some notion of what Lady Constance meant.

Well, it hadn't.

Stian stayed close beside her, his breathing ragged, his arm thrown over his eyes. She lay on her back and looked up at the cave ceiling. The furs beneath her were soft. She was comfortable enough, all things considered. She didn't actually want to move, and she wasn't sure she could. Stian had hurt her; her nether regions felt as if they were on fire. She hoped he didn't expect her to jump up and offer him sweet-meats and a flagon of mulled wine. No, probably not. Lady Constance had said that such bedroom activities were a civilized ending for the act. Stian of Harelby was anything but civilized. Besides, they weren't even in a bedroom.

Eleanor closed her eyes again. She was so tired.

Slowly, Stian became aware that the musky scent that lingered about them was tainted with another familiar odor. There was the smell of blood in the air, and this struck him as passing strange.

Until memory came storming angrily back into his thoughts. The sated pleasure of his body was completely forgotten, replaced by an ache in his gut as guilt twisted through it. He'd drunk too much. Again. So he'd faced a fine lady and his father's strong will with raw temper and raw nerves and done and said things that made no sense to his sober, sensible mind. There'd been a feast, and vows made by candlelight, and for some stupid reason he'd kidnapped his own—

"Oh, sweet Jesu," he whispered raggedly.

He rolled onto his side to look down at the girl he'd just bedded. He could barely make out her form in the shadows of the cave, but he knew her.

He still couldn't remember her name.

He touched her shoulder, trying to be as gentle as a rough simpleton like himself could be. She didn't move.

"Are you my wife?" he asked.

7

She was asleep.

Stian knew not whether to be grateful or annoyed that his lovemaking had such an effect on her. He wondered if she was hurt. He had never bedded such a highborn woman before, nor had he ever had a virgin. He wondered if the combination might prove fatal to the gently bred lady.

He rubbed his aching shoulder as he watched the naked woman sleep. He could make out a bite mark on one fine breast, but thought that perhaps she had given as good as she got or his shoulder wouldn't be hurting. Perhaps she was not so delicate after all. He prayed so. For it was not his habit to satisfy his lust with the pain of his companion.

Stian sighed and decided not to worry himself unduly over the act. She was his wife; she had done her duty by lying with him. He'd taken her maidenhead, but there had been no sin in the fornication. Perhaps he'd even planted a babe with the act.

"Hubert will be pleased that I've managed to go a few hours without bringing some sin down on my head," he murmured as he reached out to run his hand down the length of his wife's shapely thigh.

Much to his surprise, his wife opened her eyes and answered, "Hubert is a very odd priest."

Well, at least she had lived through their rough coupling. Stian moved to sit back on his heels. "Hubert is a good lad."

His wife turned her head away. Her body went stiff with tension. "My lord," she said. "You are naked."

He put his hand over her breast. It fit well against his palm. "What of it?"

Eleanor gave a weary sigh and murmured, "Aye, indeed."

His hand stayed on her breast as she sat up. She was tempted to push it away, but she had grown cold and the spot where he touched her seemed to radiate the only warmth in the whole cave. She found herself overcoming her momentary shame as curiosity drew her to look at her husband once again.

He looked disheveled and wild, but not so fierce as she remembered. When he smiled at her he showed too many teeth for comfort's sake, but she didn't actually think she was in danger of being eaten alive. Yesterday death and dismemberment at this bad-tempered, red-pelted lout's hands had seemed like a real possibility. What he had just done to her had not been worse than death, despite its unpleasant moments. It seemed entirely possible to Eleanor that she would certainly survive repeating the act—she just hoped it wouldn't be too soon. She found herself glancing down from her husband's face to his groin in hopes that there was nothing stirring there that she was going to have to deal with immediately.

"There's food if you're hungry."

Stian's voice was a rough, not unpleasant, rumble in her ear. She jumped at the sound of it. Blinking, she asked, "What?" His hand was still on her breast. She noticed only because when he spoke the sensitive peak grew suddenly tight and hard.

He must have noticed, because he moved his hand away. "You're cold," he said and pulled a fur covering up over her shoulders.

Eleanor wrapped the fur around herself, grateful for the warmth and to cover her nakedness. Stian left the cave. She found herself studying the play of muscles in his back and buttocks and strong legs as he strode out into the daylight. She noticed not only that he was well made, but took note of the white lines left by several scars. The evidence of battle showed the young knight had obviously earned his accolade. *Or possibly he's been betrothed before,* she thought as she recalled her reaction to having been tossed on a table and nearly ravished by the stinking beast.

She couldn't help but smile at the memory and wonder at her own change of attitude. Yesterday she had been sure she'd have nightmares from the incident for the rest of her life. Why was she feeling mollified toward the man who had abducted her to this dank place? Had he done anything to prove that he was safe to be with? Had he brought her here, away from Lord Roger's protection, to beat and starve and break her at his leisure?

When he came back he was dressed. He put a large bag down in front of her. "There's bread and cheese." He tipped a bulging water skin to his lips and drank deeply. "Ale, too," he added as he passed the skin to her.

It would seem that Stian was not planning on starving her, at least.

"You'll want to bathe after you've eaten," he added. "The water's cold, but it might keep your muscles from stiffening anyway."

He chuckled after he spoke, though the words themselves were essentially helpful. Perhaps he did not intend to beat her, either. He also had a smug look on his face that told her how proud he felt at having just taken her maidenhead. The gaze that raked her was as possessive as it was smug. If she hadn't been so hungry her stomach might have knotted with fury at his cocksure attitude. As it was, she put indignation aside in favor of breaking her fast with the food he'd brought her.

Stian ended up taking most of the meal, assuming, she supposed, that his larger size made him the hungrier of the two of them. He was wrong. He was right about bathing helping her stiff muscles, though. He watched her with an amused and randy eye the whole time she splashed in the water.

Since he was intent on looking his fill anyway, Eleanor set about her ablutions in as slow and provocative a manner as she could manage. In truth, she felt like a wanton fool as she practically caressed her damp breasts and thighs and belly when she'd have preferred a good, brisk scrubbing.

Stian watched the girl whose name he couldn't remember with a trapped, rapt fascination. She seemed to be putting her charms on display just for his sake. It was the most amazing thing he'd ever seen.

He was growing hard again. He wished he wasn't,

because a girl who'd been a virgin not an hour before might not welcome being taken again quite so soon. Or would she? He didn't know much about virgins. He knew the sight of this woman, with her soft brown skin, full breasts, and rounded hips, was the most rousing thing he'd ever encountered. Perhaps he should ask her what she intended, but he'd managed about as many words as he could just getting her fed and cleaned up. He didn't know what to do.

Finally, he jumped into the pool with her.

Eleanor screamed in surprise when Stian grabbed her around the waist. He dragged her out of the water and carried her to the furs inside the cave. He covered her wet body with his, warming her skin with his heat. She stopped screaming when he kissed her. Her fear calmed as he ran his hands over her. It was replaced with wonder at the tingling sensation left by Stian's rough caresses. She'd brought this on herself, she realized. He was only reacting to her shameless posing before him.

Still, she pushed at his shoulder, turned her head away from his kiss. Never mind what she'd done to deserve this, she couldn't go through with the act again. Not yet. It just hurt too much.

"Please, my lord," she begged.

His answer was a grunt, and his mouth descended around one nipple.

As he suckled and nipped at it she continued to try to push him away. Her insides were beginning to ache and throb uncomfortably. She felt his hardness against her belly. She just wasn't ready to bear the pressure of having him inside her yet.

"I can't. I won't. Please, no. No."

She had soft hands, did this wife of his, and a soft voice, but her words had the ring of iron in them.

Stian wasn't used to being told no. Peasant girls didn't know the word, nor did the castle servants, nor the tavern wenches who expected coin for a few minutes of their time. She was his wife, wasn't she? She had no right to say no.

Still, Stian sat up and glared down at the cowering woman. What was it she wanted from him? Why didn't she want him? Why had she mocked him by flaunting herself in the pool?

He pounded his fist on the cave floor beside her. Frustration and hurt made his voice rough. "Damn you!"

Her dark eyes went wide with fear as he spoke. She squeaked with fear and scrambled away from the furs. She pulled on a chemise while he sat on the floor of the cave. He fought down both arousal and anger as he watched her hasty movements.

"Mouse," he said, remembering what he'd called her the day before. "Ugly little gray mouse." By all the saints, he'd been drunk indeed to see this lush-bodied creature as ugly.

Stian's words struck Eleanor harder than any blow could have. She couldn't bear to look at him. Her throat clogged with tears she refused to shed. All she could do was cover the body that she'd so recently displayed in the full light of day as if it was worth looking at. She could only pray her husband would speak no more of how ugly he found her.

She knew she was no great beauty like Edythe, with her long, slender waist and high, round breasts. A Provençal poet had once compared Edythe's breasts to apples he longed to taste. Other poets called her an angel, a creature of air and light. Eleanor was brown as the earth under Edythe's dainty feet.

She was no mouse as Stian claimed, but she was a

creature of mud. Sometimes it was good for her pride to be reminded of her shortcomings. She would have to remember her husband in her prayers for that, she told herself as she laced up her overdress.

Stian saw no more use sitting around the cave naked after his wife was dressed, so he went outside to find his own garments. Once dressed he saddled the horse. He swung onto the horse's back as she came out of the cave. She was wearing his cape, the saffron wool trailing the ground behind her.

Stian was left shaken and breathless for a few moments as an image of the girl lifting her arms and letting the cape fall to the ground played through his mind. His body tightened with renewed need that he made himself ignore. Her face was expressionless as she came toward him. He tried not to let his hunger for her show.

"My lord?" she asked, turning her face up to him as she reached the horse. She held up a hand in entreaty. "You would not leave me in this desolate place, would you?"

Stian looked around him. Desolate? This was the most beautiful place in all the Cheviot Hills. Where had this courtier woman come from to call his private place desolate? And why would she be afraid he'd leave her? It wasn't a long way back to Harelby, but he hardly expected a stranger to know the path.

He grunted and leaned down to grab her hand. It was easy enough to haul a small thing like her up behind him on the mare. He waited until she was settled behind him with her hands firmly clutching him for balance before setting off for home.

He spent the whole way back to Harelby trying not to think about the softly feminine body pressed against his back, or the small, clever hands at his waist.

*　　　*　　　*

"You're back early."

Stian ignored Lars's cackle of laughter. "I've things to do."

"Wasn't she worth your time?"

Stian looked past his grinning cousin to where his wife stood with her sister and the other women, warming her hands by the hearth. He could still feel the pressure of those hands against his flesh. The ride back to Harelby had been silent. She'd pretended he didn't exist.

Her willow-slender sister had run from the hall as the horse reached the inner bailey. The mouse was off the horse and in the willow woman's arms before he'd even dismounted. The sisters had gone into the hall without giving him a backward glance. He'd been left to walk into the room full of curious, amused castle folk all alone. He wasn't pleased that his wife shunned his presence on their wedding morning.

Lars's question did nothing but rankle him more. "I've had her," he said. That was all Lars needed to know.

"Good." Lars clapped him on the shoulder. He passed Stian a wooden tankard of ale. "Welcome to the marriage bed. Let's go hunting."

Stian considered the suggestion while he gulped the strong new ale. Lars's companionship was far more familiar than the silent, confusing company of his wife. He could be himself with his cousin. With his wife he had no idea how to act from one moment to the next.

Better the devil he knew, he decided. "Aye," he said after he finished the ale. "Let's go hunting."

*   *   *

"You are not leaving this castle!"

Stian took a belligerent stance in front of his father. "Why not?"

"There's a shire court meeting in two days. I need you here."

"There's a shire court to be fed as well."

Eleanor tried not to listen to the argument going on between Lord Roger and Stian, though she stood only a few feet away. Edythe's arm was around her shoulder, and she was surrounded by the other household women. This was her place, she told herself, among the women. Still, her attention was unwillingly concentrated on the men who faced each other beside the high table.

"Not with the King's deer there isn't," Roger went on, his deep voice booming throughout the hall. "It's a shire court, boy."

"Then I won't hunt deer." Stian's voice was just as deep and just as loud.

Eleanor found herself drawn to the conversation despite not wanting any further involvement with her husband. Her curiosity would always get the better of her sense. What was a shire court and why shouldn't Stian hunt deer? She looked at Dame Beatrice hoping the chatelaine would answer her questions. But before she could open her mouth, Dame Beatrice tucked her hands in her sleeves and stalked over to where father and son were arguing.

"Oh, let the boy go, Roger. Better he do something useful in the woods than stay stinking drunk at home."

Eleanor slipped away from her sister's gentle hold to watch as Roger broke away from glaring at his son to round on Beatrice. "He's not getting stinking drunk, either. Not under this roof."

"Then we'll find another roof to get drunk under."

It wasn't Stian who had spoken. Eleanor vaguely remembered the young man standing next to Stian. He was shorter than her husband, more compactly built, with a sensual cast to his lips, and had a very willful look about him. Eleanor looked questioningly at her sister.

"Lars," Edythe answered with a sigh. "Something must be done about Lars," she added thoughtfully.

Before Eleanor could ask what she meant, Roger roared, "Do as you like, boy! Stian stays right here!"

"Why?" Stian bellowed back.

"This!"

The next thing Eleanor knew, Roger had swept down on her. He grabbed her by the arm and thrust her toward Stian. She landed with a thump against his hard chest. He caught her by the arms before she fell onto the rush-covered floor. She was so shocked by Lord Roger's action that she could scarcely breathe. She found herself looking up at Stian's rage-reddened face. She was even more surprised by the concern in the quick flick of a look he gave her before he went back to the argument.

"You've never minded my leaving Harelby before."

"You've never been a bridegroom before."

"What's that got to do with it?"

Eleanor couldn't help but notice that Stian was not letting go of her. In fact, despite his attention being concentrated on his father, he had shifted her so she was tucked close to his side with his arm around her shoulder. Edythe had been holding her the same way a few moments before, but that embrace had felt completely different. Yet Stian's touch felt no less protective. Eleanor didn't understand it.

"Marriage has everything to do with it," Roger told Stian. He pointed toward the stairs. "The only place you're going is to bed with your wife."

Stian's arm tightened around her as he protested, "I've been to bed with my wife."

"Well, bed her again."

Eleanor couldn't help but stare at her husband as his face went from red with anger to brighter red with embarrassment. Her face flamed as well, and she cringed inside and out from Roger's blunt words. Everyone in the hall was staring at her and Stian. Many were laughing, with Lars's braying sounding the loudest.

"I want grandchildren!" Roger's voice rose above the laughter and murmurs.

"I'll bed her in my own time." Stian's voice sounded composed and reasonable in contrast to Roger's shouting. At least he sounded deadly calm. The arm around her felt like a band of cold iron.

Roger didn't take any notice of Stian's reaction. "You can't bed your wife if you're not at home."

Stian growled, a low, thunderstorm rumble. Eleanor felt the sound more than heard it. "Father."

Roger pointed toward the stairs again. "Go on," he commanded. "Spend some time with your wife." He beckoned Edythe with his other hand. He offered his son a wide smile as Edythe hurried to his side. He took Edythe by the hand. "Make love to your wife, and I'll do the same with mine."

Eleanor was amazed at the easy way Edythe smiled and fluttered her eyelashes at Lord Roger. Here she was burning with shame at the man's words, while Edythe looked eager for the act he suggested.

Stian stood planted in place, as unmoving as a piece of red granite. "Who'll mind Harelby while we frolic?"

"Dame Beatrice, of course," Roger answered easily. He spared a fond look for the frowning chatelaine. "As ever."

"Aye," she agreed. "As ever." She turned her narrow-eyed gaze on Stian. Her expression was annoyed, but her words were gentle. "Mind your father, lad. And you," she said to Lars as she shoved him off the dais and toward the door. "You can go hunting. I'll have a dozen rabbits for the cookpot before I'll let you back in this hall."

Roger spoke to the gaping household over the sound of Lars's blasphemous protests. "Have you no work to occupy you? Come, my lady," he added, "we'll follow Stian and Eleanor up the stairs."

Stian hesitated a few more moments. To Eleanor he still looked like a thunderstorm preparing to break, but he seemed to relax a bit as the people in the hall hurried away from the confrontation. Roger looked more amused than angry, and Edythe looked sublimely serene.

Eleanor felt relieved just to have the confrontation over with when Stian grabbed her hand and hustled her up the stairs. So relieved that she didn't think to be concerned about what would happen once she and her husband were once more alone.

8

"Now what?" Eleanor asked, amazed that she was becoming more annoyed than frightened by the situation.

Stian put his hands on his narrow hips and glared, not at her, but at the heavy wooden door. " 'Tis all a jest to him."

"Lord Roger?" she asked, and he nodded. "What is all a jest?"

Instead of giving her an answer, Stian laughed. The sound had very little humor in it. "Life is a jest," he declared, then threw himself onto the bed and said, "Come here, mouse."

She knew she should obey instantly, that she should cozen and cater to him, that she should continue taking Edythe's sensible advice. Instead, Eleanor set about exploring her surroundings.

She knew that she should be used to the idea of living with someone other than Edythe by now. The fact that she and Stian had a room to themselves at all amazed her. Privacy was hard to come by, a privilege Eleanor was neither used to nor expected.

It was so unexpected that she looked around her in wonder at the curtained bed, the chests, small table, and chair that made up the furnishings. A tapestry of faded green-and-white stripes covered the cold stones of the room's outside wall. There was a small window in one high corner, and a thick tallow candle on a shelf next to the bed. A book, bound in red leather, lay on the shelf next to the unlit candle. Her bags were piled on her clothes chest beneath the window.

The sight of her things sitting in such a commonplace way in what had been a private chamber made her forget any sense of wonder or dread at having to share the room with Stian of Harelby. Since this was now her home, she decided, she might as well unpack.

"Come here," Stian repeated as she picked up an inlaid box.

Annoyance tightened in her as she looked around for a flat surface that would do. "We'll have all our lives to couple," she told her husband. She decided the small ivory-and-ebony set would not take up too much room on the little table by the head of the bed.

Stian sat up as she put the box down. "What is that thing? This is my room. What are you doing, mouse?"

She might have answered him politely if he had not called her mouse. The word pricked her painfully, so she ignored him and continued. She carefully unwrapped the layers of oiled cloth and soft kidskin from her three precious books. These were her treasure, one she thought a far better dowry than the lands her father had presented to the Lord of Harelby. This was a marriage gift she could both have and share, though she doubted her surly husband had any interest in reading.

He wanted to go hunting with his friend, or, once that pleasant diversion was canceled, to bed her to pass the time. "I wished you'd gone hunting," she said as she passed where he sat to reach the shelf.

He was standing by the time she'd carefully placed her books beside the one already there. He put his hands on her shoulders as she turned. "My father ordered me to give him grandsons," he told her.

She confronted his hard hands and annoyed expression with an effort to be reasonable. "You are a dutiful son, my lord, but I would—"

"I'd rather take you on the bed. Up against the wall will do if you won't lie down." He pushed her backward as he spoke, until her shoulders were pressed against the thick tapestry.

Eleanor shoved against his chest. It was no more effective than trying to move a mountain. "You crude—vile—"

"I'm a dutiful son." His gaze never left hers as he suggested, "We could use the floor."

The cold indifference of his tone should have frightened her. It sent hot anger through her instead.

"Or the table in the hall? Or a cave?" she asked as he pressed her against the wall. "Have you no decency?"

"None. I can take you where and when I will. You are my wife," he reminded her.

"Aye," she agreed hastily. "But is once a day not enough to satisfy your lust?"

"Not when I've nothing better to do."

"That's all I am to you then, husband? A way to pass the time?"

Stian didn't know why he was bothering to argue with the mouse. Or why her words disturbed him. Women were to be enjoyed. That was what his father was doing with his wife right now, so why should he not do the same? Though when his mother had been alive there had been more to do than hunt and bed the castle women.

In truth, he felt no particular urge to take the mouse just now, on the bed or the floor or against the wall. It was just—something to do. And a way to stop her from rearranging his room, invading his one private place in the castle. He knew that he could be roused and have her beneath him quickly enough, which would pass no more than an hour. Then after they coupled she'd probably just go back to unpacking.

"Well?" she asked.

He didn't know how long they'd been standing with their gazes and wills locked. He did take a step back, but snagged his arm around her waist when she would have moved past him. "Hold," he ordered, drawing her against him. "Are you a mouse or a terrier?"

"Neither, my lord," was her cold reply.

"Are you obedient or scolding, then?"

"Meek as milk, my lord," she answered, lowering her gaze from his. Then she looked up at him from beneath thick, dark lashes. "About half the hours of the day, that is."

It was true. Her moods seemed as changeable as the weather on the moors. He tried not to smile at her words. He tried to sound as stern as a husband ought to. "I prefer you obedient."

"What man does not prefer women so? I will do all I can to please you," she added.

"About half the hours in the day?" He couldn't hide his smile this time.

Eleanor didn't know why she found the brute appealing all of a sudden; all he was doing was smiling. She should be surprised that he even knew how to smile. He had been nothing but ill tempered and surly since she'd met him the day before. Had it only been the day before? How could the world have changed so in such a short time? She found herself wanting to trace the outline of his lips, to explore the wonder of Stian of Harelby smiling.

But the smile disappeared before she gave in to the impulse. He loosened his hold on her as well. As he stepped away from her, he said, "I'll have all your obedience, wife."

"You deserve no less, my lord."

Stian heard no mockery in her words, nor did he see any in her expression, though he searched it carefully. "Stian," he told her at length. "Stian will do in private." He gave permission for this intimacy in hopes she would tell him her name. He was too proud to embarrass himself by asking. But, of course, she thought he knew what she was called. He should have known. Only a drunken fool would not know his wife's name.

Eleanor told herself it was ridiculous for her to take such delight in this informality from Stian. In Poitiers she had called many a young man by his given name. Custom lay lightly upon the ladies of the court at Poitiers. Here, in the wilds of Britain, she feared custom could be a heavy burden for a mere woman. Stian had lightened it a bit for her with the gift of his name.

"Stian," she said. "It is a fine name."

He blushed as red as his hair at her compliment and looked away, but she thought he was pleased. She did not think it would be wise to flatter this rough-mannered man over much, so she sidled by him and continued her unpacking.

No one had ever praised him for something so simple as his name. Stian told himself it was a foolish thing to be pleased with, but the pleasure stayed with him as he watched her move purposefully about the room. He wanted to complain at her for making herself so at home. He wanted to, but didn't. Instead, he found himself sitting on the edge of the bed, aghast at the notion that he was never to be alone again. He supposed he should be grateful she hadn't brought in a half dozen serving women to help her with the task of unpacking.

Eventually, she dragged the chair under the window. She sat down and took a piece of embroidery work out of a bag. Without another glance for him, she began stitching away on a piece of blue fabric. Stian told himself he should be glad she was ignoring him, that here was his chance to occupy his time as he chose without some interfering woman harping at him.

The only diversions that came to mind were prayer or taking a nap. Neither held any interest. Perhaps he should have bedded the woman after all.

"What's that?" he asked after he had watched her nimble fingers plying the needle for a while. He wondered how nimble those fingers would be when unfastening his clothes. Well, his father had sent them here to work on making a grandchild. Before she could answer his question, he said, "Never mind. Come here."

She left the work without a word of protest. "How may I serve you, my lo—Stian?"

The eagerness of her question killed his annoyance. He leaned back on the bed and leered up at her. "Entertain me," he ordered.

With a wide smile, she turned and snatched up the inlaid box. "Do you know the game of chess, my lo— Stian?"

"No," he lied, trusting she would set the board aside and think of some more pleasant amusement. He held his hand out to her to draw her down beside him on the bed.

"Then I will teach you," she declared, ignoring his gesture. " 'Tis played on the same board as draughts, but the pieces move differently."

She wanted to play games, did she? he thought as he sat back up. What sort of games? he wondered mistrustfully. He watched her set up the board on the bed between them from under lowered brows. She was proud and headstrong, he decided. The thought of humbling her pride a bit brought a wolfish smile to his lips.

"Teach me this game, then," he said. "Once I've learned the rules, we'll wager on it."

"A true knight would not strip a lady down to her chemise on a wager."

"Why not?" Stian asked.

" 'Tis most unseemly."

Stian glanced over his wife's small form. She was indeed wearing no more than her thin linen chemise. While the drawstring that held it closed over her shoulders was still tied, his next move should take care of untying the knot.

As for himself, the lass was a fine enough chess player to have relieved him of his surcote and tunic, but his father had taught him this game brought back to Christendom by crusaders very well. He did not hear her complaining that he was bare chested, though he did catch her studying more than the board upon occasion.

He reached out to move his knight, but her hand grasped his wrist before he could pick up the piece. As their eyes met over the chessboard set between them, she said, "Would you take every stitch of clothes from me?"

He grinned.

Her grip tightened as her eyes grew wide. "A true, kindly, gentle knight would not treat a lady so. The knights of Poitiers strive only to please ladies."

He had every intention of pleasing her once he had her naked. "I know not the customs of foreign knights," he told her. He shook off her grasping fingers and moved his chess piece. The maneuver took her pawn, endangering her king. "Strip."

She glared, blushed, and balled her fists in her lap instead of obeying. Stian didn't mind modesty, nor did he mind helping her undress.

"I think you have lied to me," she said as he undid the drawstring. "I think you have played this game before."

"Not like this," he said and pushed the chemise down to reveal her breasts.

"A true knight does not lie."

He knew not what she meant by a "true" knight. Had he not knelt in the chapel through a vigil night? Had he not been dubbed with the sword? Been given his spurs and warhorse by his father? Had he not fought the Scots to protect his liege's lands?

"Every man lies," he answered her. "That is why we have confessors."

She shook her head. Then she noticed that she was naked to the waist and raised her hands to cover herself. It was Stian's turn to grab her wrists.

"Don't."

Warmth rushed through her at his word, even though the room was cold and her skin was bare. It was as if his voice alone, commanding and possessive, roused the heat from inside her. Embarrassment fled, and Eleanor wondered what Lady Constance would do in such a situation, alone and unclothed with a man, on a bed. It took only a moment to realize how ridiculous her question was.

"I'm going to catch a chill this way," she said as her skin began to prickle with sensation.

Stian still held her by the wrists. His face was lit with amusement, and eagerness burned in his eyes. He drew her toward him, ignoring the chessboard.

As the ivory and ebony pieces scattered, he said, "I'll warm you."

There was no mockery in his amusement. His grip was tight, but not painful. He was large and alien, with his fiery Northman's hair and pale skin, but he did not seem ugly to her, as he had the day before.

"Aye," she told him as the tips of her breasts came in contact with his chest. "You are warm indeed, my lord."

"Stian," he reminded her as he released her hands. His arms slid around her.

The embrace made her feel small as his broad palms splayed across her back and waist. She put her hands on his shoulders as he bore her backward on the bed. The mattress was thick, covered with soft furs. It would have been deliciously comfortable but for the chess pieces on which she landed.

"Ow!"

"What?" Stian demanded as the girl began to squirm. When she tried to push him away, he pressed her down on her back as his quick temper flared. He loomed above her. "I'll not take no from you again."

She pushed on his shoulders, nails biting into his skin. "Move," she said as he held her down with one hand and began working her chemise off her hips with the other. "I'm not telling you no. It hurts."

Stian rolled away to kneel beside her. "What?" he roared.

The girl flinched away at his shout. As she scrambled to the other side of the bed, he saw black and white chessmen, jagged as stones, scattered where her back had rested. The room was growing dark as daylight faded, but there was enough light for him to see the look of fear on his wife's face. Chagrin at his too-quick temper drove the words from him. He didn't mean to frighten her. He hadn't meant to hurt her.

Grown dumb and clumsy with his own stupidity, he did reach for her, expecting her to run. She did not run, but she trembled at his touch.

Before he could think of a thing to do to gentle her fears, the door banged open and torchlight spilled across where they knelt on the disordered furs.

"Ah, good. I see you're going about the business," his father called cheerfully from the doorway.

A new wave of embarrassment, hot as iron in a forge, flooded through Stian. He whirled to face Roger of Harelby, but not before tossing a piece of his wife's discarded clothing to her so she could cover her nakedness.

"What do you want?" Stian asked his father as he got off the bed.

He had to fight hard to keep from grabbing up the sword that lay within reach of his hand. While it was Lord Roger's right to enter any room in his castle, Stian was angry enough to dispute that right. It took all his control to keep still and look the grinning older man in the face instead of erupting into violence.

"I've come to wish you well," his father said. He still had most of his teeth, and they glinted out of his bearded face in a bright smile. "How goes the project?"

"How am I to sire you grandsons if you don't leave me in peace?" Stian asked.

Roger laughed. Stian envied his father his easy, laughing way. Roger pointed toward the window. "You've had near all day, lad. It's time you ate, to keep up your strength. Get you dressed, and bring Lady Eleanor down to supper."

Stian forgot his annoyance, and his father's presence, as he heard the name. He turned around to look at his wife. She'd pulled up her chemise and was putting on her red underdress. All he saw for a few moments was the billowing of rich cloth. As her head finally emerged above the embroidered neckline of the dress, she raised her face to look at him. To Stian it seemed as if he was seeing her for the first time, dark eyed, dark haired, and lovely.

"Eleanor," he said. "Your name is Eleanor."

"You don't even know my name!"

The girl would have slammed the door behind her if he hadn't shouldered his way inside. She backed into the bedroom as he slammed the door himself, then leaned against it to peer blearily at her retreat. Servants had scurried out just as they'd come up the stairs from the hall, leaving the covers turned down and a thick hour candle burning on the table next to the bed.

"Eleanor," he said as the girl moved into the gold circle of candlelight.

Her eyes blazed with the same fury that had been in them all through dinner. She had turned her gaze on him rarely during the meal, but when she had he'd been scorched by the intensity of her unspoken rage. They had shared trencher and cup but no words while all eyes stared openly at them. The ale had been new, and he'd called for plenty of the strong, fresh drink. Eventually, his awareness of the watchers had grown fuzzy, though he hadn't been able to drink enough to take his attention off the woman beside him. She had left the table for the tower stairs as soon as the meal ended, long before coverfire was called to put an end to the day. He'd followed on her heels with a curse, and much lewd laughter ringing in his ears.

Now that they were alone he took a step toward her, staggering a bit, hands reaching, and said again, "Eleanor."

"Aye," she said bitterly, "now you know my name. But yesterday you did not. Or today."

It was true, so he nodded in acknowledgment. "What matter if I—"

She threw the folded chessboard at his head before he had a chance to finish. He ducked and lunged for her.

"What matter?" she shouted as she dashed around the bed to avoid his grasp. "What matter? How often do you bed strangers, my lord? Daily? Nightly?" He shrugged, and she threw something else. The slop pail, he supposed, when he heard crockery break against the wall behind him.

She had spent the day being meek enough, but he remembered now that yesterday she had bitten his tongue when he'd done nothing more than greet her with a kiss. "Vixen!" he snarled and dove across the bed to grasp her around the waist.

"Bastard!" she replied as her small fists pounded against his back. "You took me! You used me! You married me! And you didn't even know my name!"

Her words made no sense, nor did the sob that followed. She shouted other things, but Stian paid the words no mind. His head was full of ale and his hands were full of a well-made woman. She writhed against him, flailed at him. Her fighting did her no good; instead, it roused him and set fire to his blood.

When he kissed her he tasted tears. After a while, it was she who was kissing him, and, along with the anger and hurt, he tasted passion.

9

"*I don't think I've ever seen* anyone look so . . . well, used."

A giggle followed Edythe's words, and Eleanor adjusted the veil she'd fastened over her braids, hoping to hide a blush. She tried to ignore her sister altogether and concentrate on the Mass as rain pounded on the roof and windows of the small building. She pulled her cloak closer around her while rushlights and altar candles swayed in a cold draft, mixing shadows and smoke among the folk gathered for the daily service.

Father Hubert mumbled in sincere but nearly incoherent Latin as he lifted the host above his head. Not that it was easy to hear him over the conversations taking place among Lord Roger's household, crowded into the chapel. So Eleanor recited the correct words to herself and watched the young man's fine, long-fingered hands as he went through the sacred motions of the service. She wondered where he'd found the tattered cassock he was wearing.

"I think you were well pleasured last night," Edythe said as the communion began. She was obviously not going to let the subject alone. Eleanor sighed and looked at her sister.

Edythe said, "You look drugged with sex. And you walk differently this morning, with a sway to your hips. Like a woman."

"I can barely walk at all," Eleanor whispered. The reply escaped before she could stop it.

While Edythe giggled Eleanor looked around furtively to see if anyone else had overheard. Dame Beatrice was standing nearby, along with several other gentlewomen of the household. The chatelaine was seemingly lost in prayer after returning to her place from taking the host, but a pair of red-haired girls were openly staring at her and Edythe. The girls were so alike they had to be twins.

Eleanor couldn't help but wonder just who all these people were, even as she took a step away from them. Her natural curiosity was asserting itself at last, even while her body was still reminding her of all the attention her lord husband had paid to it last night.

As for her lord husband . . . She cast a bitter glance to the front of the chapel. She located him near the altar, talking to his yellow-haired friend. Stian stood with his hand casually resting on his dagger, his clothes rumpled, his hair uncombed—and her scratch marks marring his cheek.

"If you keep mauling him like that," Edythe whispered in her ear, "he'll beat you."

Eleanor ducked her head, then looked up at her fair sister through her lashes. "I think not," she murmured. "He liked it."

Edythe did not answer with a giggle, but with a

soft, throaty laugh. "As did you, I think." Edythe put her arm around her sister's shoulder. "Who would have thought the brightest wit of the Queen's court would have a taste for that rough barbarian?"

Who indeed? Eleanor wondered. As she looked at him in daylight, she felt nothing for Stian of Harelby but the same righteous anger that had set her to attack him the night before. She knew that she meant nothing to him, nothing at all. She was a body he eased his desire with, a nameless body. A faceless body, for he had blown out the candle and had her in the dark. He'd called her mouse and rat and vixen, so if he thought of her at all it was as vermin rather than as a woman. But in the dark an animal part of her had stirred. Her responses to him had been primitive, wild, as demanding as—

"Oh, dear." She crossed herself and vowed to make quick confession to Father Hubert. For surely the wanton feelings rushing through her were sinful to have in church. "He is a brute and I hate him," she added with a glare toward her husband. And, despite all that had passed between them the night before, she knew it to be true.

We shared passion, Stian thought as he caught a basilisk look from Eleanor out of the corner of his eye. His body tightened with wanting her, but he feigned indifference as he thought, *Passion will do, and nothing else matters.* He remembered how she'd bucked and clawed and bit—and how they had both enjoyed it. *I'll just sleep with my dagger by my side,* he thought with a feral smile, *until the wildcat is tamed and breeding.*

He felt her gaze still on him, hot and accusing. He couldn't understand why he felt as guilty as he did sated, so he turned eagerly to Lars when his cousin tugged on his sleeve.

"Lady Edythe shared her trencher with me at dinner last night. Did you notice how she smiled at me?"

Stian had not noticed. He had paid attention to no one at the high table last night but his own wife. He was surprised that his father had allowed anyone to take his place at the willow woman's side. "Oh?" he questioned. "How came you to such honor?"

"'Twas at the lady's own request." Lars preened, puffing out his chest and running his fingers through his long, fair hair. "Lady Edythe told me it is the custom of the Queen's court for ladies to choose a knight from their lord's household to be their special champion." He nudged Stian in the ribs. "She wants me."

Stian gave his cousin a cold look. His voice was equally cold and dangerously quiet when he said, "You speak of my father's wife."

"I know that well enough," Lars hastened to tell him. "The lady is all that is good and honorable, I swear by St. Olaf. She spoke only of the customs she knows, of courtesy and gentle knights. If she wishes me for her champion I'll gladly serve her like a knight from her precious Poitiers." He put a hand firmly on Stian's sword arm, then glanced longingly at the golden-haired beauty standing serenely beside Eleanor. "Who would not do anything for a smile from a woman like that?"

In truth, Stian thought, *who would not?* He gave Lars a nod in reply while his gaze sought out his young stepmother. Once his attention was caught by Edythe, it was hard to notice that Eleanor was standing at her side. Edythe was all that was light and grace; nothing of earth, like her small, dark sister.

Stian was glad that today he could look at Edythe and feel nothing but a faint trace of longing for her burning inside him. Even that, he hoped, would soon go away, for she was strictly forbidden to him by all the laws of God and man.

He wanted to be able to appreciate the beauty who moved among them without any taint of lust coloring his observance of her. He had no idea how to idolize without touching, for Edythe was certainly no Madonna come down to walk on earth. Perhaps such detachment was what Eleanor meant when she spoke of true knights. Perhaps there were lessons to be learned from the foreign court where the sisters had been reared.

"Tell me," he said to his cousin, turning them both firmly toward the altar and away from the tempting sight of Edythe, "what did you learn about courtesy and gentle knighthood?"

Eleanor saw how Stian looked at her sister and felt no more than a small stab of pain pierce her heart. She knew the look on his face well, and she did not blame him or Edythe for it. All she could do was sigh.

Her feeling sorry for herself was interrupted as Edythe said, "Lars is in love with me."

She had never heard such cool calculation in her sister's voice before. As the Mass ended, she watched Lord Roger gather up Stian, Lars, and several older men and leave the chapel. She watched them go as she tried to get over her surprise at Edythe's matter-of-fact words.

Finally, she looked at the softly smiling Edythe. "Oh?" she asked.

Edythe nodded. She bent her head close so they would not be overheard by the women who moved past them to return to the keep. "I've noticed that Stian listens overmuch to his cousin," Edythe told her. "So I will set myself to taming Lars, which will help you tame my lord's great red lion of a son."

Tame Stian? By all the saints, that was an impossible task. Eleanor nearly laughed at the very notion of civilizing the brute she'd been wed to. Still, she couldn't help but smile and hug her sister tight, grateful for Edythe's efforts, even if they were destined to come to naught.

"You are so good to me," she whispered as they held each other close for a moment.

Edythe touched her cheek. "We must care for each other in this barbaric place. Perhaps, in the end, we can make it a little like our home."

"Aye," Eleanor agreed reluctantly. "Perhaps we can."

Edythe gave her a quick kiss on the cheek. "All will be well. Now," she said, stepping away from Eleanor's embrace, "I must see to my lord, for this day will be long and hard on him."

Eleanor wondered why the day would be hard on Lord Roger as she watched Edythe hurry away. Then she remembered mention being made of something called a shire court. She would have to find out just what that was. There was so much about the doings of Harelby she needed to find out. She also wondered if she should make sure Stian broke his fast and washed his face—or whatever nursemaid tasks were considered wifely.

"Ha," she concluded after only a very brief contemplation. "I'll see to such wifely duties when wolves fly to the moon."

Instead of returning immediately to the hall, she

approached Father Hubert to make confession of all
the sins she'd managed to commit in only a day or so
of marriage. She feared that, for herself, matrimony
was not a holy state at all.

"A word with you, Dame Beatrice?"

The chatelaine turned so quickly Eleanor had to
jump backward to avoid a collision. Not that her
moving out of Dame Beatrice's way did her any good.
She only ended up bumping into a servant who was
busy raking up old rushes from the hall floor. Eleanor
ignored the laughter from a group of men-at-arms
who loitered by the hearth.

"What do you want?"

Eleanor contrived to get her temper under control
in the time it took her to right herself. She managed a
smile as she turned back toward the chatelaine. It was
brittle, but it was a smile. She had not come here to
make an enemy, despite the woman's impatient hostility. Dame Beatrice had stepped up onto the dais
while Eleanor was occupied with the servant, so now
she had to look up to address the woman who was
already several inches taller. Eleanor greatly misliked
such a maneuver on the woman's part, but she chose
to believe that Dame Beatrice had merely moved to
get out of the sweeper's way.

"What do you want?" Dame Beatrice repeated, her
tone even more annoyed this time.

Eleanor gestured at the bustle around them as the
hall was prepared for the arrival of many visitors.
"Father Hubert told me people will soon be arriving
for something he called a shire court. Can I be of any
help? I hope that I—"

"Help?" the woman cut her off sharply before she could finish. Dame Beatrice bent forward. Squinting, she looked Eleanor square in the face and gave a caustic laugh. "What do you know but embroidery and lute playing, little girl?"

"I—"

"Roger had no business bringing court-reared women to Harelby. What's a border castle to do with ornaments like the pair of you? What use will you be in a siege? You're nothing but a pair of extra mouths taking up warm places by the fire that would be better suited to proper women."

Eleanor fought hard to keep her temper even as she was stunned into silence by the woman's attack. It was true she was a courtier, which meant she was used to viciousness being disguised with honeyed words. Dame Beatrice's blunt statements were hurtful, but almost bracingly refreshing. Which didn't make Eleanor any less tempted to bite Beatrice's work-reddened finger when it was shaken under her nose.

"Dame—" she began, only to be cut off once again.

"What use will you be when the Scots next besiege Harelby? Know you how to nurse the sick or deliver a babe? Do you know a kitchen garden from a midden? Know you the reeve from the hayward?" Dame Beatrice rattled the ring of keys she wore on her belt. "Keep your sister company in the bower, girl, and leave the running of this castle to me."

"Happily will I leave the castle to you," Eleanor answered.

As the chatelaine was so eager to point out, she was court reared. She could speak gentle and fair to a princess who slapped her for no better reason than that she was closer than the servant who had spilled the wine. So she could speak fair and gentle to a chatelaine who feared losing her power to inexperienced outsiders. She could deal pleasantly with anyone, she thought, except Stian of Harelby.

"It is true I know little of English ways. I would but learn from you if you will allow it, Dame Beatrice," she added as the chatelaine began to turn from her.

Her conciliatory words brought nothing but a sneer to the chatelaine's attractive face. "I've no time to teach a grown woman how to run a household."

"I did not mean—"

Beatrice waved toward the tower stair. "Be gone, girl. Keep to the bower with your sister and her ladies and out of my way."

Eleanor decided it was just as well to give up the field to this intransigent woman. She sighed, tucked her hands—hands that were balled into tight, tense fists—into her sleeves, and walked past the snickering guardsmen toward the stairs.

As she went she heard Dame Beatrice complain bitterly, "I told Stian he would do well to marry Nicolaa Brasey. The lad should have followed his own mind and gotten Roger's permission afterward."

The woman's rancor scraped Eleanor's already raw senses. Fresh pain squeezed at her heart for no reason she could understand. She wanted to run away.

Instead, she turned before going up the stairs and said, "How could Stian follow his own mind, Dame Beatrice? He doesn't have one."

"Nothing is going right today. I've jumbled up the pattern."

Eleanor threw down her embroidery and looked at

the half circle of women sitting beneath the window in Lord Roger's bedroom. Along with Edythe, there was Blanche, the gentlewoman they had brought with them to Harelby. There were also the red-haired twin sisters of one of Lord Roger's neighbors, seventeen-year-olds named Morwina and Fiona. The girls had been placed in Dame Beatrice's care, she'd been told, not long before her and Edythe's arrival. Eleanor had noticed furtive looks from the pair, but had yet to hear a word out of them. She only knew their names because she'd heard Dame Beatrice address them the day before.

Eleanor did not like not knowing things, such as names and functions and all the doings wherever she found herself. Since she'd come to Harelby she'd had little time to indulge her curiosity. Through all the tumult of the last few days she'd hardly had time to breathe, let alone ask questions. But what questions she had asked had met with lies from the castellan, rebuffs from the chatelaine, sweet inanity from the chaplain, and surly silence from her husband. She felt totally out of control of her life. Everything just seemed to be going on around her while she spent her time being tossed about by her husband. She was finally at the point where she thought she was going to burst from the frustration.

So, as all eyes turned to her when she threw down her work, she told off the litany of her ignorance. "I know not what a shire court might be or what guests are due to arrive. I know not the workings of Harelby, or even more than a few names of the household. I know not who will be our lord's friend or foe in the company. Or the duties expected from the ladies of the house. I know nothing of use," she added as everyone stared. "And," she added, "most annoyingly,

I know nothing of this Nicolaa Brasey that Sir Stian might have married!"

The twins bent their heads together and giggled and whispered. Eleanor couldn't help but be reminded of herself and Edythe during happier times. She exchanged a smile with her sister, who no doubt saw the resemblance as well.

"Nicolaa Brasey," one of the girls—Eleanor had no way of knowing which was which—finally found the bravery to say, "is the widow of Hugh Brasey. She holds land bordering Harelby for her son, Bertran. For now. Poor Bertran," she added.

Before Eleanor could ask what she meant, the other twin spoke up. "Courts are when the sheriff and all the knights of the shire and villagers gather to hear lawsuits and such."

"And judge those who break forest laws," the other twin added. "Bertran—"

"But what about Nicolaa Brasey?" Edythe cut in. "What do you know of this lady who will soon be our guest?"

Eleanor squirmed at the teasing look her sister gave her. She was already regretting bringing up the woman's name. Why should she care if the Widow Brasey was Stian's long-time mistress and dearest love? It was nothing to her. The priests were right; curiosity was a wicked flaw in a woman.

"Well," Morwina or Fiona began after the girls had giggled and cast furtive looks her way for a while, "Nicolaa's marriage rights are in the gift of Lord Roger, but she's managed to evade every suitor he's presented to her."

"She's much sought after," the other twin hurried on. "Even though she must be at least twenty-two or three."

Eleanor had heard as much as she wanted about this Nicolaa Brasey. It didn't matter. Learning about Harelby was far more important than gossiping about a neighbor.

She stood and said, "I left some embroidery thread in my room."

"I'll fetch it for you," Blanche offered.

Eleanor waved the woman back in her seat as she started to rise. "'Tis no trouble to fetch it myself. I'll be right back," she said and left, not intending to come back at all.

But when she reached her room she found that Stian was there before her and her mind was immediately set on flight. He stood by the bed and watched her under lowered brows as she sidled toward the chest by the wall. He didn't say anything; he just looked at her. Finally, she noticed that his expression held as much curiosity as it did hostility. She wondered what he was thinking. Instead of hurriedly snatching the thread and fleeing, she found herself looking at him as well.

Stian was stripped to the waist, and his dirt-crusted braccos clung in damp patches to his thighs. His hair and chest were wet with sharp-smelling sweat. His sword and a heavily quilted tunic lay discarded on the bed. He looked as if he had spent the whole day practicing his skill at arms. Not only did he look sweaty, he looked tired.

After a few moments, Eleanor obeyed her impulse and turned decisively back toward the door. She spotted a servant on the stairway and called out, "Fetch a tub and hot water for my lord's bath."

When she turned back, Stian's grimy hand was reaching for one of her precious books.

"No!"

She rushed forward to snatch the book from him. Stian only laughed and held it out of her reach. He pushed her, so that she stumbled back to sit on the bed.

"Stay!" he ordered.

She jumped up. "That's mine!"

"Sit!"

She did, unable to resist the crack of command in his voice. "But—"

"What's this?" he asked as he opened the heavy leather cover.

"Could you at least wash your hands?" she pleaded. "That's a book, not a wineskin."

Sir Stian peered at the first page of the book and said, "*The Dove's Neck-Ring.*" He looked at her. "What sort of book is this?"

Eleanor was struck speechless for a moment. He had pronounced the title in Latin far purer than Father Hubert's. Then she burst out, "You *can* read!"

His expression turned into a deep, familiar glower. "'Tis no sin. For a man." He balanced the book on the palm of his hand as he continued to glare. "But for a woman . . ."

Eleanor would not be cowed. "All the women of Poitiers read," she told him. She folded her arms defiantly before her. "We read and we write poetry and sing the songs of the troubadours. Poitiers is the center of all that is civilized, noble, and fair."

And she was homesick, terribly, terribly homesick. Stian could see it in her eyes, hear it in the catch in her voice. His own annoyance vanished at his realization of just how unhappy the girl was in this strange, foreign place.

He set the book gently on her lap. "This is yours," he agreed as she cradled it close to her breast. "But what is it?"

Before she could answer, the door opened. A trio of servants came in. One carried buckets of steaming water and cloths for washing and drying. The other two brought in a shallow bathing tub. Stian gave Eleanor a grateful look for the hot bath, for he had worked hard training the men today and his muscles ached. He stripped off the rest of his clothes while the servants went about filling the tub, and Eleanor carefully didn't watch him.

"What is the book?" he asked again after the servants were gone. He settled onto his knees in the tub; in this position the water just covered his hips. He reached for the washcloth, but, much to his surprise, Eleanor crossed the room and picked it up before him. It was his turn to avoid watching her as she dipped the cloth in the water and carefully wrung it out across his shoulders.

The wet heat was a blessing raining down on his tired body. The hands that began to scrub his back were even more blessed.

"Eleanor?" he said after the steady, massaging pressure of her hands had soothed away all the day's cares.

"Yes?" the answer came eventually. She sounded shy.

"Is this the custom?" he asked. "In Poitiers?"

After a long hesitation, she answered, "It is custom for men and women to treat each other with courtesy, my lord—Stian."

"So Lars tells me."

"Lars?"

"Your sister has spoken of the ways of the knights of Poitiers to my cousin."

And Lars had spoken to him. At length. He thought that perhaps his cousin had been drunk, or too mad with desire to hear properly, for much of what he said Lady Edythe told him seemed like utter nonsense. Perhaps Eleanor's explanations would make some sense of this so-called "Court of Love" and its complicated rules.

She sighed. "The knights of Poitiers are all that is good and gentle."

Stian sighed as well. He began to fear that Eleanor's explanations would not make any sense either. "Men don't go around scrubbing naked women in Poitiers, do they?" he asked suspiciously.

She gave a soft breath of laughter. "I know not what ladies might do with their lovers and husbands, but no one has ever given me a bath."

"Good."

"It is the custom for ladies to bathe their guests," she explained. "And husbands and lovers, of course. It is considered a mark of honor."

Stian arched like a cat under her touch. " 'Tis a mark I like."

Husbands *and* lovers? Were they not one and the same? he wondered. He remembered the way Lars looked at Edythe, tried to forget the way Lars looked at Edythe, and decided not to ask any questions about some of the customs of Poitiers just now. The point was to learn how to control improper lust for Edythe, for the sake of his soul and the peace of the household.

His eyes were closed as he reveled in the twin delights of hot water and Eleanor's touch. Now, here was proper lust, or a pleasant prelude to it. He found himself reveling in the sound of her voice as well, deep for a woman's, with an accent that made him think of sunlight and music. He liked her voice, he decided.

He opened his eyes to look at her when she moved to kneel in front of him. As she leaned forward to soak the cloth in the water again, he took it from her. He could not deal with the idea of a woman washing him all over as though he were a babe. She looked embarrassed about it herself, as though perhaps she had not had much practice at this particular custom in her beloved Poitiers.

"I'll finish this," he told her. He glanced toward the bed, where the book lay waiting. He had not forgotten her precious book despite this pleasant diversion. "I'll wash, you read to me."

Much to his surprise, she gave him a delighted smile and hurried to do his bidding.

As she picked up the book, he added, "But only if it tells of the conduct of *true* knights."

She tilted her head thoughtfully to one side for a moment. "It does," she said. "For it speaks of attraction and devotion between men and women."

"And what do 'true' knights need to know of such things?" he asked skeptically. "Knights need to know horses and swords."

The eager smile she turned on him was as full of sunlight as her voice. "Why, these gentle emotions are the most important things in the world!"

He was doubtful, but didn't say so. "Read to me then. And teach me all these rules Lars says chivalrous, properly behaved men are supposed to know."

10

"By the rood, it's good to see you!"

Stian returned his cousin Malcolm's hardy embrace and asked, "What the devil are you doing here?"

Malcolm held him by the shoulders and grinned. "Don't you remember? I'm English this year."

"Jesu, did the border shift that much in the last war?"

Malcolm gave a firm nod. "It's a fluid, almost imaginary thing, this border between the Scots and the English. I know not who to bow to between one day and the next—or who's collecting my taxes."

"To think the English would win a war just to get you," Stian said in mock disgust.

"Aye. Me, and the ransom for the King." Malcolm leaned close and whispered, "Rumor runs high that your father received a share of that bounty." Malcolm's gaze shifted briefly around the crowded hall before he went on. "There are some who resent his loyalties, and covet his gold."

Eleanor didn't understand what the men were saying. Her head ached from lack of sleep, and it wasn't helped by the noise in the hall. Never mind hearing Mass or attending the opening of the shire court; she wanted only to break her fast and retreat to the silence of the bower. Stian had kept her awake through most of the night with his questions. He'd paid no mind to the dinner hour, calling only for some cheese and bread as the evening drew on. He hadn't even shown any interest in bedding her.

He'd wanted to be read to and to talk instead. Talk. She hadn't thought the man capable of more than grunts the day before. And in truth, he had strung no more than five words together at a time through most of the long night's conversation. But he had talked. Now, here he was chatting amiably away with a new, blonde-pelted brute in what she guessed to be the native language of these border lands.

This stranger was shaggy of hair and beard, dressed in leather, chainmail, and roughly woven wool. He was as tall as Stian, and his eyes were as blue. Though he was thinner of lip and sharper of nose, there was a distinct resemblance. If anyone would dare to give him a shearing, he might even be handsome.

She was surprised when Stian remembered her presence at his side long enough to say in Norman French, "My cousin, Malcolm Erskine of Ballyhane."

She looked up at him questioningly. "How many cousins do you have?"

He gestured around the room. She followed his movement and noticed many a red- and gold-haired man and woman in the crowd around the fire and the trestle tables set up for breakfast. "I see," she said.

"Malcolm's my father's sister's son. Lars is cousin from my mother's family."

He pointed at a particularly surly-looking young man who was speaking to Dame Beatrice. This stranger's hair was even thicker than Malcolm's, and the bright color of new copper. He sent an ugly look Stian's way, but was forestalled from any action by Dame Beatrice putting a hand on his arm.

"That," Stian said with no great enthusiasm, "is David Kerr of Ayrfell, kinsman of my aunt Beatrice. There are many more here, besides, that I call kin." Switching his attention back to Malcolm, he added, "This is Eleanor."

While she was still registering pleased surprise that her husband remembered her name, Malcolm switched easily out of his own barbarous tongue to say in not too heavily accented Norman, "So this is the bride I heard tell of. Too bad I missed seeing the wedding night. I'll have to make up for lost time."

The next thing Eleanor knew, she was picked up by the waist and a firm kiss was planted on her lips by this new cousin.

"Careful," she heard Stian say, "she bites."

Malcolm's chainmail rattled as he dropped her to her feet as quickly as he'd snatched her up. Malcolm gave a deep laugh. "And scratches, too, from the looks of you."

"Aye," Stian said shortly.

Malcolm slapped Stian on the shoulder. "Lord, lad, sorry I am to have missed the wedding feast."

"Where were you?" Stian asked as he drew her to his side.

She would have excused herself and gladly left them to their talk, but Stian's hold on her waist was tight, and it was not unpleasant to be sheltered in the warmth of his embrace in the early morning coolness of the hall.

"Hunting reivers," Malcolm said. "Some damn Scots came over the border and burned one of my villages."

"That might explain why Ayrfell missed the wedding as well," Stian said quietly.

Malcolm gave a slight nod. "It might, but I've no proof. I had to hunt the raiders down and get back my cows. I got back the cows, but—" Malcolm looked suspiciously around the hall. "I never did find out exactly who the bastards were."

"So there's no one you can accuse here in the hall."

Malcolm acknowledged the warning in Stian's voice. "Nay. I'll keep the peace of God while the court's in session."

"So will we all."

This new voice belonged to Lord Roger. He came up to them with a smile on his face. He looked handsome and vibrant, but Eleanor saw the serious look in his eyes. He wore a fine scarlet surcote and a gold chain of office hung around his neck. There were jewels on his sword hilt and heavy rings on his fingers. He looked every bit the great lord.

Eleanor found that it bothered her that Stian's simple attire did not compare well to his father's impressive appearance. She could only take some comfort in knowing that Stian had at least run a comb through his hair, while his cousin Malcolm might have a fox den in his tangled mane for all she could tell.

"I bid you good morning, daughter," he said as he took Eleanor's hand.

Stian loosed his hold on her waist as Lord Roger

drew her toward the table. Stian and Malcolm followed close on their heels. Eleanor noticed that by moving the group to the dais there was no chance of any conversation being heard by anyone else.

"What's Ayrfell want?" Stian asked as they reached the table.

Lord Roger paused to offer a cup of wine to Eleanor, then said, "Trying to talk Beatrice out of her dower lands again." Stian gave a contemptuous snort as Lord Roger went on. "He claims he should be named her guardian and the lands that came to us through my brother should be returned to the Kerrs. He plans to plead his case before the shire court."

"The court's not likely to find in his favor," Malcolm said.

Stian said, "Aunt Beatrice won't go back to the Kerrs."

Lord Roger looked over at his sister-in-law. "I don't know," he said thoughtfully. "It seems to me she's been unhappy of late, though I can't think why."

Eleanor nearly choked on her wine. He didn't know why his chatelaine was unhappy? Was the man blind? Probably, she supposed. Men were generally blind to the lives of women. She wondered if she should try to explain, but kept silent. It wasn't her place to speak, but she would ask Edythe to explain to her husband about Beatrice. Even though she had had no kindness from the woman, Eleanor did feel some charity toward her.

The men went on talking about the cases to be called before the shire court, frequently lapsing into the language she supposed was Scots. Eleanor ate bread and sipped wine while she listened. When she couldn't understand she turned her attention toward the crowded room, looking for women from outside the household. Which one, she wondered, was Nicolaa Brasey?

Eventually, her attention settled on a well-dressed woman who stood by one of the trestle tables. She had a serving woman with her and a half-grown boy by her side. She wore a cape and was modestly veiled, but Eleanor could make out a fine-boned, attractive face in the circle of her wimple. Father Hubert went up to talk to her, and the woman lowered her eyes and clasped her hands before her when she answered him.

Modest, Eleanor thought, *attractive*, and *pious. I hate her already.*

She looked away from Nicolaa Brasey and found Roger gazing at her. "Yes, my lord?"

He put his hand on her shoulder. His touch was gentle and affectionate. "My lady Edythe is not well today," he told her. "Might I ask a favor?"

"Anything, my lord," she responded quickly, as her heart sank. She already knew what he wanted. She was about to miss whatever excitement this day promised.

"Edythe craves your company."

Eleanor sighed, but there was no way she could deny her sister her request, or anything for that matter. Ah, well, it wasn't as if the day held the prospect of a tournament or a competition of troubadours. She was disappointed, but she managed a smile. "Of course, my lord."

As she turned to leave, Stian put his hand on her arm for a moment. He seemed reluctant to let her go; she thought she saw a look of hunger in his eyes, adding confusion to her disappointment. Whatever he might have said was lost as his father spoke to him

and he turned his attention to the Lord of Harelby.
Eleanor cast one more unhappy glance at Nicolaa
Brasey, then made her way toward the stairs.

"I thought you said you were ill?"

Edythe set aside her sewing with a laugh. "Of
course I'm not ill. When have I ever been ill?"
Sunlight slanted in through the window across from
where she sat, illuminating her beauty with gold light.
She looked like a smiling angel, bright eyed and rosy
cheeked; her gold hair was spread around her like a
mantle while Blanche worshipfully brushed it.

It was true, Eleanor realized as she came to sit on
the chest at the foot of the bed, across from Edythe.
"You never catch a chill or a fever. But if you're not
ill, why aren't you going to attend the shire court?"

Edythe laughed again. "Because my lord told me
all about it. It will be nothing but peasants and
foresters quibbling over their petty rights in a language we don't even understand."

"It wouldn't hurt us to learn it," Eleanor said.

Edythe waved her comment away. "We'd be bored."

"Probably. But everyone will want to meet the new
Lady of Harelby. You should put in an appearance."

"Oh, no!" Edythe gestured Blanche away and
leaned forward. "Dame Beatrice would not like that
at all," she confided. "It is she who is used to presiding among the guests at these courts."

"But you are the lady here. Dame Beatrice must
acknowledge it sometime."

"And she will," Edythe said in her calm, reasonable
way. "But she's still bitter over our coming. I'd rather
give her her head for a while, let her preside where

she can. It will do my standing no harm, and she will not be given offense."

"I see." Eleanor nodded her agreement.

It amazed her how being married had changed Edythe. She had always been kind and thoughtful; now it appeared she was also learning cunning. First in the matter of taming Lars, and now she'd turned her thoughts to Dame Beatrice.

"How very wise you are, Edythe. You are right. Anything for peace in a household." She fetched the embroidery she'd left behind in the bower the day before and took a seat under the window. "I'll stay, of course, because it would do well for the heir's wife to stay out of her way as well."

Edythe put her hand over Eleanor's. "I thought it best. Besides, I do crave your company, sweet sister."

One of the twins came in while Edythe spoke. She walked over to them and said, "I asked Nicolaa Brasey to the bower, as you wished, my lady, but she said she would spend the day with her son instead. Poor Bertran," she added.

"You've said that before," Eleanor snapped. She didn't know why hearing the Widow Brasey's name mentioned made her waspish. "What's the matter with poor Bertran?"

"Nothing's the matter with him," the girl answered. "He's to go on trial."

Eleanor recalled the boy she'd seen with the widow, and how worried the woman had looked. "On trial? What is the lad accused of?"

"Breaking forest law."

Before Eleanor could ask for further explanation, the other twin came in, her arms full of freshly picked wildflowers.

"From Lars," she said through a giggle. "For Lady Edythe."

"Lars?" everyone but Edythe said at once.

Edythe said, "How sweet."

The twin with the flowers went off in another fit of giggling. By the time she got herself under control, Blanche had taken the bouquet from her and was sorting through them.

"He must have gone far afield to find all these," the gentlewoman said. "For spring's not so far along that there's fields of flowers waiting for the honeybees."

"Or would-be lovers," Eleanor added in a whisper to her sister.

Edythe's face was alight with pleased amusement. "Well, hunting wildflowers gave the lad something to do. Though I'm sure Dame Beatrice would rather he was hunting rabbits."

"At least we can dry the petals for the summer rushes," Eleanor added as Blanche set about finding a container for the flowers.

She noticed that the twins were giddy at the notion of someone being given flowers. They whispered and giggled together by the door. Edythe was, of course, quite used to it and perfectly calm, receiving them as her due. She didn't even bother giving the blooms a close inspection. Eleanor knew the proper way to acknowledge such gifts was with feigned indifference. She felt no jealousy, just wry amusement at the image of the likes of Lars hunting through the wilds for delicate blossoms for his lady fair.

She laughed. "I can't imagine Stian doing such a thing."

"I'm sure it's only a matter of time," Edythe answered, placid and assured.

Eleanor laughed again. What an odd notion to contemplate. Flowers from Stian, indeed! "There will certainly be wolves on the moon before that day dawns," she told Edythe.

But, still, it was a pleasant notion.

"You've been sober too long," Lars complained as he threw his arm around Stian's shoulder. "You're too serious when you're sober."

Stian grunted in reply and took a swallow from the drinking horn Lars had been holding. The wine was sharp and bitter, near the dregs of the barrel and very potent. He passed the horn back to Lars.

Serious. So he was, Stian knew, but when he was drunk he hated himself, the world, and everyone in it. There were only two things that made him get drunk: when his father wasn't home, and when he was. When Roger wasn't home Stian found little to interest him. When Roger was home Stian often found life far too interesting. So far, Roger hadn't been home long enough to irritate him into a serious bout of drinking. Of course, now he didn't have just his father to irritate him—there was also Eleanor.

Eleanor. He evaded Lars's comradely arm to take a look around the hall. Where was Eleanor? It was near the dinner hour. He'd been wanting Eleanor all day. If his father hadn't sent her up to the bower he and Eleanor could have broken their fasts, briefly greeted their guests, then spent a good part of the morning rolling about on the bed. He'd been looking forward to spending the morning bedding his wife.

Instead, he'd had to spend the day in company with his quarrelsome cousins, his needs unsatisfied.

He'd had to keep the peace between them and their men when he was as itchy for some sort of release as any of them. Malcolm and David had finally ended up with a pair of willing servant girls.

Rather than join their sport, he and Lars had gone out to the bailey to attend the court session. They'd acted as jurors in one of the minor land disputes. The afternoon had seemed to drag on forever, but at least the weather had held fair.

Lars had spent much of the time looking up at the bower windows as though he might catch a glimpse of his lady in her chamber. Never mind that his lady belonged to Lord Roger. And Lord Roger noticed.

"Lars," Stian said now, "you're a fool."

"But I'm not sober," the Dane replied. "Nor should you be," he added and called for more wine.

"And what's this I hear about flowers?" he added, quietly, for he did not mean to tease and there were many people about who could overhear. "Morwina told me you picked flowers."

Lars shook his head as he drew Stian toward the hearth, where Dame Beatrice and many of the guests stood waiting the call to dinner. "What? No. I didn't pick any flowers." Stian thought Lars's voice was louder than he intended, for all eyes turned their way. "Who ever heard of a man picking flowers?"

"Then it's not true the—"

"I sent your squire to pick them."

"My squire?" Try as he might, Stian's voice rose as well. "You sent Ranald to—"

"Lady Edythe said women like such gifts. It's the sort of thing *gentle* men do."

"It's the sort of thing Queen Eleanor taught Poitevan men to do," his father said as he joined them by the fire. "Sing songs and spout poems and make posies. Women like it." There was derisive laughter from some of the men, until Roger added, "The Poitevan knights still fought hard enough when King Henry decided to put an end to his wife's rebellion. There's nothing wrong with gentle pursuits," he went on. "In moderation, of course. No harm to pleasing the womenfolk in some things." He smiled upon the attentive crowd. "We please them, and they make life more comfortable for us."

David of Ayrfell stepped forward. His face was set in its usual scowl. "Is that what you want, then?" he asked Roger. "A soft life?"

Roger tilted his head and gave a mild answer. "A bit of comfort is not such a bad thing. Nothing wrong with soft pillows and bright tapestries—"

"Or a beautiful new wife," someone interrupted.

Roger laughed, and many folk joined with him. "Aye," he agreed. "It's good to have a young wife to lie on those soft pillows with. Her sweet body is the finest luxury I possess. Far better than a new tapestry or silver plate."

Stian moved away as the laughter this time grew louder, accompanied by bawdy and lewd comments. He shook his head, unable to understand why his father would speak about such a private thing as his marriage. It seemed Roger was not only willing to boast about what went on in his bedroom, but to allow others to joke about it as well. Stian just hoped the joking didn't turn his way. What he did with Eleanor was no one's business but theirs.

Dame Beatrice didn't appear to approve of the conversation either, for she soon announced that the meal was ready, though it was earlier than the household normally sat down to dinner. Stian turned to a servant to send upstairs for his wife, but his aunt stopped him with a hand on his arm.

"What?"

She favored him with her sweetest smile, the one she used when she wanted him on his best behavior. "Nicolaa has had a most worrisome day. This waiting for Bertran's trial is hard on her."

Stian glanced at the woman who lingered by the fire. Her hands were held out to it for warmth; her expression was closed. "Aye," Stian agreed with his aunt. "Where's Bertran?"

"I sent him to eat with the squires." She turned her smile on him again. "I thought Nicolaa might sup with you."

Stian looked up at the two seats left open on the bench to the right of his father's high-backed chair. The lady of the house's chair was also empty, but Stian supposed it would be improper for Nicolaa to sit next to the man who was the chief judge in her son's trial tomorrow. Nicolaa was a friend, she was a guest, and Eleanor was nowhere in sight. Eleanor would even approve; such hospitable gestures were the way *gentle* men behaved.

"Very well," Stian said to his waiting aunt. "It will please me greatly to share my trencher with the lady."

"We really ought to go down for the feast."

Edythe continued to rummage through her jewelry box. "Tomorrow. We'll let Beatrice head the table this one last night."

Eleanor didn't want to let Beatrice head the table. Actually, she didn't care what the chatelaine did. She wanted her supper. And she wanted—well, she wanted to be out of this room and exploring the little world that was Harelby. She'd never been so restless before. She wanted to know the doings of the shire.

She wanted to know the doings of Nicolaa Brasey.

"I'm hungry," she said, and started to pace.

Edythe merely looked up from sorting her jewelry to ask, "Have you seen my garnet brooch?"

"No," Eleanor answered. Was Stian with Nicolaa? Not that it mattered, of course. But was he?

"I can't remember when I wore it last." Edythe sighed deeply. "It's such a pretty thing. A gift from Renard d'Anesye. Do you remember him? Such a handsome lad."

"I remember him."

Stian was not a handsome lad. He was too big and long-limbed and rangy. His hair was impossible, and she'd never liked men with mustaches.

She turned toward Edythe. "Perhaps you lost the brooch in the hall—at table or among the rushes."

"Perhaps."

Edythe looked particularly lovely in the soft glow of evening candlelight. Lovely and dreamy, as if her mind were no more on a conversation about a lost brooch than Eleanor's was. Her gaze settled on the bouquet of wildflowers. She'd been acting all day as if Lars had sent her the first roses of summer.

"Shall I go look for your brooch?" Eleanor asked. "It would be no trouble."

"Would you? How sweet. Yes, run along."

Edythe waved toward the door, and Eleanor needed no more urging.

Once beyond the shielding of the thick door, Eleanor could hear the revelry even though the hall was two stories below. The stone stairs were narrow, but well enough lit by rushlights that she had no qualms about hurrying down them with her skirts hiked up around her ankles.

The tower stairs were directly across from the raised dais where the high table sat, so Eleanor had no trouble seeing who sat in her place when she came down the stairs. Of course, by the time she could see Nicolaa Brasey sharing a trencher with her husband it was too late for her to flee back to her room without being seen. So she schooled her features to neutrality, stiffened her spine, and slowed her speed to a decorous pace.

Stian's gaze was on his lady of the evening, so he probably took no note of her regal entrance, but she told herself it mattered not. What mattered was that anyone who might care to notice would see her indifference to the situation. There was less chance for gossip when a wife took her husband's dealings with his concubines with good grace.

She wished Dame Beatrice had never told her about Stian wanting to marry Nicolaa Brasey.

Stian hated David Kerr of Ayrfell, who was seated on his left. He'd hated him so long and for so many things, both petty and great, that the hatred was too ingrained for him to outright kill the man. Ayrfell's presence was like the familiar ache of an old wound on a rainy day. It was something he was used to and didn't think he could do anything about.

They were of an age, Malcolm and David and himself. All three of them were eldest sons of border lords, though Malcolm and David had come into their inheritances already. Being cousins, they'd spent much of their youth together. Along with Lars, they'd learned the profession of warfare, the managing of estates, the ways of women, and the ways of the hunt.

Loyalties shifted along the border, so sometimes their families were on different sides. In large matters the lords of Harelby always supported the interests of the kings of England. In small, everyday things, supporting one's neighbors often took precedence, and invisible borders disappeared. It had never mattered to Stian and Malcolm which side they fought on on any particular day; they were always fast friends. David of Ayrfell was no man's friend. He was a quarrelsome braggart with more temper than sense. He would argue with any man, just for the sake of his own contrariness. While Stian preferred to hide his mind in silence, Ayrfell was eager to share his vitriolic opinions with all who would listen.

It made having him for a dinner partner less than pleasant.

Stian ignored him through most of the meal, though Ayrfell grumbled loudly and often about everything and nothing. He had little to say to Nicolaa, either, but she seemed to prefer her own thoughts to any words from him.

Eventually, it became impossible to ignore Ayrfell when he grabbed Stian by the arm and demanded, "Who does that wench think she is, the Queen of England?"

Stian followed the man's gaze to discover Eleanor coming slowly down the stairs.

Before he could answer, his father leaned past Dame Beatrice to speak to Ayrfell, four seats away. "Not the Queen, boy, but her goddaughter and namesake.

Speak sweetly of Eleanor of Harelby. Or"—he gave one of his expansive smiles—"I'll let Stian cut out your tongue."

"'Twould be my pleasure," Stian responded. At the same time he was thinking, *She's the Queen's goddaughter? I'm bedding the Queen's goddaughter?* Then he remembered that the Queen was no longer in favor, which somewhat eased his sudden awe of his wife.

"'Tis but Stian's mouse," Lars spoke up, shouting from the far end of the table. His voice was slurred with drink. "Or was that a biting rat you called her?"

Perhaps it was Lars's tongue he was going to cut out—never mind Ayrfell—though the comment caused him to hoot with laughter. But then, Stian realized, Lars was only repeating his own words back to him. He only hoped Eleanor heard none of the conversation over the noise in the hall.

"She's beautiful," Nicolaa said.

This served to focus Stian's attention back on his wife. It struck him again that she truly was lovely. It was just easier to notice her dark good looks without the incomparable contrast of her sister's presence.

"It's not fair," he said.

"What?" Nicolaa asked.

There was no way to explain, not without Edythe being there for Eleanor to disappear in her shadow. "Nothing," he said.

Dame Beatrice, seated next to Nicolaa, touched the widow's sleeve and said, "It's not fair he had to marry her."

"One marries where one's father chooses," Nicolaa said before Stian could make any protest.

"Thank God my father died before any bride was

forced down my throat," Ayrfell spoke up. "I'll choose the woman who'll bring *me* the most profit."

Eleanor paused at the foot of the stair to look around. The room was crowded with a half dozen trestle tables, full of smoke and noise. Stian watched her looking about through a veil of smoke. He'd half risen to go to her, when she gave a gracious smile to a group of wildly gesturing boys and went to join them at their table.

"Squires? Pages?" Dame Beatrice asked. "What's she doing eating with them?"

"Looking for a bed partner, perhaps?" Ayrfell suggested.

Stian was about to round on the foul-mouthed bastard when his father said, "She's being a proper hostess. Court ladies are taught to make one and all feel welcome, from the youngest to the most exalted." Roger gave everyone at the table a look that brooked no denial. "Lady Eleanor is merely doing her duty to *my* guests."

Not even Ayrfell dared to snicker at his host's words, and dinner resumed while Stian lost himself in a red haze of fury. He did not know how long it was until Nicolaa put her hand over his. It was only then that he noticed his eating knife was clenched tight in his fist.

"David's never been more than a stinging midge," she leaned close to whisper. "Perhaps your Eleanor is with the squires because there's no place for her at your side," she suggested after a while. "Perhaps she's jealous."

He heard the smile in Nicolaa's voice and laughed outright himself, though the laughter was used to cover a twinge of emotion that was something like hope and something like denial. For who would be jealous of him?

"No," he told his friend. "Courtiers have different ways. My father understands them. I don't."

He wondered if he should tell her of all the rules and strange practices Eleanor had told him of the night before. Then again, who would believe such nonsense as "Courts of Love"? It was ridiculous to think a man might bow and prance and play the fool just for the sake of pleasing a woman.

Though such foolishness might be useful for cajoling another man's wife into bed, he had to admit. Lars certainly seemed to think so. Well, Edythe's chastity was more his father's problem than his own, he decided. Eleanor, who preferred the squires' company to his, was his immediate concern.

Let him have Nicolaa, Eleanor found herself thinking as she got to talking with the young men around her. What she was having with her dinner, she decided, was much more entertaining. For at last she had what she wanted, information. The boys were talkative and eager to please, and a few of them even spoke Norman, though she had to listen carefully to cut through their thick accents.

It all went very well, she thought, even if she did lose the thread of the conversation sometimes as an inadvertent glance toward the high table would steal her attention away from the lads. Of course, she also gradually put names and histories to the people sharing Lord Roger's table. So it wasn't just Stian who distracted her, despite catching an occasional scowl from him when she did look his way. She didn't know why he looked at her so, when he looked at her at all. She did nothing to disturb his meal. Not even when young Bertran's mother huddled close with him in privy conversation. Though why she had an urge to dump a pot of ale over the man's head when that happened she did not know.

She ate little, but drank several toasts of both wine and ale with the lads. She grew tipsy, she knew, and that was not wise. She recognized that several of the older squires were bent on trying to seduce her. And, though she was more amused than offended, she knew how unwise it was to offer them any encouragement. She could not linger long at table, especially not when the drink began to warm her and loosen her tongue. So, before the last of the meal was cleared away, she excused herself and went back to her room.

Stian watched Eleanor go, her hips swaying beneath her deep blue gown as she walked slowly up the stairs. He watched, and knew that he was being watched in turn by all his ribald, teasing cousins. To follow her immediately, as his body urged, would bring too many jests from them tomorrow about his lusty, rutting night.

He supposed he shouldn't mind. He was a bridegroom. He was expected to follow after his bride as if he was eagerly on her scent. He shouldn't have dreaded the jokes. He should learn how to laugh with them, at himself. But he couldn't make himself run after a woman who had completely ignored his presence. She was a courtier; she obviously cared nothing for him and his country ways. He would not give her the satisfaction of trailing after her like one of her "true" knights.

So he finished his meal, then joined in a game of tables with Malcolm after the trestles were cleared away. He lingered for hours, though he drank little, wanting a clear enough head to bed the woman properly and thoroughly when he decided to come to her. He was one of the last to leave the hall to the guests, who were bedding down for the night.

Sober he might have been, eager he might have been, but when he pulled back the bed curtains he found Eleanor sleeping soundly. When he tried to rouse her, she mumbled and turned over. So he shed his clothes and climbed in beside her. To sleep. The worst part was when she turned back over and cuddled against him, all soft and warm.

No, the worst part was when she sighed contentedly and said, "Good night, Edythe."

11

"*Did you find my brooch?*"

As if that was all she had to worry about! Eleanor shook her head as she hurried down the stairs past her sister.

By all the saints, where was Stian? Hadn't the man even come to bed last night? She needed to talk to him, and in private was best. But no, he'd probably drunk and wenched the night away, for he certainly hadn't been in the room when she woke up. Worst of all, she'd woken up late. For all she knew he'd slept peacefully by her side, then rose with the dawn and went about his business.

"I should never drink more than a cup of wine," she complained as she entered the hall.

She wondered if sleeping too soundly from *almost* drinking too much was a sin of some sort. Not that Father Hubert would know. Young Father Hubert didn't seem to know much about the Church at all.

Still, she found that being near him was oddly comforting, for all his untutored ways.

"Where's Sir Stian?" she asked the first servant she saw.

"At Mass," he answered. He gestured around the jumble of bedding and crockery littering the nearly empty hall. "With everyone else," he added.

Mass. Of course. Why wasn't she at Mass? Why wasn't Edythe? Why had her sister lain abed, and let her do so as well, when the care of their souls was at stake? In Poitiers they'd always been very faithful to attend morning service. It was when the best bits of gossip from the night before could be freshly garnered.

Eleanor wondered if her sister was too bored with the less interesting service offered in the chapel of Harelby to attend regularly. Or if she just intended to spend another day out of the sight of the Lord Roger's guests. *It matters not what Edythe intends*, she thought anxiously. She needed to speak with her husband.

She had to push her way through a thick crowd to reach the front of the chapel, but she found Stian there with his father, Dame Beatrice, and a great horde of hairy male cousins. Most of the cousins were more red-eyed and disheveled than the day before, looking as if they'd gotten well and roaringly drunk last night. Stian looked positively civilized beside them. At least his surcote was clean and his cheeks and jaw looked freshly shaved. She supposed she couldn't hope for much more in this wild place.

When she made her way to his side at last, he put his arm around her shoulders. The gesture seemed automatic, as his eyes never left the altar. For some reason Eleanor found the embrace more comforting

than restraining despite the snickers and bold looks it
received from the numerous cousins. He left her only
to take communion.

She followed him, accepted the host, and returned
to her place to kneel and pray. After she'd stood for
the rest of the Mass, she tugged on his sleeve.

"What about Bertran?" she whispered when she
had his attention.

"Bertran?" he whispered back. "What about the
lad?"

"He's on trial today."

"I know that."

"They say he could lose his hands."

"That's the law, yes." Frowning, he drew her into
the nearly unpopulated shadows near the baptismal
font. "He shouldn't have gotten caught," he added
when they were alone.

"But he'll be crippled. For taking a deer? He's a
boy."

"It was the King's deer."

"He says he didn't do it."

"The foresters found Bertran near the deer."

"He says he found the carcass—"

"It had an arrow in its side, and Bertran carried a
bow."

"But he didn't necessarily kill the deer. If he came
across some other poacher's kill he—"

Stian took her by the shoulders. "We all kill the
King's deer. We're all poachers in the King's forest."

Eleanor was not to be put off. "Does that mean
you'll let one person pay for all your crimes? Is an
occasional sacrifice for everyone's transgressions
what the law demands? That deer could have been
killed by anyone."

He gave a frustrated glance back toward the crowd milling around as the service finished. "I know."

"I've talked to him. He's a good boy."

"I know."

"His mother's only child."

"I know."

"I like him." Stian looked at her in surprise, and kept looking at her in a way that made her uncomfortable and disturbed. "Is 'I know' all you have to say?" she questioned after the silence stretched out for a while.

"No. How came you to like Bertran?"

"Last night. When I ate with the squires," she reminded him. "I talked to him. He's fair spoken. Unlike most I've met at Harelby," she added. "The others teased him, but they all seemed worried about him as well. Stian." She reached up and tugged hard on the neck of his surcote. "You must do something." She hesitated, then added earnestly, "For Nicolaa's sake, if nothing else."

The chapel was emptying. Stian looked around them while he tried to understand his wife's sudden concern with those who were strangers to her. He knew the shire court would be in session soon, and Bertran's case would be brought before the judges early. Of course he cared for Bertran; he'd known the boy since he was born. Of course he was concerned about Nicolaa Brasey, and the fate of her lands if her son was maimed or put to the horn. The most either he or his father had been able to do for the boy so far was keep the sheriff from locking him away in a dark cell between the arrest and the trial.

"What can I do?" he asked.

"I don't know," his wife answered. Her grip tightened on his clothes. "I know nothing of law," she said, "but chopping off a child's hands for a crime that no one witnessed has nothing to do with justice."

"Aye. That's truth." He shook his head. He pried her hands loose and took them in his own. "Come, wife. Let's see what this day will bring for poor Bertran Brasey."

She went with him reluctantly. "You'll want to be with Nicolaa," she said when they were outside.

It looked as if it was going to be a bright day. The sun was well up, the sky was clear, and the breeze was more crisp than cold. There was green grass on the hills beyond the castle walls, crops were up, and buds were starting to open on the trees. There were flowers in the sheltered places at the base of the wall.

"Spring at last," he said sniffing the air. "True spring. It's too good a day for bloodshed," he added as he led Eleanor across the bailey.

There was a group of women gathered by the entrance to the hall, Beatrice and Nicolaa among them. He dropped his wife's hand and pointed toward the women. She gave him a worried, demanding look, but went to join the group without any protest. He sighed in relief, thankful that she sometimes knew her proper place.

"Do something for Bertran," he muttered as he watched her go. "Aye. I would if I could, but the lad says he's not guilty." Stian ran his thumb along his jaw, then looked up at the sky and let out a hoot of laughter. "By St. Andrew, why didn't someone think of it before!"

He gave Eleanor one more look, then hurried off to find his father and the priest.

＊　　　＊　　　＊

Edythe asked, "What's going on?"

Eleanor registered her sister's arrival and her question, but she couldn't take her eyes off the man standing in the cleared space before the judges. He stood tall and straight, wide shouldered and dressed for war. The sun glinted in his burnished copper hair and off the polished helm tucked in the crook of his arm. The crowd watched as well, and, for the moment, they watched in hushed silence.

Stian stood alone, surrounded on all sides, by the judges in front, the rows of jurymen to both sides, and the onlookers crowded together behind him. He felt every pair of eyes, friend and foe and stranger alike. The concentrated regard very nearly crushed him. Still, the thing needed to be done and he was the best person to do it. He could bear the attention for a little while. Soon the matter would be settled in a familiar way he could deal with.

He looked at the men presiding over the shire court. His father, alert, unsmiling, studied him with interest and a hint of encouragement in his dark eyes. Michael, the kind old abbot of St. Randolf's, who had been a frequent visitor to Harelby in the days before Stian's mother died, waited impassively for him to speak. Michael had also been his first teacher. The abbot had a pair of monks with him for the court, scribes seated at tables to write down the charges and judgments of the trials. There was also Sir Edwin Stoks, the sheriff whose foresters brought the charge against young Bertran. Sir Edwin looked irritated.

"Well?" he demanded as the crowd began to murmur questioningly. "Why have you approached this court dressed for battle, Sir Stian?"

"I've come to do battle," Stian answered, surprising

himself when the words came easily. He pointed to the boy who stood nearby, his mother on one side of him, Hubert on the other. "Bertran Brasey claims his innocence. He has sworn his innocence before the altar to Father Hubert. I claim his innocence." He turned around, raking a fierce look across all the men present as he spoke, loudly and slowly. "I challenge any man who thinks Bertran Brasey guilty of taking one of the King's deer to trial by combat."

Watching her husband, Eleanor found herself wondering if Michael, the angel of battles, had ever looked so splendid as Stian did proclaiming the justice of Bertran's cause. It was a ridiculous notion, of course, for archangels were creatures of light in armor of gold.

Stian wore no wings of dazzling white; in fact, the quilted collar of the padded cote peeking above his chainmail was sweat stained. There was a tear in the chainmail, a ragged circle of rings missing where the heavy metal armor rested on his right thigh. It was a wonder that she noticed such small details. She even noticed that the sunlight was burning the tip of his nose a bright pink.

Well, he might not be as beautiful as an archangel, but Eleanor thought him surely as brave as one. Who could doubt the right of Bertran's claim of innocence when such a brave warrior championed him?

Her answer came in a moment as a harsh, mocking laugh rang above the murmurs of the crowd. The reddest tressed of the bright-haired cousins stepped before the judges. She remembered him from yesterday, David Kerr of Ayrfell.

"I'll accept the challenge," he announced loudly. "For the English King's honor," he added with a sneer.

"For the joy of rousing trouble, you mean," Lord Roger answered.

Ayrfell laughed again. He turned to Stian. "What matter why I fight? It's the fighting that matters."

"It is who wins that matters in this instance," the abbot pointed out sternly. "This fight is for justice, not pleasure."

"If the combat is allowed at all," the sheriff put in. "A trial by combat is a grave matter." He looked from one man to the other.

"I claim Bertran's innocence," said Stian.

"I claim his guilt," Ayrfell said with equal stubbornness.

"And you are willing to do combat to prove your claims?" Roger asked. Both men glared at each other, then nodded. Roger turned to the sheriff. "Let them do it." He gave Stian a fierce smile. "I've no doubt the boy will be proved innocent myself." Stian returned his father's smile.

"God will decide," the abbot said. He nodded gravely. "Yes. Let them do combat."

The sheriff sighed. His reluctance was obvious, but he gave way to the other judges' wishes. "Very well." He stood. "I'll act as marshal." He looked at the antagonists. "One weapon each. First blood to decide."

Stian saw the disappointment on his cousin's always-scowling face. He supposed it was a pity that they wouldn't be allowed to kill each other today, but saving Bertran was more important to him just now than killing David of Ayrfell. "Very well," he agreed. "First blood."

"Coward," David muttered, but gave a terse nod when the sheriff looked at him for his assent.

"Let the lists be cleared!" the sheriff called out. The space before the judges widened quickly as the spectators moved back.

Small as she was, Eleanor very nearly lost her place as people milled about, changing position at some order from the judge who seemed to be acting as referee in the duel. Despite their rank, she and Edythe had to push and prod the people surrounding them to be able to have a decent view of the lists. By the time she was firmly entrenched at the front of the crowd, Stian and David of Ayrfell were facing each other. Instead of shield and broadsword, each man held the much longer greatsword, heavy enough that it had to be used with two hands. Though the men were not very far from where she stood, Eleanor could not make out the expression on either face, for the cheek and nose pieces of their conical helms hid most of their faces from view. She could see their eyes, equally blue, alert, determined, fierce as hunting hawks. And, if she wasn't mistaken, there was a glint of humor in Stian's gaze as well. She didn't understand it, how a man could find humor in such a desperate situation, but for some foolish reason she found that hint of bravado endearing.

She was grateful he'd done what he could to save Bertran. She also wished she'd known he was going to challenge the shire court to combat over the boy's innocence. She wouldn't have tried to stop him, but she would have liked to offer him some token to take into battle, though she supposed if any woman should have offered him her favor it was the one whose child he was defending.

The thought was unexpectedly painful, and she found herself looking at Nicolaa Brasey as the fight began. Though her hand was on Bertran's shoulder, the boy's mother had eyes only for Stian. It was a look full of worship and hope. Eleanor couldn't look at her for long. Besides, as the clash of metal upon metal rang out, her stomach clenched with fear and all her concern focused on her ragged archangel.

My archangel? Sweet Jesu, when did he become mine? she thought as Stian parried an overhand blow. How could Stian be hers? Was he not fighting for Nicolaa? He was her husband, but he was another's champion.

In the sophisticated court of Poitiers such a situation was perfectly normal. It was even the ideal, for all knew marriage was nothing but a financial arrangement. But this wasn't Poitiers, and Eleanor wasn't feeling particularly sophisticated. Her hands clenched in tight fists as she watched the fight, and she found it hard to breathe. She barely noticed Edythe's arm around her shoulders, or her sister's encouraging comments. All she really saw were two very sharp weapons coming together again and again.

The men circled in a quick, scuttling, sideways dance, then Stian swept his sword toward Ayrfell's thigh. His opponent jumped back and aimed a blow at Stian's head. Stian ducked and came up under the other man's guard.

The greatsword was a slashing weapon, and chain-mail was meant to deflect chopping sword blows. Stian ignored the accustomed roles for both weapons and armor and used the heavy sword to stab at Ayrfell's upper arm. There was a grating screech as the tip of the blade penetrated the rings of the chainmail. The thrust didn't pierce far before the armor deflected it, but it did as much damage as Stian wanted.

He laughed as he jumped backward.

Then he called, "Hold!" as a thin trickle of blood seeped from the puncture wound to stain Ayrfell's armor. "First blood!" Stian declared. He looked toward the judges as he lowered his sword.

Ayrfell roared with anger and rushed forward, ignoring the small hurt as he swung his blade at Stian's head. Stian knew he might have been in trouble if the sheriff hadn't tackled Ayrfell from behind, bringing him down heavily on the dusty ground. Then sat on him.

"Hold!" the sheriff shouted when Ayrfell struggled to throw him off. "Curse your temper, David; the fight's over! The lad's innocent. God has made his choice, now yield and be still!"

It was some time before David of Ayrfell finally gave up the fight, but Stian left him to the sheriff. He could have stood over his fallen cousin and gloated, and he was tempted to savor the victory that way. But all thought of doing so left him when Nicolaa Brasey threw herself into his arms, snatched off his helm, and pulled his mouth down to hers.

The excitement of battle was still in him, and she was full of the energy of pent-up fear. The kiss they shared was fierce and hungry. For a while he forgot the reason for the fight, the fight itself, that he was surrounded by a laughing, cheering crowd, and the woman for whose sake he'd actually brought the challenge of trial by combat.

As soon as he tasted the salt from Nicolaa's tears he remembered himself, why they were there, and that they shared nothing more than friendship. He let her go, and she immediately turned to her son. He looked around for his wife.

He saw Edythe, but for once Eleanor was not standing unobtrusively in her shadow. He made his way over to Edythe, though it took some doing. First he had to deal with Malcolm and Lars. They slapped him, hugged him, shouted in his face, and thrust a tankard of ale in his hands. After he drank it down gratefully, he let them help him take off his chainmail.

Then he shook sweat-soaked hair out of his face and roared, "Where's my wife?"

Ayrfell's people had taken him away. Nicolaa and her son were standing before the judges. Hubert was shepherding a large portion of the crowd toward the chapel to give thanks. Dame Beatrice was marshaling the household to prepare for a celebration. A great deal was going on. Everyone was busy. The abbot was gesturing for him to come before judges and jurymen. Eleanor was nowhere in sight.

Edythe made her way to his side. He asked her, "Where's my wife?"

She gave one of her dazzling smiles, and Lars sighed. She said, "She remembered that I loaned her my garnet brooch for her wedding. She said she thought she must have left it in the bower where you took her on your wedding night. She said she thought she remembered the way and that it is not far." Edythe smiled again. She said to Lars, "Would you escort me to my lord, good sir? The crowd will part easily at your command."

Lars leapt forward like an eager puppy. With her hand on his arm they started away.

Stian called after Edythe, "Eleanor is at the cave?" She neither replied nor turned around, nor even seemed to hear him. Stian turned his puzzled, annoyed gaze from Edythe and found Malcolm watching him.

"Eleanor is at the cave?" he repeated to his remaining cousin.

"It would seem so," was Malcolm's response.

"I just fought a battle."

"A small one," Malcolm pointed out.

"For her."

"For justice."

"Aye. But she talked me into it."

Malcolm laughed. "Let her go, then. Or beat her. It's not like you to let a woman talk you into anything."

"Why would she go alone to the cave?"

"Why would you kiss Nicolaa Brasey before the world—and your woman?"

Stian had been growing angry, but Malcolm's comment brought him up short. "Oh." He rubbed his hand thoughtfully along his jaw. "Think you she saw? Think you she's jealous?"

Malcolm's boisterous laugh briefly blocked out all other noise in the bailey. He clapped Stian on the shoulder. "I know she saw. She certainly looked jealous."

"In truth?"

"By the rood and all the saints," Malcolm swore, hand on heart. He gave a sly smile. "Why don't you go find out for yourself."

"I will. 'Tis not safe for her to go into the woods alone," Stian said.

"Liar." Malcolm made quick work of his lame excuse. He pushed Stian in the direction of the castle gate. "Go on, then." Stian went, and his ears grew red as his cousin added loudly, "If you're not home for dinner we'll know the reason why."

12

As he came into the clearing he saw the animal first, then Eleanor kneeling in the mouth of the cave; her cloak pulled tightly around her. She was pale; her dark eyes were wide, staring in terror.

"Eleanor?"

Her voice was too calm when she answered, "It's a wolf."

"I know it's a wolf," he said. He walked boldly toward the black-and-gray creature. "She's my wolf. I raised her from a pup."

"She's going to kill me." Eleanor's voice was barely above a whisper. She wondered how she could manage to talk at all, she was so frightened. She wished Stian would at least draw his sword.

Stian stopped a few feet away from the wolf, between it and the mouth of the cave where she huddled. "Wolves don't kill people. Not usually."

"That's no comfort." She looked him in the face

for the first time. "What do you mean, you raised her? You mean she's tame?"

The wolf growled as Eleanor spoke. The animal was standing stiff-legged, with her head down. Her teeth were bared, looking bright and sharp against the black fur of her muzzle.

"Your wolf doesn't sound tame," Eleanor pointed out in her too-calm voice.

"She's not tame."

"You said you raised her."

"Then I set her free. Sometimes she comes back to the cave. Sometimes she lets me near her, but that doesn't mean she's tame."

"Oh," she said as the wolf growled again. It took a stalking pace nearer to Eleanor. Stian carefully moved closer himself.

As he came closer to the cave mouth, Stian could see that Eleanor was trembling. If she broke and ran the wolf just might attack. She hadn't been around any human but him for a long time. "You can't show weakness to a wolf," he told Eleanor. "You'll have to show her you're stronger than she is."

"Why don't you just kill her?"

"No," he answered flatly. "Show her you're braver than she is and you'll come to no harm."

"I'm not brave."

Stian took a step back. "Then perhaps she'll maul you."

He didn't know why he was doing this. It would have been easy enough to drive the wolf off. Maybe it was because he considered the cave and pool to be his and the wolf's territory. Perhaps Eleanor needed to show she deserved a place in the world they occupied. Perhaps he just wanted to show her that she could outface a wolf.

"Damn you." The words were a hoarse, terrified whisper, but the anger underlying her fear pleased him. She looked as though she might faint at any moment, though.

He asked, "How long have you two been like this?"

"I don't know. Forever."

It wasn't like the wolf to confront humans. It wasn't like her to be threatening. "She just came out of the woods?"

"Yes."

"Then what?"

"Every time I move she growls at me."

Why would the wolf behave like this? She was usually shy of any human but him. It made him wonder, and then it made him laugh. The wolf's ears flicked at the sound, but she didn't take her yellow-eyed gaze from Eleanor.

"What?" Eleanor demanded.

"She probably smells me on you. She won't like that."

"Won't like?"

"She thinks I'm a wolf, I think. Her mate. Wolves fight for their mates," he added. "And the winners mate for life."

"Don't expect me to fight a wolf for you, Stian of Harelby."

"I'm worth a fight," he told his wife. "Don't you want to mate for life?"

"Stian, please! I'm frightened."

He moved swiftly to her side. Squatting beside her but not touching her, he said, "She knows she's frightening you. Don't let the beast win. Stare her down. That's all you have to do. Look her in the eye.

Don't blink. Don't look away. Dominate her with your eyes. Do it, and she'll leave you be."

Stare her down? That was all she had to do, stare down a wolf? Eleanor wanted to laugh, but her throat wouldn't work to make the sound. She could feel Stian beside her, the heat and scent of him. She could sense the size and power of him. She knew he could save her if he chose, but instead he was forcing her to save herself. What would he do if she lost? Would he interfere? Would he take the part of the wolf he'd loved enough to raise and free? Or would he take the part of the wife his father had forced on him? She thought she was more frightened of the answer than she was of the wolf.

"You're strong, Eleanor," Stian told her. "Always remember that you're strong enough to conquer a wolf."

His voice held so much confidence she almost believed it herself. Since he gave her no other choice, Eleanor forced herself to look the beast in the eye. At first she thought she was looking into the face of the devil himself.

"You're just a big old flea-bitten dog," she heard herself say after a while.

She'd forgotten to think. She'd forgotten time. She'd discovered that this was indeed a dominance game. Stare and stare and see whose will crumpled first. She'd actually seen King Henry and Queen Eleanor confront each other like this on the road outside Poitiers. Their fury with each other had been palpable, crackling like lightning between them. The Queen had looked away first, and she'd ended up a prisoner in Salisbury Castle. Compared to what humans did to each other, Eleanor thought, wolves were nothing.

She glared. She refused to blink. All she saw were the other's gold eyes. Eyes that seemed to be filling with uncertainty.

"You probably got the fleas from Stian."

"Aye," came a soft voice beside her. "That she did."

The wolf whined. Then she lowered her head, whined again, and rolled onto her back. Eleanor could have sworn the expression on the wolf's muzzle was hopeful.

She looked at Stian. "What?"

"You've won. When they expose their bellies it's a sign that they're defeated." He moved forward, approaching the wolf on his hands and knees. When he was beside her, he looked back at Eleanor as he began to rub the wolf's thick coat. "It's also a sign they want their bellies rubbed."

"Dogs like that," Eleanor agreed.

"Wolves, too. This one does, I know."

After Stian had given the wolf a thorough scratching, cooing and growling playfully all the while, the animal jumped to her feet. She circled the clearing, gave Stian one long look, then loped away, back into the woods.

Stian went back to where Eleanor still knelt. He put out his hand to help her up, but she shook her head. She was still trembling from the aftershock of facing down the wild, or nearly wild, animal.

"I don't think I'll ever get to my feet again."

Stian dropped down beside her. His blue eyes were full of mischief. "If you can't get to your feet," he told her, "it'll be easier to tip you over backwards whenever I desire."

He put his hand on her shoulder, and Eleanor,

quite abruptly, collapsed against him. She didn't know where the tears came from so suddenly, but they flowed like water. She couldn't stop them and she couldn't let go of Stian even though she smelled the dry mustiness of the wolf's coat on him as he held her close.

When she stopped crying she began to laugh. Stian preferred the laughter to the tears, though they both had the same wild sound to them. He just let her have her head, let her get out all the emotions until she was drained and exhausted. He just held her, giving her his warmth, not knowing anything else he could give.

It was Eleanor who finally found words, though it seemed to him like the sun had shifted far to the west before she was able to find her voice. When she did speak, it was with her head pressed to his chest, so he had to strain to make out the muffled sounds.

"No," he said after he was sure he'd understood. Then, "Yes. You are a fool." She looked up slowly. Her dark eyes were red-rimmed, brimming with tears again. "Not for coming here," he added, hoping to keep the tears from spilling over. "This is a good place to come."

She raised her head a bit more. "We should go back to Harelby. You'll want to be with Nicolaa."

He didn't see any reason for either. "Why?" Her veil had long ago slipped from her head. Stian pushed strands of hair from her face. "I can't carry you all the way home," he added, though that was probably untrue. She probably weighed less than his armor.

Her expression changed from miserably bleak to curious. "Why would you carry me home?"

"You told me you couldn't walk."

"I didn't mean—"

"Isn't a gentle knight supposed to serve his lady?"

"I'm not your lady," she protested, pushing her small hands against his chest. "I'm your wife."

She was upset. She truly was jealous. He couldn't keep himself from teasing. "If you're not my lady, then whose are you?"

"I'm no one."

Her answer shocked him into seriousness. It occurred to him that she hadn't answered him at all, but that she had spoken what was hidden in her heart. And he understood exactly what she meant, for in this they were very alike. He held her face between his hands. Hers was a small, delicate face. His hands were big, red, and rough from swordplay, scarred and freckled and altogether unlovely. He held her gently, even so. He caught her gaze with his and dared her to look away, just as he'd made her dare the wolf. She didn't flinch. She blinked as tears spilled down her cheeks, but she didn't look away.

"You are Eleanor," he told her. "Wolf mistress. Lady in the shadows, aye, but a power in your own right. You think no one sees you for Edythe, and mostly you are right. I see you, Eleanor," he told her. "Though you have to kick and bite and scratch me to get me to do it, I see you. I've lived in the shadow of a celebrated man myself. It's not such a bad place, much of the time."

"It's full of mice."

He couldn't help but chuckle. "It's a brave mouse, you are. You ran here to be alone, didn't you? When you couldn't stand it anymore? Not just Nicolaa's kissing me, but being at Harelby? Being in Edythe's shadow? You needed to get away from all of it for a while, didn't you?"

He waited a long time for an answer. "You were kissing Nicolaa," was what she finally said. "Not just her kissing you."

"You should have moved faster than she did," he teased.

"I won't come between the two of you," she said. She tried to pull away, but he wouldn't let her go. "I understand these things."

"Do you? Then you'd best explain them to me."

"You wanted to marry her."

"Aye," he agreed. He found himself massaging her temples with his thumbs. Her eyes were wide, studying him earnestly. He went on. "Aunt Beatrice thought it a good marriage. I had no objections. Better to wed a friend than a stranger, I thought."

She looked away. "I'm sorry you were made to marry a stranger."

"It's done me no harm." He waved her apology away. "I may have a few scars from it. I'm a warrior. I can live with scars."

That he recognized her own scars, the ones Edythe had never meant to inflict, the ones Eleanor hadn't admitted existed until he spoke of them, was a marvel to her. He was a marvel to her.

Tentatively, shyly, she reached up to touch his face, to run her fingers along the red fringe of his mustache.

"Tickles," he said.

"Earlier today I thought you were an angel."

"Can't be an angel," he said. "I'm not dead."

"Then, with the wolf, I thought you must surely be a demon."

"In time, I will be. I doubt even Hubert's best prayers will serve to save me."

"You are a barbarian."

"I'm a man," he said and kissed her to prove it.

She had thought all her emotions spent, but eagerness kindled in her as his mouth took possession of hers. It was only moments before she wanted more than just a joining of their lips and tongues. She wanted all she could get of Stian of Harelby. She suddenly craved his flesh next to hers, his strength covering her, his seed making a new life in her. She hungered for everything that could join them.

She hadn't known how lonely she was until now, how incomplete. It was Stian's touch that gave her hope for completion. It was Stian's presence that made her feel whole. His touch, the heat of his mouth, the tang of sweat and wolf on his skin, the sweet memory of his words, all these things combined into a longing for him that would not be denied.

She heard herself moan and strained against him as his lips moved to her throat. His hand touched her breast beneath all her layers of clothes, then moved to unclasp the pin holding her cloak closed. Her hands found his thighs, running her palms up the long, muscular length of them to find the place where his braccos were tied at the waist.

They stood together without any consultation. Their hands worked together with no need for consent or directions, unfastening, untying, pulling off, and pushing down until all their clothes were heaped in a colorful pile on the cave floor. Then they came together again, all skin and heat, fair and dark, male and female fitting exactly. Touching, they were gentle and fierce in turn as they explored and claimed each separate part of each other. It was a long time before they lay down together.

A longer time still was spent kissing and caressing

and finding wooing words for each other, words that included "mouse" and "wolf," "angel" and "demon." Half the time Stian spoke in the dialect of the Border, half the time Eleanor used the soft tongue of the poets of Poitiers. Neither had any trouble understanding the other.

As night drew down, urgency overcame the use of words. If the spring evening was cool, they didn't know it. They knew nothing but the warmth they gave each other, the surcease of loneliness, the intensity of pleasure.

When Stian entered her, Eleanor understood the songs of the troubadours for the first time. She had known some pleasure, born of angry passion, the last time they had had sex, but it had been feeble compared to this coupling. This was passion born of gentler emotions, yet the feelings were stronger.

Now they were one being, moving together, sharing pleasure instead of taking it from each other. Her head reeled as though she'd been drinking strong wine; her blood was pure fire. Her body strained to meet each thrust, to give herself and take all of him. She panted and moaned and clutched at the straining muscles of his back, then drew his head down to capture his mouth. It went on and on, until finally whatever their bodies did was forgotten as the pleasure they built together consumed them both.

The ecstasy was bright, indescribable, ephemeral, and forever. It left her feeling both sweet and a little sad, lost and yet complete, exhausted and elated, heavy of body and light of head. It had been wonderful, and she wanted more than anything to find that bright moment once again. But not just yet. She was sated, spent, satisfied. Happy.

Gradually, as the world came to include more than just herself and Stian, she also realized that she was shivering from cold in the spots where his body didn't cover hers. It was a warm, fur-lined cape she wanted more than another indescribable experience.

"Cold?" Stian asked before she could summon energy to speak.

It left her wondering if he had absorbed a part of her with their lovemaking. Had she absorbed a part of him?

"Cold," she agreed. She found she was too tired to manage more than the one word.

Stian's answer was a grunt, but he managed to roll off her, find their cloaks, and tuck the cloth around them. She rolled gratefully into his embrace and had no idea why he said, "Maybe now you'll know I'm not Edythe," as she fell happily to sleep.

Roger wished Lars would stop looking at Edythe like that. The feast was done, the tables cleared, the wine and ale were flowing freely. Roger wished that Stian was in the hall, and that he hadn't broken his lute over someone's head in a drunken brawl. For music would suit the company well tonight. His guests were full of laughter and sated from their supper. It was a festive time, and Roger felt well content with the world. Except for the way his nephew looked at his wife. Not that he blamed the lad for worshipping at her lovely, delicate little feet. Edythe was a great prize, the perfect toy, a lovely ornament, and damned hot in bed.

But that was not for anyone but him, so young Lars could just stop sniffing around her skirts. Roger scowled at his nephew as Lars followed Edythe away from the hearth. Lars took no notice of him, so Roger got up from his chair and went down to join the circle of people Edythe was forming for a game. He noticed that even Beatrice was taking part in the merriment.

It cheered him, for his sister-in-law had not been her usual pleasant self of late. He'd watched Malcolm cajole and tease her all evening, and she seemed to be in as good spirits about Bertran's freedom and her nephew's comeuppance as everyone else in the hall. It was good to see her remembering her love of games and frolic. For it was Beatrice who had brought some joy back into his life after the death of his first wife.

"What's this?" he asked, displacing Lars from his present wife's side. "What sport are you planning?"

Edythe held up a square of cloth, a clean napkin Roger had watched her request from a serving page earlier in the evening. "Hoodman-blind, my lord," she announced. She waved the cloth airily above her head as she called, "Who will be the first to seek the quarry?"

"What token is the prize?" Malcolm asked as he joined the group.

"Why, a kiss, of course," Edythe answered with a bright laugh.

Malcolm looked around the group. "But what if I take the challenge, then capture my uncle? Must he kiss me, then?"

Beatrice slapped Malcolm playfully on the arm. "Just be sure to capture something in skirts, then, you fool," she told him.

"That would be simple," Malcolm said. "If I hood only one eye."

"But that would be cheating," Roger announced. He took the cloth from his wife. He looked about with a grin. "We can't have cheating. I'll just have to show you how it's done. Form the circle."

He waited until he and Edythe were standing alone in the center of a cleared space between the hearth and the dais. The players included Malcolm and Beatrice, Morwina, Fiona, Hubert, two squires, and Lars. It was a goodly number for a game of hide and seek. Lars looked eager for a turn, for the hooded man had much license to grope and fondle the captured prey to try to guess its identity in the dark. Roger knew his wife would be much sought after tonight, but he intended to find her first, then whisk his lady off to bed while their guests continued the game.

With thoughts of that pleasant future in mind, he bent down to let Edythe tie the cloth snugly over his eyes. Then she turned him around until he was nearly dizzy before retreating into the anonymity of the circle of players. Roger lunged after her.

He felt a swish of skirts against his legs, heard the chime of her laughter, caught a whiff of her scent, but Edythe eluded him easily. He turned the way he thought she'd gone and stumbled forward. He grabbed at the air and heard a girlish giggle. Morwina or her twin, he supposed. He turned again. There was much laughter drowning out his hearing. People circled him in the dark. He felt their movements, now and then a touch on his shoulder or backside. He followed after the circling players. He followed one laughing lady in particular, feeling the heat when the game moved near the hearth. Then the air on his skin grew cooler as his prey retreated toward a wall.

One more quick lunge and his arms circled a slender waist. He didn't need sight to draw her willing form to him and extract the prize of the touch of her soft lips. As the kiss deepened, it was her tongue that searched his mouth, her hands that held him fiercely to her voluptuous body. His hands roved over her, from breast to thigh to rounded buttocks. Ah, but she was a wondrous handful!

He was breathless, his passion rising, by the time he lifted his head to whisper, "Edythe, my sweet."

The hands holding tightly to his back grew talons that dug into his shoulder blades. Before he could protest the sudden pain, the hood was snatched from his eyes. It mattered little that he now had eyes to see, for the corner where they stood was deep in shadow.

"You were ever a fool," a voice came from the darkness, husky with unfamiliar emotion, yet very well known to him. He caught a glint of pale eyes, the set of her angry mouth, the proud lift of her chin.

"Beatrice?" he asked as though he'd never before seen this woman he'd known for near twenty years.

Her hands had dropped from his back. She was leaning against the tapestry-covered wall. He knew he should move away from her, take a step back at least and look to see what the rest of the people in the hall were about. He didn't move. He didn't care if the whole world were watching. For the moment, the whole world consisted of himself, his dead brother's wife, and the shadows of Harelby keep.

He put his hands against the wall on either side of her shoulders. He felt the texture of the embroidered tapestry, rough against his palms. "Beatrice," he said again.

For some reason, even knowing who she was, he found himself still wanting her. He supposed even the thought of wanting her was a sin. She was his brother's wife!

"He's been dead a long time," she said, as though she knew his thoughts. Or as if she were having the same thoughts herself.

Roger lifted her chin with his fingers. They were looking each other in the eye when he said, "When did you become such a beauty?"

"I'm no beauty. It's just dark over here, you randy old fool."

Randy? Yes. Old? Yes. Fool? Oh, most certainly. A fool for years and years. Why had he never seen before what was so clear here in this nearly night-dark corner? Because it was convenient to accept her fealty, to let her raise his son and care for his home without questioning what price she paid with her service. Because if he had turned his thoughts toward her as a woman he would have betrayed God, his brother, and the wife he had loved. But the brother and the wife were long dead. There was only God to worry about now. And Edythe, whom he loved not at all.

"Oh, my dearest Beatrice," he whispered. "Whatever is to be done?"

She pushed against his chest, shoving with all her might until he took a step back. "What's to be done?" she asked, her voice as harshly irritated as it had been since he'd brought his young wife home. "What do you think's to be done?" She moved past him and took a few steps toward the light and noise in the center of the hall. He watched her with a growing ache in his heart.

He wasn't surprised when she stopped long enough to look back at him and say, "It's time you found a new chatelaine, my lord."

around his narrow waist. She was no more than chin high on him, but of late his size seemed more protective than threatening to her.

"I was laughing at myself," she told him. "Remembering my days at court, and missing them not at all. Except my mother," she added. "Her heart was ever with the Queen, but she spared as much affection for us as she could."

"It's hard to miss a mother," he said and ran his hands through her unbound hair.

She thanked the saints the squire had brought a comb the day before. Probably at Edythe's suggestion. Eleanor was certain her elder sister would never go without the comforts of life, no matter what wild adventure befell her.

"Do you miss your mother very much?"

She asked the question gently and wasn't surprised when he stiffened in her embrace. For a moment, she expected him to push her away, but sighed with relief when he drew her closer instead.

"I miss her," he said.

She knew from his tone that it would not be good to ask any more questions on that matter. She suspected his father's relationship with her sister had something to do with it.

"I'll miss my aunt as well."

"Dame Beatrice?" she asked. She looked at him questioningly.

"She's leaving Harelby."

Eleanor wasn't surprised, but she didn't say so to Stian. "Where does she go? With David of Ayrfell?"

He shook his head. "No. He tried to get her to leave with him, I'm told. She's chosen to enter Honcourt Abbey instead. That's five miles or so from

Harelby," he added before she could ask. "Five miles closer to the border, though."

Eleanor would not be sorry to have Beatrice go, but she hated the thought that it was she and Edythe who had driven the woman from her home. "When does she leave?"

"Tomorrow morning."

So, the idyll was to be over even sooner than she'd hoped. Eleanor stepped away from Stian to look around at the cave mouth, the pool, the trees with their fresh, spring green leaves, the fire where the smoke was heavy with the scent of cooking meat. She thought she could make out the dark fur of Stian's wolf cautiously watching them from back in the trees.

"This is a pleasant place to be," she told her husband. "But we'd best go back in time to say good-bye to Dame Beatrice."

He put his hand on her shoulder. "We'll come back soon," he told her. "This is my place. Our place now."

She smiled up at him. "Soon," she agreed. "And next time we'll bring a pallet."

He laughed. "Weakling." He drew her toward the fire. "Come, let's have breakfast."

"What think you of a garderobe?"

"How can I think of something when I don't know what it is?" Beatrice snapped back.

Roger refused to be rankled by her tone, but smiled benignly over her head. The hall was empty but for the pair of them, standing near the foot of the tower stairs. It was time for morning Mass, but he'd wanted to have a few minutes alone with his sister-in-law before she left.

He heard footsteps and turned as his daughter-in-law came down the last turning of the staircase. "You're rising late, my dear," he told her.

"Aye," she agreed, ducking her head as her cheeks reddened with embarrassment. "And Stian woke just as I was leaving," she added. "I should hurry. It's been days since I heard Mass."

He put out a hand to stop her when she would have slipped away. "Stay a moment, and answer a question for Dame Beatrice."

She looked inquiringly at the other woman. "Yes?"

It was Roger who said, "Explain to her about garderobes. It was Edythe who reminded me of their existence," he added and got a mighty scowl from Beatrice for his words.

Eleanor continued to look embarrassed as she tucked her hands in her sleeves. "'Tis like a slops pail, only more so," she explained. "A small chamber, with a seat with a hole in it, where one sits and—relieves oneself, you see."

Beatrice shook her head. "I don't want to see. It sounds disgusting."

"Not if it's built properly," Roger said. "I've used them in French castles. If the hole's deep enough to reach a moat everything gets washed away."

"And where would you dig such a hole at Harelby? In the hall, perhaps?"

Roger refused to lose his enthusiasm in the face of Beatrice's harsh questioning. "No, no. It will be simple enough to construct this garderobe in the spot where the tower joins the curtain wall. It'll take a bit of work and rebuilding, but by fall we'll have the thing done." He glanced toward the hearth, letting his gaze travel up to where the smoke failed to exit through the roof louvers. "Then perhaps we'll consider this new thing called a chimney."

Eleanor smiled at his comment, but Beatrice only frowned all the more and said, "Thankfully I'll not be here to see such changes. I like Harelby just the way it is."

"All things change, my dear," Roger reminded her softly.

Eleanor was surprised at the depth of meaning in Lord Roger's words, but she tried not to show her feelings. What was between these two people was no business of hers, especially since Beatrice would be leaving to take up residence in the abbey within the hour. She did think she should leave them to their private farewell.

When she began to move away, it was Beatrice who said, "Stay. I've something to give you."

This time Eleanor did not conceal her surprise. "Yes?"

Beatrice handed her a heavy pouch. When Eleanor looked inside, she discovered the ring that held all the keys to Harelby's storerooms. She stared blankly, first at Lord Roger, then at Dame Beatrice.

"Well?" the older woman demanded.

"Shall I give these to Edythe?" Eleanor asked. "She is the lady of—"

"I said they were for you, did I not?"

Eleanor looked imploringly at Lord Roger. "My lord, I—"

"Will make a fine chatelaine." He patted her on the head. "Edythe certainly thinks so." He grinned. "She says she'd rather concentrate on caring for me instead of every soul at Harelby."

"Hmmph," was Beatrice's comment to this. "It

matters not which court girl takes the post," she went on. "Neither knows anything of responsibility."

Eleanor's hand knotted around the keys as she fought the temptation to throw them in the woman's face. She'd heard such words from Beatrice before and not challenged them. Now, she wanted to strike her.

Instead, she said, "I think I can find my way around the undercroft well enough. *Queen Eleanor* makes certain the damsels under her tutelage are trained to manage their own households. *My mother* was in charge of such training in Poitiers."

Beatrice was unmoved by her words. "This is not Poitiers, girl," she answered coldly.

"So I have noticed," Eleanor replied through clenched teeth.

Stian had told her that the woman was normally cheerful and kind. Eleanor hoped life at the abbey would help restore Dame Beatrice's good nature, for the sake of peace among the nuns, if nothing else.

She weighed the keys in her palm and found that she was glad that she'd been given this responsibility. She was glad that Dame Beatrice was leaving, that Edythe wanted none of the duties that went with her rank. Eleanor relished the chance to be useful, to be out of the shadows. With Beatrice's departure she felt as if her own life was just beginning.

"I'll do my best," she promised Lord Roger.

He patted her on the head again. "I trust you will." Dame Beatrice gave a sour frown and strode away toward the hearth. Lord Roger looked after her, but he lingered by Eleanor to ask, "So, how will you start as chatelaine?"

Half of her attention was on Stian, whom she

heard humming as he came down the stairs. She answered Lord Roger's question as her husband came into view. "First I think I shall write my mother to tell her all that has passed since we left our father's care."

Lord Roger looked at her in grave silence while Stian came up and slipped his arm around her shoulders. She leaned against her husband, easy in his company. They exchanged a smile, then she looked back at the Lord of Harelby. His brows were drawn down in a frown.

"Yes, my lord?" she asked. "Is something amiss?"

He was silent a while longer before he said, "I think it would be unwise for you to write your mother, child."

It was Stian who asked incredulously, "But why?"

Eleanor understood, though the knowledge pained her. "My mother is with the Queen, and you are the King's man," she said to Roger. He nodded, and she sighed. "Aye, my lord. As you wish."

"But—" Stian began.

"Eleanor can contact her mother when times are less chancy," Roger cut his son off. "We'll not discuss it."

Eleanor showed Stian the chatelaine's keys as Roger went off to join Dame Beatrice. "This will keep me occupied enough," she told him. "In truth, it doesn't matter," she added as he continued to glare his displeasure at his father's back.

"It matters," he said.

She thought for a moment that he was going to follow his father to start a confrontation on her behalf. She shook her head, grateful but not wanting to be the source of tension between father and son. He gave her a long look, then nodded.

"Lars is seeing Aunt Beatrice to the abbey," he

said. "I think I'd better inspect his men and horses before they go. The Dane's so addled by your sister it's likely he's had the men saddled and the horses issued new armor."

She nodded her amused agreement as she ran her fingers through the assortment of keys. "And I must introduce myself to the steward," she told him. She craned up to kiss him on the chin. "I'll see you at dinner, my sweet," she said and hurried away, both embarrassed and elated to have spoken an endearment to him for the first time when they were both standing up and fully dressed.

"The damn Muraghs are over the border!"

Roger looked up from the board game he was playing with Stian as Lars's shout rang through the hall.

Stian jumped to his feet. "Thieving bastards!" he shouted.

"How large a raiding party this time?" Roger wanted to know.

"Sounds like the whole clan's out for blood and plunder," Lars answered. "I met a messenger from Malcolm on my way back from the abbey. I sent him and the men I had with me back to help guard the abbey. Then I rode on with the message myself."

Eleanor was seated behind the high table, where a large frame was set up beneath the window. She'd been working on the embroidery with Edythe and the twins when the angry shout shook her out of a contented reverie. Though only a few hours had passed since Dame Beatrice had gone, a peaceful aura had seemed to descend over the household. Now, here was trouble.

She looked up, a chill of fear coming over her as

the men gathered in the center of the hall around Lars. She stood, but when she would have gone to Stian, Edythe put her hand out to stop her.

"This is the men's concern, my dear."

That her sister was right didn't soothe Eleanor's tension any, but she did take her seat once more. "Aye."

It didn't help when Edythe went on, "I'm afraid we're in for a border war. My lord has told me of the Muraghs. They, and some of the other Scots marcher lords, have vowed to have revenge for the capture of their King. My lord thinks it's just an excuse to loot their neighbors of all they own. Which is what any war is, really, for all the sense I can make of it," she added with a sigh.

"Aye, that's true," one of the twins said softly.

The men would be going off to fight within a few hours, Eleanor realized as she watched and listened to the plans they made. It wasn't as if she hadn't lived all her days among men who went off to war, it was just that she never before had been married to one of them. Just as she was getting used to having Stian in her bed, in her life, he was going away. Into battle.

She stared at him in open horror. He could be killed. There he was, laughing his fierce laugh, slapping Lars on the back, talking strategy with his father, and totally unconcerned about dying. He was a warrior, of course; he'd been trained to this. Even the most gentle knights of Poitiers were more in love with battle than with their ladies. She could see from the wild look of him that her husband was eager to be away, to be in the fight.

He doesn't see me, she thought. *Doesn't need me, or want me, now. He wants his squire, his armor, his sword, and his horse. Women are for the waiting time between battles.*

As the thoughts came to her, it was as if she had not known the truth of them all along, as if she was a stranger to her own world. It was as if she had never watched by a bedside as a wounded man breathed his last. It was as if she hadn't been in sieges, hadn't heard word of a brother dead in Antioch, hadn't ever seen a sword drawn in anger or blood spilled on the ground. She closed her eyes and all she saw was Stian, not as the sunburned angel of the trial, but as a man in a tattered mail coat, his blood washing away as he lay in some Border stream. Of all the warriors in the world, only Stian mattered to her in that moment, and the thought of losing him choked her with tears.

Then she opened her eyes and saw him still laughing, and she couldn't bear the sound or sight of him. Of anyone. She desperately needed to be alone. So, even though Edythe called a question after her, she picked up her skirts and fled for the stairs.

Stian wondered at Eleanor's hurry when she left the hall, at what business the new chatelaine had that took her from her needle. Then he saw the worry on Lady Edythe's face when he looked her way and thought that perhaps his wife had gone away because something had upset her. He rubbed his chin and ignored a comment from Lars as it occurred to him that Eleanor might actually miss him when he was away. Perhaps she would worry about him while he was gone, pine for the sight of him.

"Such as ladies do for gentle knights," he murmured, and couldn't help but chuckle at the notion.

"What of gentle knights?" Lars asked, having overheard him.

To divert his cousin from any more questions, Stian put a hand on his shoulder, turning him in

Edythe's direction. "Gentle knights," he said, "seek tokens from their ladies before riding into battle." He gave Lars a slight shove, but the man was eager enough to approach his lady fair. "Why don't you see if she'll give you a bit of her embroidery to wear on your sleeve?"

And I'll try to work up the courage to ask the same from Eleanor, he thought as he headed toward the stairs.

He found her in their room, standing by the bed, looking at nothing, and wringing her hands with nervous energy. She was not crying, he was relieved to see, for a woman should be brave when her man went into battle.

Her man. Yes, he was, wasn't he? And she was his lady. He found himself glancing toward the bookshelf as he hesitated in the doorway. A few days ago he'd suffered with the frustration of wanting Edythe. He'd thought he could learn to control such sinful urges with learning about men who put women on pedestals to worship from afar. Well, he was willing to wager those men put women on pedestals just so they could look up their skirts. He didn't need the poets of another land to tell him how to forget Edythe. Edythe was merely lovely; Eleanor was his.

He went to her, took her in his arms, kissed her, then sat her on the bed. He stepped back carefully, for he didn't have time to lie with her now, no matter how tempted he might be.

"Tonight," he said, and she smiled a little. "We'll make tonight so fine and wanton you'll remember me while I'm gone."

"I won't forget," she promised, and he accepted those words as all the token he needed.

He went to his chest and brought out a box which he took to her. "My mother's," he told her after she'd opened it and looked at the sheets of vellum and quills and inkstone. "She used to write her family sometimes."

"I see."

Eleanor's voice was soft, but the look on her face was full of wonder. The look, he realized, was for him, not the tools for writing. It made him feel warm, content, as if he was basking in summer sunlight.

"You should write your mother," he said, "if that's what you want to do."

"But, your father—"

"You are my wife, not his. I give you permission."

She ducked her head then looked up at him through her thick, dark lashes. "Thank you, Stian."

He nodded. "When you write, send the letter by Hubert to the abbot of St. Randolfs. He'll see it reaches your mother."

"I see," she said again. "Thank you."

Stian tilted his head to one side and teased her, "You could throw yourself in my arms with gratitude."

She put the writing box on the bed and stood up. "You have more important things to do right now," she reminded him. "I'll throw myself into your arms tonight."

He took her words for a promise. He also saw that for now she wanted to be alone. He understood wanting to be alone. So he contented himself with cupping her cheek in his palm, drawing in the warmth and softness of her for a moment. Then he went away.

14

"How did the birthing go?"

Eleanor trudged up the last steps to the bower door and answered, as Edythe stood back to let her enter, "It went well, thank the Holy Mother. Father Hubert and the girl's mother are there to tend the babe. My presence in the hut wasn't needed anymore." She pulled off her headrail and shook out her braids. "I am so tired."

Tired, yes, but full of a wild energy as well. She'd just overseen the birth of a healthy babe, the first birth since she'd become chatelaine. She'd been called out in the hours before dawn, but she'd been expecting it and had a basket already made up with clean linens and bags of medicinal herbs. Hubert had been in the serf's hut to help her with the language, and the labor had gone quickly.

"I was told Dame Beatrice couldn't have done better as midwife," she told her sister.

"But you don't know a thing about delivering babies."

"But I looked like I did," she told Edythe as they took seats beneath the bower windows.

The morning sunlight that fell across them was bright and strong. The late spring air was growing warm despite the early hour. Edythe, dressed in dark red, her long gold braids reaching to her waist, looked cheerfully serene and well rested. Eleanor felt like a grubby puppy beside her. Grubby, but satisfied with her lot in life.

Eleanor also longed to go back to bed, but it was too late in the day for such a luxury. So she stretched and told her sister, "I was there when they wanted me there. It was the mother's mother that did all the work. I think the villagers want the chatelaine to nurse them so they'll know the people they serve care for them. And it's not as if I haven't watched babes be born before. And I know enough about herbs and simples not to poison anyone."

"That's true, my dear, and a good thing. I'm sure my lord wouldn't want you to poison his serfs."

"His serfs? By holy St. Agnes they are his, aren't they? In the twenty days I've been chatelaine I've started to think of them as mine."

Edythe wiggled her fingers as though she were counting with them. "Twenty days? Has it been so long that my lord's been away? How swiftly time moves."

For Eleanor the time had not moved swiftly at all. For twenty days the keep had been alert for an attack. She'd spent much of her time making sure there were enough provisions in case of a siege. Lord Roger had left a strong guard to mind the walls, but she'd been responsible for every other detail of the life within.

Including sending to Durham for masons to build Lord Roger's garderobe. That had been his last concern as he'd left to fight the Scots who'd invaded his lands. He'd wanted her to make sure the thing was well started by the time he came home.

"I wonder when your lord, and mine, will be home?" she asked her sister.

Edythe only shook her head without any show of concern. Edythe never worried about anything. Eleanor wished she had her sister's serene acceptance of life. As for herself, only working herself to exhaustion every day for the last twenty had kept her from sleepless nights.

Edythe might be unconcerned herself, but she was perceptive, as she showed when she leaned over and took Eleanor's hands in hers. "You need something more than the doings of Harelby to divert your mind, my dear."

Eleanor nodded. "Aye. I suppose I do. I suppose I could help Hubert with the plans for the Lady Day festival. I hope the Blessed Virgin doesn't mind that her holy day celebration is being put off until the menfolk come home."

"Well, we can't have a proper Lady Day without the young men, can we?" Edythe asked. "I'm glad I made Hubert see that. He's such an . . . odd young man, don't you think?"

Eleanor chuckled. "Odd? I'm not sure he's more than half Christian. But he's a good lad." Stian had told her that once, that Hubert was a good lad. Jesu, but she missed the red-haired lout. "Did I tell you that the babe has Hubert's long hands? And her hair is all dark curls? He said it's a pity she can't grow up to be a priest."

Edythe giggled. "What an odd place this is. I'm

sure the priests in Poitiers would call Hubert's words blasphemy."

"Poitiers is far from here," Eleanor replied. "And a good deal closer to Rome. Hubert thinks the Church was started somewhere called Iona, for that is where the monks who converted this land came from."

"Odd," Edythe repeated, then a small frown creased her brows. "There we go again, speaking of nothing but the doings of Harelby's folk. We're forgetting there's anywhere but the cold Northland."

"It does seem to be all I think about these days," Eleanor admitted.

"It's not as if this place was as interesting as home."

"No, of course not. But it's all—"

"I know," Edythe interrupted. "You said you were going to write Mother but you haven't yet. Let's spend the day composing a letter to her."

Eleanor got to her feet. "But I have things to—"

"Nonsense. Harelby can do without you for a few hours." Edythe lifted her head and said with mock arrogance, "The Lady of Harelby commands you to attend her today."

Eleanor knew her sister meant her words in jest, but they were not jest at all. It was her duty to obey the Lady of Harelby, as chatelaine and Roger's son's wife. She didn't point this out, but she did resume her seat. "Very well," she said. "I'll fetch the writing box and we'll work on the letter."

Edythe clapped her hands with delight. "Splendid. What will you write?"

Eleanor couldn't stop the teasing smile that lifted her lips. "Why, of Harelby, of course."

"Yes. What else is there, really? You'll tell her our news and then she'll write back with hers. She'll be happy to hear any news, since I doubt she has much to do in Salisbury. Any part of England is as barbaric as another, I suppose."

"Yes," Eleanor agreed. "I suppose. Shall I tell her everything? About how Stian thought you were to be his bride? About how he was drunk at the wedding? And the look on Hubert's face when I protested the marriage, and when Stian did as well? And how he abducted me? And couldn't remember my name? And the wolf? And the trial?"

Edythe laughed at all her enthusiastic questions. "By the Lady, sister, I think you are mad."

Eleanor blinked in surprise. "What? Mad? Why?"

"Because all you seem to think of is Sir Stian. If you look around you will see that there are other people at Harelby but Stian."

Not for me, Eleanor thought, but did not say so. She blushed instead and said contritely, "True. I think too much of my own doings. We must tell Mother of all that has befallen us since we saw her last. I will fetch the vellum."

As she left she couldn't think of anything but what had befallen her. She thought of it, and wished Stian would hurry safely home.

"Does your wound pain you, uncle?"

Roger glared at the young man who'd ridden up to ask the question. Lars had pushed the mail coif back on his head, baring his bright gold hair and fresh young face to the sun. The boy looked as if he hadn't just spent the last three weeks sleeping in ditches and chasing down vicious bands of Scots reivers. Lars looked, in fact, like exactly what he was, a sturdy young man of twenty summers.

Roger, in fact, felt all of his forty years, and possibly a few more. Yes, his leg pained him, though the cut was not deep or festering. The man who'd cut him was dead and roasting in hell, but the satisfaction of knowing he'd dispatched the cur didn't make the ache any less. He was well enough to ride, and he was riding back to Harelby at last. That knowledge was enough to make him ignore how he was feeling while he anticipated a roof over his head, good wine, hot meals, a soft bed, and Edythe to nurse and cozen him.

"Uncle?" Lars asked. "Are you well?"

"Am I deaf, do you mean?" Roger said to the young man riding on his left. "No, I'm not deaf. No, I'm not in pain. So don't bother to ask again." Roger looked to his right, where Stian rode, slouched in the high-backed saddle. "At least you don't pester me with questions," he said to his son.

Stian's mind was not on being a pleasant companion. He barely managed a nod to his father's comment before he returned his attention to the muddy path before them.

Soon the war party would reach the rutted track that led to Harelby; they'd no longer be riding three abreast, but single file in a long line that would take them through the deep woods between Honcourt and the castle. It would be a good place for an ambush. He didn't expect one, for most of the Scots had been driven across the border for now, but it was best to be alert for any possibility. After the woods there was only one more burn to ford, the one that fed the moat that surrounded Harelby Hill. After the ford, he had only to ride up the hill, through the double gates of the bailey, and then he'd be home.

Stian wanted a bath. Not because he was covered

in dried sweat, mud, and other people's blood. He didn't mind being crusted from toes to hair with muck; the coating helped keep the midges from biting. What he wanted was the luxury of a hot tub of water and Eleanor scrubbing his back.

They'd sent word ahead they'd be returning today, bringing their wounded and their prisoners to be held for ransom. Stian didn't care if there was a feast prepared for the victors, though the men deserved the reward for their bravery. The fighting had been hard; the Scots hadn't been the only ones with dead to bury, though they'd had more than the English. Hubert would have to say a Mass for all the souls lost to war, including the women and babes in the villages the reivers had plundered.

The praying could wait, too, as far as Stian was concerned. All he wanted was a bath. In his own room. With his wife doing the scrubbing. Then, when she was done, he'd take a turn at scrubbing her. Or maybe they could fit in the tub together. He couldn't help but smile at that thought, and Roger noticed.

"You've that newly married look to you again, lad."

For once, Stian didn't mind being teased, since his father's comment had been low enough so that no one else could hear. He just gave his father a wry look and said, "You're the one wanting grandsons. You can't fault me for being dutiful."

His father nodded. "No, I can't. I'll tell you what, you work on giving me grandsons, and I'll concentrate on giving you a brother." He rubbed his thigh. "After the leg's healed," he amended.

"Does it pain you?" Stian asked.

"Your cousin's already asked."

"Which is no answer, my lord," Stian replied. "Does it pain you?" he asked with genuine concern.

"Of course it pains me," Roger snapped. He rubbed his leg and added, "And I'm going to miss Beatrice's gift with poultices, I can tell you that."

Stian grunted in response and went back to watching the road. It wouldn't be long now until they got to Harelby.

"You'll die, Roger of Harelby," the Scots prisoner said as he was hauled off his horse. His arms were bound behind him, but two guardsmen stood watch at his side. He was a dangerous man, and a proud one. He shook long, graying hair out of his face and snarled at his captor, "There's a price on your head high enough to tempt every man on the border."

Roger really had no interest in what the man had to say. He'd heard the tales of how the Borderlords planned revenge and wasn't the least impressed. "Well, you won't be collecting the reward, Conner Muragh. I'm the one who's collecting the ransom for you." He pointed toward the undercroft at the base of the tower. "Assuming any of your relatives want to buy your hide out of my cellar."

"Better to take the Muragh's head than sell him back to his own," Stian advised, not for the first time.

Roger wasn't sure that his son was wrong, but he'd fought with Conner Muragh as many times as he'd fought against him—and wenched and gotten drunk with him as well. He'd stood godfather to one of Muragh's sons, one he'd killed himself a war or two back. If Conner had been killed in outright battle, Roger wouldn't have complained, but he couldn't bring himself to kill the old wolf once he was captured.

"I'll take the ransom," he told Stian. He clapped a hand on his son's shoulder. "It'll make a fine present for Edythe. See that our guest has a comfortable nest with the rats, lad."

Stian gave a curt nod and barely more than an impatient flicker of a glance toward the hall. He jerked a thumb and let the guards haul the chief of the Muragh clan off to sit chained up in the undercroft until his family claimed him. Satisfied with both his captive's security and his son's obedience, Roger turned his attention to the household women waiting on the hall steps.

Though he knew she wouldn't be there, Roger felt an odd tightness about his heart when Beatrice was not in her usual place to greet him. It vanished quickly enough as he caught sight of Edythe, her slender form dressed in colors as bright as summer flowers, the gold of her hair barely subdued by the covering of a sheer veil. In one hand she held a silver cup; her other hand she lifted in greeting. He stepped forward to accept the stirrup cup, though he practically had to elbow Lars out of the way to do so. His son might be obedient, Roger decided, which was all very well and good, but something had to be done about his nephew.

"Have you considered going home to Denmark?" he questioned as Lars hurried after him toward the steps.

The young man gave a hearty laugh. "Not while you need my strong arm against the Muraghs," he said loyally.

Roger made a noncommittal noise in reply, but his

irritation with the lad was soon forgotten as he lost himself in his bride's welcoming smile.

Duty to Harelby came before personal pleasure. This was the first and most important lesson Stian's father had taught him. He made himself remember it as he saw the prisoner down the ladder to the store-rooms beneath the tower. The undercroft was the chatelaine's domain, full of barrels and casks, shelves and storage chests. They used torches to light their way to the one small chamber kept for prisoners beyond all the household goods. He left Conner Muragh there with a guard and orders for his care. With this obligation done, and Conner's threats and curses ringing in his ears, Stian went looking for Eleanor.

She was waiting for him as he climbed up out of the undercroft. He took the sight of her in slowly as he came up the ladder, from the embroidered hem of her skirts on up past where a belt cinched in her waist. His gaze lingered for a moment on the rounded curve of her breasts, then finally found her face. Instead of a wide, welcoming smile, she was looking at him in complete confusion.

"What are you doing down there?" she asked as he stepped out.

"Securing a prisoner for ransom," he told her. He put out his hand. "We'll need to keep this door locked and guarded for now."

Instead of handing over her key, she crossed her arms. "It would be locked now, but the servants have been bringing up supplies for tonight's feast," she explained.

Stian understood her sudden stiffness. She was new to the post of chatelaine and thought he was questioning her competence. He suspected she'd had some opposition from the servants, who'd been so loyal to his aunt Beatrice. He knew his mouse could fight like a lioness, so he pitied the servants more than her. But he also knew it wouldn't be good if he seemed to question her as a youthful, inexperienced, interfering foreigner.

He stepped closer and put his hands on her shoulders. "'Tis good to see you," he said, leaning close so none but she could hear. "And I welcome the feast to come, though I'd sooner have it served in bed than in hall." Her lips lifted in a shy smile while her head ducked modestly. He kissed her forehead, then he straightened and told her, "I'll need a key so I can see to the man's needs, but I can borrow the steward's."

"I'll fetch it from him," she answered promptly. She looked toward the hall. "I had a bath prepared for you," she told him. "In your room, if it pleases you."

"It pleases me very well," he said.

He wondered why they were both being so circumspect and shy with each other. There were many a boisterous meeting going on between the returning fighters and their womenfolk in the bailey. Even his father had his wife in his arms. They were the only ones acting so uncomfortable with each other. *We're too new together*, he supposed, *for the habits of leaving and reunion to have taken hold.* He put his arm around her shoulders and thought about taking a kiss from her lips. They looked willing enough as she smiled anxiously up at him.

Instead, too aware of the people around them, even if most of them weren't aware of him, he said, "Come bathe me, wife. I'm filthy to the bone."

*　　　*　　　*

"I'm wetter than you are and I've still got my clothes on."

"Well, strip them off and join me," Stian answered, unrepentant for having splashed her when he jumped in the water.

She was flushed and breathing hard from all the kisses and caresses they'd shared as she'd helped him undress. She was soaked. She was dripping. She should get back to her duties. She had so much to do. People would say she shirked her responsibilities.

He held out his arms to her while she stood locked in indecision. "Well, woman, what are you waiting for?"

Was her lord husband not her first responsibility? Besides, she wanted the man. She began to work at the wet knot of her belt, to the accompaniment of his bold laughter.

"I missed you, you scruffy cur," she told him later, after they were both clean and dry and their passion was satisfied. She lay with her leg thrown over his, her head on his shoulder, naked on the softness of the bed. He made a faint noise in reply and stroked her loosened hair. The day was waning. She knew she should go. She didn't want to.

A knock on the door settled the decision for her. She sat up and Stian followed suit. "What?" he called out gruffly while she hurried to pull on a chemise.

It was Fiona who answered, her young voice muffled by the wood. "The cook, my lady—"

"Oh, the cook!" Eleanor remembered as her head emerged from the neck hole. "I must speak to the cook."

"Yes, my lady," Fiona called out. "And Father Hubert says the bonfires are ready. The alewife—"

"Yes, yes, I'm coming." Eleanor opened the door enough to look at the girl, whose eyes were bright with merriment.

"Are you done bedding him yet?" Fiona asked. "I waited as long as I could, but the cook would have come himself soon."

"I'm done," Eleanor answered. She tried to look disapproving and formal, but she couldn't help but smile at the merry girl. "Just wait until you've a husband of your own," she whispered, and Fiona giggled.

"I pray it's soon. Will you come, lady? Or should I tell the cook to—"

"Tell the cook I'll be there directly."

The girl nodded and hurried away. With a fond smile, Eleanor watched her disappear down the stairs. Fiona had become her chief assistant in dealing with the servants. Assistant and translator, and champion as well. The girl was betrothed and eager to learn the duties of running a keep, while her twin was proving good company for Edythe.

She closed the door and turned back to her husband, who was still sitting naked on the edge of the bed. "I do have to go," she told him.

"Hubert?" he said. "Bonfires? May Day is long past."

While taking a fresh overdress from her chest she explained. "Hubert said we needed the menfolk to celebrate properly, so it was easy for Edythe to talk him into holding off the holiday. Where I come from," she added, "the day celebrates the Holy Virgin. Here, apparently, it has more to do with the fertility of the fields." And, speaking of fertility, she smiled to herself as she added so softly she doubted he heard, "I think I have some news for you, but I'm not certain yet."

Stian stood and stretched. She tried not to notice as she finished dressing. For his nakedness was of deep interest to her, and she feared all her efforts at putting on clothing would come to nothing if she watched him too closely, since she would probably go from looking to touching to tumbling under him once more with very little encouragement.

While he scratched his flat, hard-muscled stomach she hurried to find her shoes. She scurried out with them in hand, and he called after her as the door closed, "Then we'll jump through the fire together tonight, you and I."

Jump through the fire? she wondered as she made her way down the stairs. What did the man mean about jumping through the fire? Perhaps she'd heard wrong.

"A pity Lord Roger's wound pained him too much to attend the celebration."

"I should have stayed with him."

Eleanor heard the words spoken by Lars and Edythe, but she didn't detect any great feeling behind either comment. She was really more interested in Stian, who had found her lute and brought it to the feast in the moonlit meadow. Not only found it, but was playing it, and well, for a group of dancing youths and maidens. Since she didn't want to join in the dancing with anyone but her husband, she was standing next to a food-laden table keeping Edythe company when Lars joined them and spoke.

Nearby, a bonfire blazed. The flames seemed to reach halfway to the star-laden sky. The full moon shone brightly as well. In fact, the meadow was nearly as bright as day, glowing gold near the fire, and frosted with silver moonlight as well. The earth was still sun-warmed, fragrant with green grass and the flowers crushed beneath flying feet.

Everyone was there from the hall and the nearby villages. It was a laughing, singing, happy crowd, full of ale and meat—and something more. Something of the earth's own fertile magic permeated the place. Eleanor could feel it in the air, see it in bright eyes and openly hungry expressions. There was a glistening, pulsing fervor in the air, passing between men and women, growing with the promises of ever-bolder embraces.

It was a warm night. The fire roared with heat and everyone seemed stripped down to little more than braccos and shifts, skirts hiked up for dancing. Everywhere there were glimpses of flesh, soft shoulders, jiggling breasts, hairy chests. Everyone, from the swineherd to the lady of the hall, seemed beautiful, seductive, willing. Eleanor wished Lord Roger had come to the fire festival, or that Edythe had stayed steadfastly by his side. For Eleanor could see by her sister's expression as she looked at Lars that Edythe was caught up in the mood of the night.

Eleanor could feel the pull of it herself every time she looked toward Stian. She trembled when their eyes met over the fire, barely able to breathe from the longing that shook her. She wanted to go to him, lay down with him, there and then, in the field. Many another couple were straying off into the darkness after first linking hands and jumping through the fire. Now that she knew what he'd meant when he spoke of leaping the fire, she knew she'd willingly jump through it with him. But she could not leave Edythe's side. Duty kept her staunchly on her side of the fire, acting the chaperone, while her husband played the lute for other lovers on the opposite side of the blaze.

Stian wanted Eleanor to come to him. At first he thought the music might draw her, for he knew he was a fair musician. He did not like playing before others, but he'd brought the lute to please her. The dancers loved it and praised him loudly when he added his playing to the drum and pipe played by two of the villagers. Eleanor merely stood by her sister and sometimes looked at him. Oh, she was all hot-eyed and panting, but her feet were unmoved by this form of wooing. For a while, the yearning look on her face was enough for him, but it grew more frustrating than promising when nothing came of it. It became tempting to toss the lute into the fire just to see if that would move her, but that was something he could not do to the lute, never mind to Eleanor.

Eventually, it occurred to him that perhaps his wife's being so steadfastly planted at her sister's side had something to do with Lars. It seemed to him that perhaps the Dane was doing more than acting the faithful guard for the Lady of Harelby. Oh, he was loyal all right, Stian decided. A devoted cur sniffing eagerly around Edythe's skirts. Stian found himself growling like a dog himself when he realized what was going on.

"Why don't you find someone to bed?" he demanded as he marched up to his cousin.

Lars's look was all innocent surprise. "What?"

Stian handed the lute to his wife and grabbed the arm of the swineherd, who lingered by the food table.

"Hulda would be happy to jump the fire with you. Wouldn't you, Hulda?" he asked as the girl looked at him in astonishment.

"Uh," she answered, and jerked her thumb toward a tow-haired, buck-toothed youth nearby. "I've a husband now, if it please you, sir."

Stian let her go. "Oh." While Lars gave a loud laugh, he asked, "When?"

"On Beltane proper, sir. Father Hubert said you wouldn't be wanting the bride night with me since you'd had plenty of nights with me already."

The hurt look on Eleanor's face was far worse than the sting of Lars's amusement at Hulda's words. "Go on." He pushed Hulda away, toward her husband.

"Congratulations!" Lars called after her.

Let his father mind his own wife's chastity; he had his own life to deal with. Stian spared a glare for his cousin as he stepped to Eleanor's side. "Are you hungry?" he asked her. "Thirsty? Will you dance with me?"

Eleanor had already decided to bury the pinprick of hurt at Stian and the peasant girl's conversation. When he asked her to dance the pain of knowing he was no better than any other man dissipated completely. What matter if he'd tupped every woman in the countryside? That had all been before they'd met. He was by her side now, and he wanted her to dance.

"Gladly," she told him and handed the lute off to Edythe.

He took her hands, and soon they were whirling around the fire, laughing and lost in each other like any other couple at the fire festival. In fact, she was so consumed with Stian's presence that she barely noticed when Edythe and Lars leapt, with hands entwined, through the fire.

15

"Wake up, lad, you're going to York."

Stian recognized the voice, but he didn't know where he was. At first all he knew was that his head was resting on a woman's soft, linen-covered bosom. When he opened his eyes he thought for a moment that he was blind, but when he scraped his hand across his face he found that his eyes had been covered by a thick fall of black hair. Wonderfully soft, flower-scented black hair.

"Eleanor," he said, sighing as he remembered who he was with and what they'd done through most of the long night. He still didn't know quite where he was, though he recognized the moisture covering him was most likely the morning dew. He was glad Eleanor had insisted they cover themselves before lying down beneath a tree to sleep. Ah, so that's where they were, beneath the tall oak on the north edge of the pasture.

"Lord Roger!" It was Eleanor who spoke before

Stian could turn over and face his father. "Good morrow, my lord."

As she spoke, Eleanor searched the face of the mounted man above her. He was looking cheerful and far better rested than she felt. Not a sign of anger or disappointment emanated from his smiling, relaxed demeanor. In fact, there was a bright twinkle in his eyes as he gazed benignly down on them. From this, Eleanor decided that her sister had made her way safely and chastely home. She sent up a swift prayer of thanks to the Holy Virgin for that and made up her mind to have a firm talk with the Lady of Harelby.

"Well, lad, get up," Roger said as his horse pawed the ground. "Or do you want Jupiter here stepping on your backside? Good morning, my dear," he added to Eleanor while Stian got to his feet. "You look as if you enjoyed last night's celebration."

Eleanor didn't have the shame to blush; she grinned widely instead. "It was a passable affair, my lord," she told her father-in-law. "Far different than the customs of Lady Day in Poitiers."

"Perhaps you'll have the chance to compare the celebrations with old friends while you're in York, my dear."

Stian gave her a hand up as she said, "York, my lord?"

"What's Eleanor going to do in York?" Stian asked, gazing questioningly up at his father.

"Visit the merchants with my lady Edythe," Roger answered. He pointed at Stian. "While you, my lad, attend our liege, the Earl of Lincoln. As I recall, you've yet to swear fealty to him as heir to Harelby and Kirksted."

Stian wanted to rinse his mouth with a flagon of

ale; he wanted fresh clothes. He did not want to go to York to present himself to an earl as a good and loyal vassal. The less association he had with the great men of the realm the happier he'd be.

"You're the one who likes courts," he said to his father. "You go."

Roger shook his head and touched the bandage that bulged beneath his clothing. "I can barely ride."

"Hubert will hear your confession for that lie," Stian answered.

"And there's the new building to oversee. I've a mind to keep an eye on the workmen tearing up my walls. I'm sending you to York," Roger said in a tone that brooked no argument.

Of course, Stian argued anyway. "I've no business with the earl. You go if you want to sniff around the doings of the powerful. Besides, you know the man. I've never met him."

"It's time you did."

Stian took a firm stance, prepared for a shouting match with his wrongheaded father. Then he saw Eleanor's face.

"What?" he asked his wife, as he absorbed all the excitement and hope in her eyes. "Oh, no," he complained. "Not you as well?"

"Go to York?" she said eagerly. "Be presented to an earl? Visit merchants?"

Stian was not used to giving in gracefully. He didn't want to now, but the hopeful look Eleanor turned on him was more than he could take. "York," he said, and the word came out a grudging snarl. Eleanor nodded, grabbed his hands, and bounced like a child yearning for a promised sweet. How dull she must find life at Harelby. "Must we?" Stian asked.

"Please!"

He looked back at his father, who sat on his horse with a look of smug satisfaction. "York. With messages and parleys and ceremonies as well, I suppose?"

Roger nodded. "There are a few things I need you to do. I'll instruct you before you go. Oh," he added as though it were an afterthought, "there'll be a tournament, as well. You might enjoy that."

Stian grinned, suddenly full of enthusiasm. Typical of his father to save the one thing that would entice him for last. "A tourney, eh? I could use some new armor and horses." He put his arm around his wife, clasping her tightly to his side. "Peace, mouse, we're going. When do you want us to leave, Father?"

"If it weren't for you, I'd be spending the night with my wife."

"If it weren't for you, I'd be getting a sound night's sleep," Lars countered. "You snore like a bear."

"That's Ranald," Stian told him, pointing at the squire curled up on a pallet by the tent flap. "I don't snore."

He sat up with his blanket pulled around him. It was a cool night, and raining besides. The tent kept them dry, but the dampness in the air was uncomfortable. The squire was snoring, and so was the servant huddled next to him, while the guards they'd brought patrolled their watch in the rain. The tent wasn't that large and it was full of bodies, none of them the right one. He would have appreciated having Eleanor to cuddle with.

"No need to complain about me," Lars said. "It's not my fault your wife's with Lady Edythe. Her charge is to attend her lady."

Stian thought Edythe had quite enough company, what with Morwina, Blanche, and a maidservant also accompanying the party. True, properly speaking, Eleanor was chief lady-in-waiting to the mistress of Harelby; sleeping in Edythe's tent was what she was supposed to do. Stian knew that it was indeed propriety that kept her constantly at her sister's side, but it was Lady Edythe's chastity that concerned her more than her comfort.

And that concern was Lars's fault. Stian wished that either Edythe or Lars was back at Harelby. But Roger had insisted, to Edythe's delight, that his wife enjoy the pleasures of the town. And Stian had wanted Lars for participation in the upcoming tournament, for the Dane was one of the finest fighters in all the Border country. So Eleanor spent her time with Edythe, and he spent his time with Lars—just as they had all done as children before they'd ever met. He could hardly wait until they reached their destination.

If Stian had had his way, he would have set his wife pillion behind him on his horse and ridden off without delay, paid homage to the earl, fought in the melee, and come straight home again. No journey with women was ever that easy, of course, and they'd been days longer than necessary on the road. They had carts and chests and servants—and Eleanor had been brazen enough to look speculative when he sarcastically suggested they bring along the cook and the midwife as well. Then she'd saucily told him they didn't have a midwife, but she'd do her best if the need arose. He'd been too annoyed at all the fuss to laugh at her comment until hours after she'd made it.

By the rood, how he did enjoy her company, he thought now as he tried to get to sleep. If only he had her company, it would be much easier to find some rest on the thin pallet beneath him. His consolation was that come morning he would have her riding pillion behind him again. She'd lean against him with her arms wrapped snugly around his waist, and they'd ride at the head of the cavalcade, mostly in companionable silence, throughout another long summer day.

With that pleasure to anticipate—even though the morrow would probably be as rainy as the night, making the traveling a long slog through churned-up mud—Stian finally drifted off to sleep.

"You're not wearing that, are you?"

Stian looked at the surcote in his hands, then at his frowning wife. This was a question he'd never heard before, so he didn't quite take her meaning. "These are my best clothes."

"I know," she said easing the cloth out of his grip. "But you look absolutely awful in that shade of red." She folded the surcote and stuffed it back in his traveling chest.

"I like red." He looked around the tent seeking help, but he and Eleanor were alone.

She was dressed in her richly embroidered black kirtle and red underdress, her hair covered by a modest veil. He had to admit that she looked every bit of what she was, a lady from a queen's court. Beside her elegance, he looked every bit of what he was, a rude, backcountry knight without a grain of polish or sophistication. Which was just what he liked to be.

About his only concession to the fact that he was about to be presented to one of the country's great magnates was that he'd let his servant shave him and trim his hair and mustache. Eleanor had come in just as he'd sent the man away. She'd watched him start to dress for court with a disapproving eye. He noticed now that she'd brought a bundle of cloth with her. She picked it up and unfolded it. What was revealed was a deep blue surcote, knee-length, with wide bands of gray-and-white embroidery on neck, sleeves, and hem. Stian studied the design, then smiled, first at the fancy work, then at his wife. The design was a repeated pattern of a stylized wolf and moon.

When Eleanor saw that he was pleased with her gift she sighed with relief. She'd brought the cloth with her from her father's castle and had planned to make it into a kirtle for herself. When she'd gotten it out to start the dress, she'd been struck by how well the rich color would suit Stian's fair complexion and bright hair. The color pleased her, but she had hoped the embroidery would please her husband. Edythe had called the design barbaric, and Eleanor had only laughed in agreement and gone right on stitching.

"Do you like it?" she asked now.

In answer he kissed her, crushing the cloth between them. It was one more barrier to be resented, for this was the first time he'd properly kissed her since they'd left for York. While she enjoyed the chance to be away from Harelby, the circumstances had proved less than ideal. It was Eleanor who broke the kiss, reluctantly, for they had no time for dalliance.

"I think you like it," she said on a breathless laugh. "There's more," she added and picked up the black cote and braccos she'd made to complete the court apparel. "Promise me you won't wear these during the tournament," she said.

"I wouldn't—" Then he realized she was joking and his frown turned into a grudging smile. "What else should I wear to please you, lass?" he asked as he stripped so he could wear her gift. "A jeweled brooch on my cloak?"

"Do you have one?"

He grumbled, then conceded, "Aye. But it's at Harelby."

With your heart, she thought as she waited for him to dress.

Outside, the day was bright, the air full of shouts and laughter. Not only had the earl brought his own large household with him, but many of the local lords and landless knights had come to pay homage and take part in the tourney. They were all camped outside the walled trading town of York, the bright tents almost as numerous at the buildings of the town. The citizens were out to watch the deeds of the nobles, and the merchants were there with all their wares.

There was excitement in the air, and Eleanor could barely wait to take part in all the doings of the day. There was much to explore and see, provisions and trinkets to be purchased, news to be garnered, acquaintances to be made. She longed to be out of the tent, but she waited for her lord, trying not to let her impatience show. For she knew he dreaded the crowds she craved.

When he was ready, he took her hand and they left the tent together. "What now, my lady?" he asked as they stood in front of the tent.

For a moment Eleanor just drank in the colors, the sights, the sounds. " 'Tis like a great fair."

"Better than a war camp," he agreed. Stian sniffed the air. "There's mutton roasting nearby." He looked to their own cookfire, where the servants were dishing up bowls of porridge. "I'm for meat to break my fast," he said as he began to tug Eleanor toward the merchant pavilions. "Let's find food before we find the earl."

"If it please you, my lord."

He could tell it pleased her, for she practically skipped as she hurried along beside him. The crowd grew thicker the closer they got to the merchant area. Stian supposed it was to be expected this early in the day. At noon the focus of attention would be the gathering of the earl's court. In the afternoon the crowds would gather to watch at the field staked out for the tournament melee. In the evening there would be a feast, with tables set up beneath starlight and torches. Tomorrow the pattern would be the same, and the day after, if the fair weather held.

Stian hoped torrents would come raining down from the clouds the moment today's tourney came to an end. He'd come to York as his father wished. Soon he'd make his homage to the earl and deliver the messages, reports, and taxes to the earl's clerks. All that would be left then would be to bash a few heads and be gone. Surely Eleanor and Edythe could spend all Harelby's gold on frippery in the time it took him to do his errands.

"You have a grim and brooding look to you," Eleanor teased, drawing him out of his thoughts.

"Nay," he answered. "'Tis only hunger that twists my face."

She laughed and drew him toward a baker's booth. It was easy enough for him to use his size to clear the way through the crowd for her. Coins were passed from Eleanor's pouch and they soon turned away from the counter, each with a gold-crusted loaf of white bread in their hands. Strips of roasted mutton were had from the next booth, and ale at the next. The alewife had set out benches for her customers. Here Stian and Eleanor settled to break their fast and watch the passing crowd.

Eleanor couldn't have been happier at the Queen's court than she was sharing simple fare with Stian. It was such a fine day she decided it was time to tell him her good news as soon as the meal was done.

Before she could speak, Stian lifted his head. He sniffed the air and said, "I smell ginger cakes." He bounced to his feet, as eager as a little boy. "I love ginger cakes."

Eleanor breathed in the rich, spicy aroma, better than any perfume. "So do I."

Stian grabbed her by the hand and they dove back into the crowd, laughing like children as they went in search of the sweet cake. It wasn't long before they rounded a corner and came upon the booth they were looking for, where a plump old woman was doling out thick slices of brown cake to another eager couple. Edythe and Lars were there before them. Edythe, dressed in shades of pale yellow and white, looked like a fresh summer bloom. Lars, wearing a green tabard over newly shined mail, looked every inch the lady's dashing champion—especially since he had braided cords of yellow and white fastened around his upper arm as Edythe's favor. Eleanor and Stian came to a halt as they spotted the pair. It was obvious that Edythe and Lars had eyes for none but each other. Neither Blanche nor Morwina was nearby as chaperone for the pair.

Eleanor looked away. She glanced at her husband, who was staring angrily at the pair. "Stian?"

He looked at her, icy with anger. "This is like the books you read to me, the tales Edythe fed to my cousin. I see now the dishonorable way people lived in Poitiers, where no man minds how his wife behaves."

Stian's right hand was grasping his sword hilt. She put her hand on his arm. "Edythe would never dishonor Lord Roger; I will swear that on my own life, if you like."

"You are not responsible for anyone's honor but your own," he answered.

"Edythe chose him as her champion with your father's approval," Eleanor hurried to explain. "To be a champion does not mean the same as being a lover. Though it might look that way," she admitted, "anywhere but in Poitiers."

And in Poitiers, she knew, it had rarely been true that a man worshipped from afar for very long. No matter how long the love games went on, the object was always to bed the lady fair and move on to the next conquest. She wondered how long Edythe would play the courtship game before bluff, untutored, rough-handed, handsome Lars beat her at it.

"I'm going to have to stop putting off having a talk with that girl," she concluded, feeling for once as if she were the older, more experienced sister.

"And I with Lars."

"But don't beat him," she advised. "The more difficult he finds the way to her bed, the more he'll want her."

I'll beat him all right, Stian thought grimly. To his anxious wife he said, "As you say."

He slowly took his hand away from his sword, but not before Lars saw him through the crowd. His

cousin smiled and waved, and pointed them out to
Edythe. The Lady of Harelby promptly ordered two
more ginger cakes and brought them over. Lars hurried at her heels.

"I've checked out the tourney field," he told Stian.

"Where are your women?" Eleanor asked at the
same time.

"I left them haggling with a cloth merchant,"
Edythe answered. "Lars met me while he looked for
Stian and escorted me as far as the baker's booth.
Isn't it a wonderful day?" Edythe asked as she looked
around them. "I wish my lord had felt up to the ride."

"I've no doubt you miss my father very much,"
Stian said coolly. Then, avoiding the puzzled expression in Edythe's incomparably blue eyes, he took Lars
by the arm. "Come, cousin. Let us see to our arms
and mounts before we're called to court."

Leaving the women to make their way to the field
before the earl's green-and-red striped tent, Stian led
Lars to the the area where the squires were readying
the horses and arms for later in the day.

Stian wasn't surprised to find his squire engaged in
swordplay when he came up to where the lad was
supposed to be working. Nor was he surprised to see
who the squire was sparring with.

"Malcolm!" he called out to his other cousin. "Well
met! He always kites his shield, Ranald," Stian told
the squire. "Use that to get under his guard."

"Thank you for your help, cousin," Malcolm panted
as Ranald followed Stian's advice. It didn't take long
before the squire landed a blow to the ribs with the
wooden sword from up under Malcolm's shield.

"My job's to teach the lad," Stian reminded him.
"And yours is to hold the shield close to your body.

You'd think it was a wing, the way you flap the thing about."

Malcolm called a halt to the combat, threw down his shield, and went up to Stian and Lars. "Don't like Norman shields and broadswords," he said. "Give me something I can use two handed any day."

"You do fine with a battle axe," Stian conceded while Ranald ran up with a cloth.

Malcolm wiped sweat off his face and neck. "You did well, lad," he told Ranald, who was also his youngest brother. "See that you keep doing well," he added before sending the squire back to his duties. Malcolm turned his attention toward Lars. "Plan on winning the jousting, do you?"

"That I do," the Dane answered.

Stian knew it was no idle boast. Nor did he mind knowing Lars was a better tournament fighter than himself. He was sure enough of his own skill to be certain he wouldn't be unseated in the melee. He thought it likely he'd be taking some other man's possessions as a prize in the upcoming contest, and one prize was all he wanted. Such a small victory would be good enough for him. Let the public acclaim go to someone like Lars, who'd enjoy it.

"I'll do my best to unseat you," Malcolm promised Lars, "if it comes down to single combat tomorrow."

"Your best is good enough for most men," Lars answered. "I'll be careful."

"Who else fights on the Borderer side of the lists today?" Stian asked. "We only arrived last night, barely in time to enter the tourney. I've no idea who we're fighting with, or against."

"Most of the Borderers are here," Malcolm answered. "In one generation or another."

"Ayrfell?"

Malcolm laughed. "No. I'm told he's out chasing cattle someone stole from him."

"Now, there's an uncommon occurrence," Stian said. There was the sound of a horn call in the distance, high and sweet. It came from the direction of the earl's tent. "That's the first summons. Damn, I've got to go bend my knee before my liege—and everyone in Britain," he added.

His cousins laughed. "By the rood, you're as shy as when you were a boy," Malcolm said. "The only time I've seen you forget yourself is on the battlefield. Are you so shy with your wife?"

"That's not for you to know," Stian answered, trying not to take offense at the teasing question. He did, however, take offense at Lars's smirk, which reminded him of a duty he needed to perform. Putting his arm around the Dane's shoulder, he said, "Come, and let us have a word in private, cousin."

Not long afterwards, just as the horn was sounding the second summons to court, Stian met his wife as he came back from the far side of the area. "Well met!" he said as she rushed up to him. "Have you come to fetch me to the earl?"

"In part," she answered. "Have you hurt yourself?"

Stian realized that he was rubbing the aching knuckles of his left hand and stopped. "No, no. I am well. In part to fetch me, you say?" he asked as they joined hands and walked along. "Why else did you come looking for me? Did you miss my handsome face?"

Eleanor paused long enough to study his face, then they walked on. "It's not such an ugly face," she said. "Nowhere near as bad as I thought at first."

"Familiarity renders it acceptable, does it?"

"Oh, indeed, my lord." In truth, she'd come to think that he had a rough, raw handsomeness that was uniquely his own. She admired his bright hair and the height and width of his well-formed body. She thought he looked especially fine in the clothes she'd made to flatter his size and coloring. "Aye," she told him, "you'll do well enough for a mouse like me."

"That is good to know. So, why else did you search me out?" he went on, trying to keep his tone light to cover his pleased embarrassment at words he found very flattering.

She paused again and took a narrow, folded piece of cloth from her pouch. She handed it to him hesitantly, with her gaze fastened on the ground. " 'Tis my favor, Stian. For you to wear. If it please you," she said and looked up at him through her lashes.

Stian unfolded the cloth, a narrow width of dark blue covered with a bit of embroidery on the ends. Studying the design, he saw that it was the wolf pattern of his surcote repeated. Only this time the wolf was crouched down, with a mouse looking up at it between its paws. Stian couldn't help but throw back his head and laugh. It was the most perfect thing he'd ever seen.

"Do you like it?" Eleanor asked once he had his mirth under control. She had a half smile on her lips. "I think you like it."

"I like it," he said.

"Will you wear it, then? And be my champion?"

For an answer he kissed her. And they got so caught up in each other that they almost missed the third and final call from the herald's horn.

*　　　*　　　*

"I mislike the sight of them together."

"Aye, so do I, but there's nothing for it. Pass the winecup, Eleanor."

Edythe was set at the high table, on the earl's right side. She was in the place of honor as the Baroness of Harelby, and as the acclaimed fairest lady of the tourney day. It wasn't Edythe's place at table that was so disturbing; Eleanor expected no less for her sister. It was the fact that Lars was seated beside her as champion jouster of the day.

The only flaw to Lars's perfection was the black eye he'd said he hadn't gotten on the melee field. Though he declined to explain how he'd gotten the injury, Eleanor didn't think she had farther to look than her husband's bruised knuckles to find the answer.

"For shame," she said as she passed him the cup. "You are a brawling lout," she explained to his questioning look.

"Aye," he said. "What of it?"

"I told you to let me deal with the two of them."

"You said no such thing." He took a sip of wine and passed the cup back to her.

Though the two of them were not seated at the high table, their rank entitled them to a silver-rimmed cup and a wooden trencher at the first table below the salt. Stian preferred the thick bread trencher the food was served on at home.

"Remind me not to eat the platter," he said to Eleanor as he picked a piece of meat up off the plate. Jesu, how he wanted to go home! "Think you we can leave tomorrow?" he asked.

Eleanor looked around the torchlit meadow where the banquet was being held. It was a well-organized affair, with roving minstrels and jugglers and an abundance of servants seeing to the needs of the guests. The earl's large household were dressed in rich clothes. The courtiers were full of clever conversation. She'd heard more gossip in half an hour from the lady seated on her right than could reach Harelby in years. She was having a wonderful time. She knew this sort of entertainment would come as a rare treat for her as the wife of Stian of remote Harelby and she wanted to savor it. But Stian was hating every moment of it.

It took an effort, but she managed to put some sort of smile on her face when she said, "Why not? If your business is done we might as well leave. But someday," she added sternly, "I'm going to make you take me on a proper *chevauchée* to your family's southern estates. Maybe we'll even go as far as the lands your family holds across the Channel."

"My father can take you," he answered. "I'll stay home and go hunting."

"You would."

"As for business," he went on, "never mind the taxes and lawsuits; our true reason for being here was concluded the moment I showed up with you and Edythe. Introducing Harelby's women to the world was all the purpose Father really wanted to serve. Your being the daughters of both Hugo and Jeanne FitzWalter is valuable, he tells me."

"I see. Of course," Eleanor concurred. "He's a clever man, is Roger of Harelby; to marry women with a parent in each royal camp in these troubled times is indeed useful politics." She glanced once again at Edythe and Lars. "Getting the two of them back home would be best, I think." Not that it was going to be easy to get them to go, she added to herself. Instead, she tried for a more genuine smile this time and said, "Yes, let us be gone as soon as may be."

Stian put his arm around her shoulders and kissed her cheek. "If we hurry," he said, "we can be at Harelby in four days."

16

"No!"

Stian was the first to see the smoke, though the shout the sight ripped out of him was enough to bring the other riders hurrying up the hill behind him. He was the first to see it because he'd ridden ahead of the cavalcade and so reached the top of the rise across the Valley of the Harl from Harelby Castle well ahead of the wagons with the women and baggage. It was a clear, bright late afternoon without a cloud in the sky. Somehow, the gentle, blue background made the rising pillar of darkness all the more ominous and out of place. It gave the lie to the atmosphere of peace that had surrounded the day until now.

There were woods, the narrow river, more woods, and the fields of the manor between where Stian brought his horse to a halt and the place he called home, but he knew without a doubt where the smoke was coming from.

"Oh, sweet Jesu," he whispered, the reins tight in his tense hands. His eyes closed as he leaned forward in the high saddle, momentarily immobilized by pictures his imagination carved from the dark column of smoke. "My home," he whispered. "My life. Harelby." Then his head came up, eyes snapping open. "Father!"

He spurred the horse forward on the word, everything else but the need to reach Harelby forgotten. Voices called questioningly behind him, but he paid them no heed. He rode hard down into the valley, and splashed through the ford without noticing the spray churned up by the horse's racing hooves. Nothing mattered to him but reaching Harelby.

He didn't notice the horseman who came pelting up from behind until Malcolm came abreast of him, shouting, "Reivers in the village?"

In Stian's headlong rush to reach his home, the words didn't register for a moment. When they did, he asked, "What?"

"Think you there's raiders after your cows?" his cousin shouted back.

The logical question brought some sense back to Stian's panic-stricken mind. At least enough for him to slow his horse down to actually look about him for any sign of approaching danger. He was glad hard-headed Malcolm Erskine had chosen to come home with him for a visit rather than lingering in York.

The path from the ford led through a stretch of woods to the village before going uphill again toward the castle. For any invader to reach that stone fortress there was the moat to cross and the motte to climb; then they'd have to go across two walled and well-defended baileys before reaching the tower built to withstand a strong siege. Malcolm was probably right; the fire had been set by raiders in the village, though that would be bad enough.

"Come on," he said and urged his horse forward again, heading for Harelby village.

It was Hubert he saw first as the young priest stumbled out of a smoking hut, his baby daughter in his arms. The priest's surcote was torn and singed, and his thin face was covered in dried blood from a deep gash. There was ruin all around them, bodies both human and animal, trampled fences. Many a hut was already gutted by fire; others were still burning, their thatched roofs sending up the dark smoke Stian had spotted two miles away.

"What!" he demanded as he rode up to the priest. "Tell me quick! Where did they go?"

Hubert shook his head. He pointed toward the looming bulk of Harelby up on the hill. "The castle," he told Stian. "They attacked the village as a diversion. While we defended the village others got into the cas—"

Stian didn't stay to listen to any more. He rode desperately for home. He cared not whether Malcolm followed or if there was an army waiting for him when he reached the gates.

As soon as she saw the smoke, Eleanor jumped out of the cart where she'd been riding with the other women. The cavalcade had come to a halt at the top of the rise, just after Stian raced away followed by Malcolm pelting madly after him. All was in confusion among those left behind. Everyone was full of questions and worry. To Eleanor what was happening was evident—the village was under attack.

She wished Stian hadn't ridden off without any warning, but she wasn't afraid of her own party being attacked. Besides Lars and their own people, Malcolm had brought a half dozen of his men with him. They had plenty of protection, even without her lord to command the guards. She was confident that Edythe could be safely gotten back to Harelby, and that was her first concern.

Standing in the dirt track surrounded by the baggage train and a great many men on tall horses, she felt very small, and more insignificant than ever. It was an image of herself she had no time to indulge in, however.

She looked toward Lars. "Take her to Harelby," she told him, pointing to the cart from which Edythe peered anxiously at the sky.

The women around her were cackling like frightened hens, but Edythe's attention was on the rising smoke. Eventually, she turned her gaze on Eleanor. "I'm cold," she said, though the day was very warm. "Something awful has happened."

Eleanor didn't try to argue with the unknown. "You'll be safe," was all she said. "Get her out of here," she said to Lars, and got a curt nod before she turned to Stian's squire. "Take me up behind you, Ranald," she ordered. "I'm going to the village."

"It could be dangerous, my lady," he answered, but he gripped her arm when she reached up and gave a mighty pull to help her onto the horse.

"I know," she told him. She gripped him around the waist. She didn't care if the reivers were gone or not. There would be people who needed nursing and bodies to bury, no doubt. She had to go where her help was needed. "Hurry."

Hubert was standing by the roadside when they

came into the village. He looked sick and stunned. Eleanor slid gracelessly off the back of the horse to rush up to the priest. "What happened here?" she asked as soon as she'd taken his babe from his arms. She automatically rocked the infant on her hip as it began to cry. "Where's her mother?"

"She'll be all right," Hubert said, sounding more like he was reassuring himself than giving information. "The reivers hurt her, but she'll be all right."

"And the others?" Eleanor asked. It was an effort to keep her voice calm. "What happened? What needs to be done?"

"Broken heads and bones," he answered. "Some women raped. Hulda's dead, and her man, and most of the pigs. She shouldn't have fought to save a few pigs."

"I'm so sorry."

"It was a diversion," he went on, his voice far too calm. "They were driven off far too easily, though they did damage enough while they were here."

"So I see. Ranald, ride to the castle. Send back my bag of medicines."

"Aye, my lady," he answered. "And I'll come back to guard you myself."

Eleanor took the stunned priest by the arm. "Come," she said. "Walk with me." She headed them into the smoke that still curled around the pillaged huts. "Show me what needs to be done, and we'll start to take care of it."

"He's dead."

The signs of fighting in the bailey were unmistakable, but those were the last words Stian had expected to hear when he vaulted off his horse at the door to the hall. It was a girl who had spoken, Fiona, standing in the doorway at the top of the stairs. He didn't have to ask who she meant.

Stian ran past her into the hall, calling, "Father!" in the unnatural quiet of the shadowed room. Only his voice echoed in the silence; he knew he wouldn't be answered.

Malcolm and Fiona followed after him. As he looked around the wreckage of overturned tables and bodies strewn in the rushes, he heard Malcolm ask, "How? What happened here?"

"A surprise attack," the girl answered. Her voice was none too steady, but she seemed sure of her facts. Stian listened with half an ear while she explained. "Lord Roger sent most of the men to fight off the reivers when they attacked the village. But that wasn't all that happened. Some men climbed up through the hole the masons made for the garderobe."

Stian whirled on the girl. "What!"

She flinched away, face full of terror. "I—"

He came after her and grabbed her by the shoulders so hard she whimpered in pain. "What happened? How could anyone—"

Malcolm grabbed his arm. "Leave her be. The girl's terrified. Were you hurt?"

Stian just barely remembered that Fiona was one of Malcolm's younger twin sisters. He eased his grip. "My father," he demanded. "What happened to my father?"

The girl went into Malcolm's sheltering embrace. "I wasn't hurt," she told her brother. "Lord Roger told the women to hide when he realized the tower was full of invaders. I hid under Lord Roger's bed. I heard the fighting, saw some of it when I looked out from where I was concealed. They'd come for Conner

Muragh," she added. "Got him, too. He escaped with them."

"But what happened to Lord Roger?"

Stian had grown angrier and more desperate with every word. He no longer cared for the answer to what had happened; he knew he was going to kill for the how and the why. There was only one thing he needed to know. "Where is my father?"

"On the tower stairs," the girl answered. "I tried to move his body," she went on, "but he was heavy."

For the first time, Stian noticed the blood on Fiona's skirts. Not her blood.

"Oh, sweet Jesu."

Maybe he wasn't dead. Maybe he was just—

Stian ran for the tower. He took the narrow stairs three at a time. He came across the first body at the turning from the second floor to the third. The dead man had been a Muragh. The second as well. He found his father at the top of the stairs, at the opening where the little room for the garderobe was being built next to the bower.

Roger of Harelby was laid out on his back. There was no doubt he was dead, for his throat had been slit.

There were a pair of dead men beside him, leaving little room in the narrow corridor for Stian to kneel beside his father's corpse. Tears streaming down his face, he kicked an enemy carcass aside and dropped to his knees. There was still warmth in the body he took in his arms.

He closed his eyes, rocking back and forth for a few moments until the grief welled out of him in a roar. His hands and arms were covered in blood when he stood once more.

He held his hands before him and vowed,

"Revenge. Every Muragh living will pay for this." He gave his father one last look, then hurried down the stairs faster than he had raced up.

By the time he reached the hall Lars was there, inspecting the carnage with Malcolm. There was a group of women huddled by the hearth. He supposed Eleanor was among them. The women were safe enough; he had other matters to attend to.

"Come on," he said to his cousins. "We're going."

"Where?" Malcolm asked, hurrying after him.

Stian headed toward the stable. "We'll want fresh horses. They've got a good start."

"They're traveling fast," Lars said. "Must be. They killed the cattle rather than herd it before them. They're not even thieves, just murdering bastards."

"They've got more than a good start." Malcolm pointed. "The light's going."

It was indeed close to sunset, Stian noticed. He didn't care. "We'll track them in the dark."

Malcolm stopped and pointed toward the north. "Look to the sky, man." Stian looked up and saw the clouds piling up on the horizon, dark and moving in fast. "There's a storm blowing in from the sea," Malcolm said. "Can we track them in that? At night? See sense, Stian. Set your castle to rights, bury your dead, and wait for morning."

Stian did no more than snarl at the man's advice. "Come with me or go home," he told him. "I'm off to kill Muraghs this night."

"I'll come with you," Malcolm said. "But it won't do any good."

It had to do some good. Killing the bastards would do him good. Someone had to pay, Stian knew that. Only death would satisfy this consuming rage clawing away at his insides. He had to have revenge, or else how could he be whole again? All he truly wanted was his father.

"Conner Muragh's head will have to do," he said. "Fetch every man who can ride," he ordered Lars. "We're leaving right now."

"I'm soaked through to the skin, and I don't even care."

Eleanor tiredly dragged off her dripping headrail and gazed upon the sorry state of the hall. Not that there was much she could see in the near-total darkness. There was but one rushlight sputtering on the wall next to the tower doorway, and the hearth fire was out. There was more illumination from the lightning almost continually flashing across the narrow windows than from inside the hall. She'd been more afraid of the weather than attackers as they came back from the village in the raging storm.

She had no idea of the hour, no idea of the state of the household. She was tired, more than tired, soul weary. She wanted only to rest in Stian's arms, but knew that longing was not likely to come to pass this night. She'd had word of Lord Roger's death and her heart ached for it, pain that was for Edythe, herself, all Roger's loyal people, but mostly for Stian. She would have gone to him, even leaving the villagers to deal with their own troubles, but Ranald had come back from the castle with word that Stian had set out to track the raiders.

She rubbed her temples and tried to find some strength to get her through the rest of the night. She'd been tired enough just from the journey. That exhaustion was long forgotten, replaced by weariness from more grisly tasks. She couldn't let herself dwell on the death and pain she'd seen. If she let herself think, she wouldn't be able to do anything but cry. She would save up her tears for later.

"Crying won't do anyone any good," she said. "A hot meal might."

"Aye, my lady," Ranald answered.

She'd forgotten the lad was at her side, though how she could have overlooked his presence surprised her. He'd been with her, loyally protective and helpful, for many hours.

She put her hand on his shoulder and said, "Thank you."

His voice came, shyly pleased, out of the darkness. "For what, my lady?"

"For just being here, lad. I truly appreciate all your help."

"'Tis no more than duty, Lady Eleanor. Sir Stian would have my hide if anything happened to his lady."

"Thank you, anyway," she said. "Think you can roust out some of the servants?" she went on, before the fondness she felt for the squire brought out all the other emotions she was carefully keeping in check. "Where could everyone be? There's much to do."

"I'll see who I can find, my lady," Ranald promised.

"Good. We need to get a fire going, and find out if there are any supplies left in the undercroft so we can get people fed."

So much to do, she added to herself as Ranald went off. *So much. Edythe. I must see to Edythe. She lost a husband this day. She must need me.*

As she slowly picked her way toward the tower doorway, she couldn't help but wonder again where everyone was. There had been a guard at the castle gate when they rode up, and a few men in the stables. Between the aftermath of the attack and the fury of the storm all life seemed to have fled Harelby. She found that she was not only chilled from the rain, but from the heavy silence in the hall. Or perhaps the silence was only of her own imagining, since the wind and thunder were a constant roar, even through the thick stone walls.

Passing below the windows over the dais, she glanced up as a white flash of lightning, more brilliant than any before it, burned across the glass. The blue-white brightness blinded her for a moment. In the afterglow she thought she saw a figure seated in Lord Roger's high-backed chair.

Whether it was ghost, man, or her imagination she didn't know, but the thrill of fear the sight jolted through her sent her running up the stairs. The stair-case was dark and smelled of blood. It was not until she reached the turning leading up to the third floor that she saw light in the distance. Unfortunately, the light also served to show her a stack of bodies on the landing that must have been cleared off the stairs. The bodies blocked the entrance to her own room. She eased past them, panting, choking out prayers, and fighting the urge to be sick.

She set her gaze on the light above and hurried on until she reached the torch set in a bracket next to the bower door. She stopped there, just looking at the fire for a moment, until her attention was caught by the sight of long gashes in the wood. It looked as if someone had taken an axe to the door. Someone probably had, but the thick old wood had given up but a few splinters for all the attackers' trouble. There was dried blood splattered on the walls as well, but she refused to dwell on whose blood it might be.

The door was ajar, letting out the sounds of wailing, prayer, and murmured conversation. She slipped inside, glad of the people and the light despite the circumstances of the gathering. Edythe was by the bed, with all the gentlewomen surrounding her. Hubert knelt at the head of the bed, mud-encrusted hands tightly clasped in prayer. The cut on his forehead showed as an ugly red line in the glow of candles set on a nearby table.

Eleanor was not yet ready to look at the body on the bed, though the man's large form was decently covered with a cloth. So she turned at the sound of men's voices to see Lars and Malcolm seated in the alcove where the women spent their days. It was a corner full of thread baskets, embroidery frames, spindles, and piles of dyed wool waiting for the loom. The big men, still dressed in mail and leather, looked like a pair of cuckoo chicks set in a sparrow's nest made of bright yarn. They were passing a wineskin back and forth between them, but their gazes were set on the bed and the people surrounding it.

Eleanor knew she should go to Edythe. She saw the tears streaming down her sister's face and knew she should comfort her. She couldn't make herself do it. Though her sister was only a few steps away, Eleanor simply could not bridge that short gap. Her own weariness weighed her down so much she wanted to sink to the floor and die.

"Or just sleep," she whispered, "and let this all be a bad dream." She had a hopeful vision of waking in

Stian's comforting arms, then forced the yearning away to concentrate on bleak reality. She went to speak with the men. Malcolm stood to offer his chair.

"You look very bad, lady. You need dry clothes and to rest."

She shook her head, but did sink gratefully into the seat. "I thought you'd gone after the reivers."

"Aye," Malcolm said. "For a while."

"With darkness and the storm there was no tracking them," Lars said. He glanced over at the bed, and Eleanor watched tears roll down his cheek. "My father sent me to Roger when I was seven. Everything I learned was at his hand, as page and squire and fighter. I—" He shook his head, then, shifting his attention toward Edythe, said very softly, "I owe him everything."

Eleanor left the warrior alone in his grief, thinking he would prefer it so. She turned to Malcolm. "I sent Ranald to rouse the servants. There will be hot food soon." As he nodded, she recalled the grisly pile she'd found on the stairs. "And I'll have those invaders buried tonight, storm or no."

"My men will help, lady," Malcolm told her.

Eleanor nodded her thanks. She knew she should get up to give the orders, but she sat back further in the cushioned chair instead. It was so tempting to rest her head and close her eyes. She did rest her head, but looked up the long distance to Malcolm's face. Looking at him in his armor and with his curls all wind tangled, a simple, obvious truth slowly occurred to her. "Stian's back," she said. "If you turned back Stian must be at Harelby."

"He's here," Malcolm acknowledged. "I hit him over the head myself to get him to come home. It wasn't easy bringing him in tied over his own saddle, but someone had to show sense."

Eleanor would have jumped to her feet, but the combination of exhaustion and wet skirts made it a struggle to rise. "He's here! He's hurt?"

"Not hurt." Malcolm put his hands on her shoulders and eased her back into the chair. "We left him with a wineskin in the hall. Let him be, girl," he ordered when she tried to stand again. "Let him grieve in his own time and his own way."

Eleanor remembered the brief illumination of a figure in Lord Roger's chair. Not a ghost, then, but her husband. She hated the thought of him brooding alone in the dark, but she also didn't think he'd want to be seen spilling his grief out in tears. He might think it made him seem weak. She thought Malcolm understood his touchy pride. Perhaps she would let him alone, as Malcolm seemed to think he needed, at least for a little while.

So she folded her hands together, trying to keep still so as not to betray her own agitation, and made herself talk to the men. "I heard some of the tale in the village, about how the Muraghs took the castle by surprise. But how they breached the defenses I'm still not certain."

"'Twas through the space Lord Roger had had opened in the curtain wall," Lars answered. "The hole was narrow but scaleable, and it led straight from the moat to the bower."

"But—" Eleanor did manage to get to her feet this time. "But what outsider knew of that?"

"Now, that, wife, is just what I've been wondering."

Stian's voice rang out loudly from the doorway, slightly slurred, full of anger. All eyes turned to him as he stepped forward. His own hate-filled gaze raked across them, and people moved back as he halted in the center of the bedchamber. He held the wineskin in one hand, a dagger in the other.

Stian couldn't bring himself to look at the cloth-covered mound on the bed. A part of him wanted to kneel and pray, to say good-bye. He could not do it. He could hear the man laughing from the shadows of the room, could hear the shouts of their arguments. It had always been a clean anger between them, maddening, but the storms never left anger in their wakes for long.

Now, he could only make one concession to his father's passing. He looked to Hubert. "He died unshriven?"

The young priest shook his head. "He made confession just after Mass—this morning." Hubert's last words trailed off into confusion. "It feels like a month since dawn," the priest said and knelt down to pray again.

Stian left him to it and turned his attention on all the staring people. "Stop it!" he snarled. He pointed to the door. "Don't look at me. Get out! I want no strangers here."

Edythe took a step toward him, her hand held out like a supplicant. Before she could say a word he rounded on her, the dagger held to strike. "Back, bitch." She shrieked. And while she scrambled back behind her women, he went on, "Was it you?" He turned toward Lars. "Or you?" His dagger pointed to Eleanor. "You?" He tossed the drained wineskin at his wife.

Malcolm caught it before it reached her. "What are you talking about?" his cousin demanded.

"Someone betrayed my father," Stian answered. "Don't you see it? Someone told the Muraghs of the weakened wall. Someone." He glared at Lars while he pointed toward Edythe. "Do you want her that badly?"

When Lars's hand went to his sword hilt Eleanor stepped in front of him. "Peace," she said. She looked to her husband. "Leave be, I beg you. I know you hurt—"

Stian just turned his cold glare on her. His eyes looked like ice, and she saw nothing in his face but hate. "Did you want the title sooner than you deserved it? Couldn't you have waited a few more years?" He gave her a mocking bow. "Well met, Lady of Harelby."

Suddenly he was on her, pressing her back against the wall with his arm across her throat. He'd moved so fast she hadn't seen it. Eleanor couldn't breathe. She couldn't cry out. She could only look into his angry face, smell the sour wine on his breath. She heard the women scream, Malcolm shouting. She felt muscle before her and the stone wall at her back, both equally hard.

Holy Mother! She'd never been so afraid in her life. "Please!" She could only mouth the word; no sound would come out. He shook his head, just once, eyes never leaving hers. Then he eased the pressure enough for her to breathe.

"Did you betray my father?"

"No. I swear!"

He raised his hand above his head. "Did you?"

"Don't strike me," Eleanor pleaded, her voice a bare whisper. "Please. Don't hurt me. I'm with child."

Stian's hand dropped to his side as though it was made of stone. Some of the cold seemed to leave his eyes. "With child?" He closed his eyes and took a stumbling step backward. "Sweet Jesu, he wanted grandsons."

Stian never saw the dagger hilt that knocked him out, but Eleanor did. She didn't try to warn her husband as Malcolm hit him on the head. She did grasp him around the waist and helped ease his fall to the floor. She went down with him and ended up with his head in her lap.

"Damn drunken fool," Malcolm muttered and nudged Stian's body with his foot. "His head's too hard for that to keep him out long, but maybe the wine will keep him asleep."

Eleanor looked up. "Why did he—?"

"And damn the wine, too," he answered. "He's mean as a wounded boar when there's wine in him."

"Aye, that's so," Lars agreed.

Malcolm knelt down and put his hand on her shoulder. "Are you hurt?"

"No," she said. *Not where it shows.* "Why would he think I'd betray—?"

"Why accuse any of us?" Lars said. He sounded both offended and petulant.

"There's an easy answer for that," Malcolm said. "I remember when my own da died. Though he died in battle, I still felt guilty. There's a curse that comes with being an heir," he explained. "You want the lands and title and power, but you come to it over another man's body. If you love the man, you blame yourself no matter how he dies." He put a comforting arm around Eleanor's shoulder. "He feels powerless right now. He wants someone he can punish, and the Muraghs are out of his reach. He blames himself, but takes it out on others. It's just grief; it'll go in time."

Aye, she supposed it would. His, at any rate. Right now, she could no longer keep herself from weeping. Stian's words, his anger, his violence, they were more than she could take. This day had been spent in purgatory until now; all of it had been just a prelude to the pain Stian had just inflicted on her soul.

"Are you hurt?" Malcolm asked again.

She wiped her face with her sleeve. "I've much to do," she said. Her voice was steady. She looked at Malcolm with outward calm. *How odd*, she thought as though watching herself from a long way away.

She gently eased Stian's head onto the floor. She let Malcolm help her to her feet. She grew dizzy when she took a step forward. The room had grown much darker. Why was everyone staring at her?

"I'll see to the servants now," she told them. She took another step, but for some reason found herself scooped up into Malcolm's arms.

She heard him say, "She needs—" but the rest of it was lost in safe, heavy darkness.

17

"My lord?"

Eleanor couldn't bring herself to call him Stian.
She wondered if he remembered last night, but
wasn't about to ask. The expression on his face was
as hard as it had been then, though she thought there
was more pain in his eyes than coldness. She wanted
to reach out to comfort him, but his stiff demeanor
warned against any contact.

"Why didn't you tell me you were with child
before?"

So, he did remember. He didn't look repentant. He
had a cup of wine in his hand. He drank it down in
one long gulp and tossed the cup away. It rolled with
a clatter down into the hall.

Eleanor's throat tightened with pain from grief and
the coldness in his voice. "I was going to, in York.
But then I thought it would be amusing to tell you
and your father together. He wanted grandsons," she

added, echoing Stian's words before Malcolm knocked him out.

Stian just gave a curt nod. He moved to step around her. They were standing on the stairs, and had met with him going up and her coming down. For once they were eye to eye.

She'd woken in her own bed just before dawn, wrapped in a fur blanket, with Edythe lying beside her. She'd come awake disoriented, and not feeling very well. She hadn't understood why Stian wasn't in their bed with her at first. She couldn't remember how she'd actually gotten to bed. What she did remember were Stian's accusations of the night before. The words, the way he'd looked at her, left her in more pain than physical blows would have. The memory of his anger left her weak and tired and unwilling to face the day. To face Stian now, though she needed to speak to him. She didn't want to talk to the husband who didn't want to talk to her, so she tried to make herself think of him only as her liege.

And why should he trust me? she wondered bitterly as they faced each other. What was she to him but the foreign mouse his father had forced him to marry? She had thought they were building a life together. She had thought he was happy with her, content, coming to care for her. She had had hopes, confident hopes, dashed now.

She had tried not to feel the pain of betrayal when she climbed out of her lonely bed. She'd tried to think only of her duty to the new Lord of Harelby, for she had much to do.

Fiona, Morwina, and Blanche had all slept on the floor. She'd quietly woken everyone but her sister and set them and herself to work. Fortunately, at least the bodies had gotten cleaned off the stairs while she'd been sleeping.

She'd met her husband on his way up while she was coming down for the fourth time in two hours. She'd wondered how he'd slept, and where, and how he was, and was angry at herself for caring. But her concern had been cut off when he'd asked about the child.

Now she said, as he tried to get past her once more, "Why are you wearing your armor?"

"I'm going after Conner Muragh."

Eleanor gave a quick glance out the nearby narrow window. Rain was still lashing down outside. A narrow trail of water had leaked down from the window casing, forming a tiny puddle in the worn step below it.

"The weather hasn't cleared yet."

"I ride out today. Woman, will you get out of my way? I need my leather cloak."

She didn't want him fetching his leather cloak. She didn't want him leaving. Didn't he know how horrible it would be for her to be alone here? Didn't he know she was frightened? Of the raiders' return. Of the responsibility. Of losing him. Though she supposed she had lost him already if he had no faith in her. She wanted to cling to him and beg him not to make her face all these grim changes at Harelby alone.

She said, "You can't leave!" and the words came out sounding harsh and commanding, though she didn't mean them that way at all. "My lord, Stian, please," she added when his eyes narrowed to furious slits.

"It is not for you to give orders, woman," he told her.

She knew she should humbly beg his forgiveness at her presumption, but since she had not meant any disrespect she tried logic instead. "There is so much to do.

So much you need to supervise. The steward was killed. Many of the stores in the undercroft were destroyed."

"They didn't destroy the wine," he said. "That's all I care about."

"Well, I care about the flour and the dried peas and the pickled meat!" she snapped back. Anger flooded her, making her forget all deference and diplomacy. "The crops were trampled in the field, pigs and sheep were slaughtered, the villagers burned out of their houses. Don't you care about that?"

"I care about finding the whoresons who murdered my father." His words were punctuated by a bright streak of lightning.

Eleanor answered in the thunder. "Well, I care about burying the man! And the steward, and the guardsmen, and Hulda and her husband. There's more to be concerned about here than one man's death. I care about Harelby even if you do not!"

It was the wrong thing to say. She knew it before the words came out of her mouth, though she couldn't keep herself from saying them. Stian wasn't ready yet to be reasonable, practical, or logical. Stian cared nothing for the things she thought important. She thought he might strike her this time. He didn't, but the stare that bored into her for a long time was almost worse than violence. She was reminded of the struggles of wolves as she looked away first, having no doubt which of the two of them was the stronger.

"Get out of my way, woman," he growled after they stood on the stairs in silence for a long time. "Or fetch me my cloak. Be useful or be silent; I don't care which."

Stian was surprised when Eleanor turned meekly to do his bidding. As she walked up the stairs he almost called out to her. He wanted her to come back, into his arms. He wanted to be near her, to rest his head on her breast and cry out all the pain that engulfed him. To tell her he'd been in the wrong last night.

He cursed his evil temper, but knew he couldn't afford that kind of weakness. There were men that needed killing, and it was easier for him to kill in hot anger than in cold blood. He wanted the pain, the anger, and the hate. He needed them to keep going. His world had been destroyed. For some reason, Eleanor thought they could rebuild it. He knew that the only thing that was left for him now was revenge, to kill Conner Muragh or be killed by him. That was all that he could let matter now.

A part of him wanted to follow after Eleanor. It wasn't easy to ignore the pull the woman had on him even through his carefully nursed anger. He had to leave, he knew, storm or no storm. The men were assembling in the bailey. Stian decided to go out and join them. It would be better to start the hunt for Conner quickly, before he was tempted not to leave the woman's side at all. His father deserved revenge more than he deserved the comfort of his wife's presence. He couldn't let himself think about being a father, or about the state of Harelby. All those things were part of a broken pattern, and he couldn't imagine any new one forming without his father there to hold it together. All that could matter was killing the man who'd smashed his world apart.

He'd send someone to fetch the cape from Eleanor.

"They stole my horses and some cows and set the stable on fire. Thank the Holy Mother the rain came so soon after they did."

Stian looked around from the back of his tall warhorse. Nicolaa Brasey's manor house and most of the outbuildings were untouched, but the gate of the tall wooden fence was smashed in. The thatch of the stable roof was blackened and partly burned away.

"No one was hurt," she added. "I can spare three men to ride with you if you're going after them."

"They killed my father," he told her.

"Then take all my men. I'll be glad to see Conner Muragh dead at last."

The widow stood with a stern, stoic face, her arms crossed. Her son and household people flocked behind her as a light fog mixed with the smell of smoke filled the morning air. At least the rain had stopped. Stian was sorry for the damage, but glad the raiders had taken time for one more foray. He welcomed anything that slowed them down.

"Which way did they go?" She pointed north, which was no great surprise. "How many?" he asked.

"No more than a dozen, several of them wounded."

"Keep your men, then," Stian told her. "We already outnumber them. I'll send back your horses," he added as he turned his horse and headed back out of the broken gate with Lars, Malcolm, and their men following behind him.

North led across a rain-swollen burn into heavily wooded country. Soon they came to a stone track, overgrown and broken in places, but still easier for traveling than cutting through the forest's bracken and brambles. Stian recognized the roadway.

"It leads to the Roman wall," he said as they stopped to examine the obvious trail left by the raiders.

The wall wasn't so much a wall anymore as it was an intermittent line of piled stones that stretched like broken teeth across many miles of countryside. Sometimes it marked the shifting border between England and Scotland. Stian had no idea just which side of the border it was on at present.

"The rain and booty are making travel slow for them," Lars reported after examining a pile of fresh horse droppings.

"Good," Stian said. A plan was forming in his mind. For all the pain, he could still think like a soldier. "They'll be bending west toward Muragh lands as they near the wall. If we ride hard I know exactly where we can be waiting for them."

They rode hard. The sky cleared and the breeze stilled as miles and hours passed. The woods grew hot in the midsummer sun; flesh inside layers of padding and armor grew hotter still. Stian sweated out the wine and the headaches brought on by drink and Malcolm's loving care of the night before.

His head grew clearer as he rode. Though he tried to think only of the fight to come, thoughts of Eleanor kept intruding at odd moments. A picture of her formed in his mind when he saw a patch of flowers the color of one of her kirtles spread over a meadow they crossed. Then again when the song of a bird reminded him of her laughter. He kept reminding himself that he had no space for such soft thoughts now, not even to pass the time. Fortunately, images of his father always came back to haunt him, sharp as the dagger that had ended Roger of Harelby's life.

They circled around the reivers to reach the Roman ruins long before them. Stian had plenty of time to set up an ambush, placing his men behind a tumble-down stub of wall and in the surrounding woods. He arranged his force so that the Scots would be surrounded as soon as the raiding party reached the open area just before the wall. By the time all was ready the first of the Scots came into view. Most were on foot; some men in the rear were driving a few head of stolen cattle before them. No more than five or six were riding. Stian recognized at least one of Nicolaa's horses. He recognized even more of the raiders. Conner Muragh was in the center of the first line of riders, and his son, Rob, was on one side. A skinny youth in an oversized, rusting pot helm rode on the other.

Conner was bareheaded, and bent-shouldered with fatigue. His braids were streaked heavily with gray, and his face lined, but Stian knew better than to make the mistake of thinking it would be easy to kill this cunning old devil. His father had been of an age with Conner. There had been enough Muragh bodies around Roger to show that he had not gone like a lamb to the slaughter, and neither would his old enemy. Which was good. Stian welcomed the fight.

It came soon enough, when one of the Scotsmen among the cattle was the first to notice the men moving up from behind the raiding party. He called out and died with an arrow in the back for his trouble. Stian gave a shout, and the rest of the men on the flanks moved in. He rode in from the front with Malcolm and Lars, leaving a trio of archers to cut off any charge by the enemy to get past the wall. He let his men look to themselves while he charged down on Conner Muragh. His war cry filled the hot air, a release for all the pain and hatred within him.

The chief of the Muraghs met his cry of challenge with a wild shriek of his own. "You're mine!" he cried as he spurred his horse to meet Stian's.

Stian liked men who talked in battle; it did nothing

to help their concentration. He never talked to his opponents once the battle began. When their swords met, he fought in deadly silence. Silence that was full of anger and determination. A learning silence, as he studied the older warrior, hunting for any weaknesses.

The most obvious were the differences in their mounts. Stian's was a trained warhorse. Conner rode a gentle palfrey from Nicolaa's stable. It shied away from the fight in terror as swords clashed, while Stian's mount moved easily into battle. Conner fought two-handedly, with a greatsword, making him unable to use his reins. The horse beneath him had never been taught to be guided by signals from knees and spurs.

It wasn't long before the palfrey reared in terror, throwing its rider from its back. The horse's head knocked into Stian's shield as it came up, knocking the round, wooden shield from his grasp.

Conner made one wild swing as he fell. The greatsword connected with Stian's left arm, hacking far enough through his protective chainmail to slice open a deep cut in Stian's upper arm.

Stian felt nothing. He concentrated on the enemy, who fell beneath his horse's feet. Conner would have tried to slice open the horse's belly, but Stian wheeled the animal quickly, and the horse's hoof landed a hard blow to Conner's shoulder as it turned. There was a heavy crack of breaking bone. Conner dropped to his knees, left arm dangling uselessly, barely able to hold the heavy sword in the other.

The man looked up as Stian rode forward for the kill. With his neck exposed that way, it was easy to take off his head.

When it was done, Stian just stared down at the

decapitated body, without any thoughts or feelings, for what seemed like a very long time. If a battle went on around him, he wasn't aware of it. He'd expected to feel gleeful, vindicated, washed free of all the sorrow and anger. But all he felt while looking at the dead man was the tiring aftermath from the exhilaration of battle.

When he did begin to think and feel again, the throbbing physical pain in his arm was the first thing he became aware of. Bloody, but not too bad, he decided after a quick look at the cut. He still hurt inside as well, but now he recognized that it was a hurt that would grow less with time. His father was avenged, and that helped. Now he could go home.

He looked around to see that the battle was over. Most of the Muraghs were dead, but a few prisoners were being rounded up. Stian guided his horse toward Malcolm, who was calmly watching two men wrestle with the skinny lad who'd ridden by Conner's side.

"By the rood," Malcolm said as he rode up, "that's Long Kate!"

The struggling prisoner's head came up at the sound of the name, and Stian saw that the tall lad wasn't a lad at all. The loss of the oversized helmet revealed the freckled face of a pretty girl.

He looked from her to Malcolm. "Long Kate? That's old Conner's granddaughter." He carefully got down off his horse to have a better look at her.

"Aye. A great bundle of trouble she is, I've heard." Malcolm leaned over his saddle to contemplate the prisoner, now standing quietly enough between the men who held her. "Seems all I've heard about her father treating her more like a son than a daughter is true."

With his wounded arm carefully held at his side, Stian went up to the girl. He gestured for the men to let her go. They stepped back, but stayed close. The girl kicked out at Stian's shins as he approached, but he used the movement to knock her feet out from under her. With an angry hiss she fell heavily onto her back.

Lars laughed, "If that's truly a female, that's the right place for her."

She glared hatred at the Dane's words but kept most of her attention on Stian. She was a trapped thing, frightened, he could tell, but defiant and dangerous with it. Stian wondered what to do about this odd prisoner. For all that she was one of the murdering thieves, she was also little more than a girl.

"She's what, fourteen, for all her size?" he asked. "She's Conner's eldest son Rob's oldest child, isn't she?"

"Closer to sixteen, I think. She's the only one of Rob's brats left," Malcolm answered. "Her brother died in last year's war." He glanced toward the pile of Muragh bodies. "Now her da's dead as well. And her grandda. Would that make Long Kate here the heir, do you suppose?" Malcolm asked thoughtfully. "I'm told she asked for a dagger once as a child after her da offered her a doll, and he laughed and decided she was really a boy in skirts. Now she'll need the training if she's to head her clan. Assuming she leaves here alive."

"Assuming that," Stian agreed.

"I'm not asking for mercy," she declared. She pressed her lips tightly together, obviously angry with herself for speaking to the enemy at all.

"I'm not asking for your opinions, brat," Stian replied.

Stian supposed that she would need to be a fighter if she was indeed the heir. Her position within her clan made what he should do with her even more complicated. Killing her might end the threat from the

Muraghs for a while, but another generation was bound to grow up to harry his own sons' lives and lands, claiming a darker blood feud than the one they already had.

His own sons? Had killing Conner really cleared his conscience so much that he could now consider the possibility of a future? It seemed that it had, for he knew that all he wanted now was to go home and make peace with his wife. And get this arm taken care of. Damn, but it hurt. First, though, there was the prisoner to consider.

Lars came up and knelt beside the girl. He grabbed her by the hair when she tried to scoot away. "Take her," he said to Stian. "You first, then all the men. Plant a bastard in her, then send her home."

"Take her?" Stian echoed. "Rape her?" His stomach twisted as Lars nodded. Some of the men laughed and cheered at the idea, but stopped when Stian turned a cold look on them.

Lars took no notice of his displeasure. "Do it. Revenge for your father." He shook the girl, like a terrier with a rat. Though she grabbed his wrist with her hands, she couldn't stop the shaking.

"Stop that!" Stian ordered. Stian stepped forward to loom over his cousin and the prisoner. "Get away from her."

"Gladly," Lars answered moving back. "You first. It's your right to take her maidenhead, if she has one."

"I don't give a damn about her maidenhead."

Lars laughed. "Fair enough. Let me at her first, then. I promise it'll hurt. Your father deserves every drop of revenge we can extract."

Stian looked down at the girl while he continued to ignore the blood dripping down his arm. She was on her knees now, looking around frantically, as though seeking a weapon or a way out. He was half tempted to let her escape, but didn't trust the girl's ability to make it the many miles back to her home despite what he'd been told about her being raised as a warrior. Why hadn't her father kept her safe in the bower even if she had grown up taller than any of the Muragh lads her own age?

Lars had a dagger in his hand and a look in his eyes that showed he was thinking about using it on the girl's clothing. The other men were drawing near, some of them looking expectantly. It was time to put an end to it before the men took the girl whether he gave permission or no.

He grabbed Long Kate by the back of her leather tunic and hauled her to her feet. "This is my prisoner," he declared, giving a warning glare to the circle of men. "To be held for ransom. No man is to touch her. Am I understood?"

There was a reluctant murmuring of assent from the men, but Lars burst out, "What about Roger?"

"Roger's been avenged," Stian said. "This girl came to rescue her grandfather. Any one of us would have done the same. I've no quarrel with her." The girl gave him a look that told him she had a deep quarrel with him, but that was to be expected. "She'll be ransomed back to her kin," Stian went on, glaring at Lars as he spoke. "She'll be safe at Harelby. Returned whole and untouched to her own land."

Lars shook his head angrily and stalked back to his mount. Stian pushed the girl toward Malcolm's horse. Malcolm had watched the proceedings impassively, but Stian liked to think his Borderer cousin would have weighed in on his side against raping the girl.

He trusted him now as he said, "Take her up behind you."

"Gladly." He looked the tall girl over carefully. "But not until the hellcat's been searched and bound. A Muragh blade in my back is not how I intend to die." Malcolm beckoned to one of his men to do the job.

Stian turned away from Malcolm and gestured for Ranald. "Help me get this armor off. I'll need a bandage." As the lad helped him with the wound, Stian asked, "Dead?"

"None of ours, my lord."

"Wounded, then?"

"Just you. It was the archers did most of the work."

"Good. Have someone see to the Brasey animals. We'll soon be back at Harelby." That was all he wanted, to get back to Harelby. "This hurts like hellfire," he added, while he thought, *Soon I'll have Eleanor to cozen and care for me. If a man must get wounded, it's good to have a woman to tend him. I want to go home,* he thought. *I want to start living.*

18

"What are you doing with my chess set?"

Morwina looked from the box to Eleanor. "Moving it, my lady."

"But why?" Eleanor asked. "Where?" She'd come to her room to change clothes only to find Morwina and Blanche there. "What are you doing?" she demanded, stepping through the doorway. "Who sent you here?" She had a horrible premonition that Stian had sent word that she was exiled from Harelby.

"Lady Edythe," Morwina answered as she waited anxiously.

Edythe? What was Edythe about? Before she could ask the women, Edythe came up the stairs behind her. Eleanor had last seen her sister in the chapel, where she'd remained after Mass to pray at her husband's freshly sealed tomb.

Eleanor turned toward her, moving from the doorway onto the landing to speak to Edythe in private. "What is going on?"

Edythe was pale, eyes red-rimmed, but she was serenely beautiful even in grief. Her voice was as gently reasonable as ever when she answered, "I'm having your and Lord Stian's possessions moved, of course."

"Of course?"

"You've been far too occupied with setting the household to rights, my dear," Edythe said. "So I thought I'd supervise this one thing for you. If you don't mind."

Eleanor looked back into her room and at the women busily packing her things. "Stop that!" she called. To Edythe she said, "Mind? Why would I want my possessions moved? Stian is angry with me, but I don't think a separation is called—"

"To the bower," Edythe interrupted. "It's time you moved to the bower, my dear. That bedchamber is where you belong now."

Eleanor stared at her sister. "You want me to move back in with you? I just got used to sharing the bed with someone else." She vowed she would not be sent away, no matter how mousy and treacherous he thought her. Though she didn't know if she was being stubborn, proud, or foolish to be so determined to stay with Stian.

Edythe gave her a brief embrace. "I would love to have your company to share my loneliness, sister. We both know that that closeness is in the past." She sighed and went on. "The bower belongs to Lord Stian and you now. I'll have my things moved in here, if you don't mind."

Edythe's tone expressed more then her usual politeness; she was asking permission. Asking her permission?

"Edythe?"

"You are Lady of Harelby now, Eleanor." Edythe

spoke slowly, as one would explain things to a child. Or to one in shock. "You've been too busy to notice the change. And I know you would be too kind to remind me of my place as Roger's widow even if the full implication of his death had occurred to you."

"What?"

Edythe gave her one of her sweetest smiles and explained, "You remember that you are chatelaine, but you do not remember that you are now a baroness."

As this truth hit her, Eleanor found that she was supporting herself by holding on to the door frame as her knees buckled in reaction. Her thoughts whirled dizzily for a few moments. She had an odd image of Stian and herself dressed in Lord Roger's and Edythe's clothes and sitting in their seats at table. It seemed ridiculous to her, but she realized that things had indeed changed. She had to acknowledge that her life was changed. The dizziness faded as she tried to settle into acceptance of a new pattern to life.

She knew Stian did not want to share his life with her and wondered how he would treat her as his baroness. Would he allow her to be at his side, or would he send her away? Would he keep a suspected traitor under guard or allow her to continue as chatelaine? Could he repudiate her while she carried his heir? Would he whether she did or no? No. She would not worry about what Stian would do as baron just now. She would deal with the truth that she was the baroness and not show her fears to others, not even Edythe.

"It is true," she finally said to Edythe, who had been patiently watching her. "I knew, but I didn't think about it."

"You haven't had time to let yourself consider the

future, my dear. You are involved with the present. While I"—Edythe waved her hand dismissively—"while I must do something not to think about what is past. So, my lady, I'll see to rearranging our living quarters for you."

Eleanor looked into her sister's slightly smiling face and shook her head. "No."

"But it is the least I can do."

Eleanor hated to disappoint Edythe in anything, but she said, "I thank you, but no. Stian must decide this."

"But this will ease the transition to his new position, don't you think? Should he not be treated as Lord of Harelby from the moment he returns?"

"Perhaps." Then Eleanor shook her head again. "Most men would welcome the change. Most men relish power, but I don't think Stian is like most men in this. He needs time," she told Edythe. "I tried pushing him about his obligations before he left. He did not take it well. We will leave everything as it is for now."

After a considerable silence during which Eleanor was acutely aware of her sister coming to grips with having to obey her younger sister, Edythe nodded slowly. "I suppose it would be best to leave the decision until Lord Stian's return. I pray it is soon."

"So do I," Eleanor said.

She didn't want to think about the chance that he would not return at all. He had been gone only a day, and she had no idea how much longer his mission of revenge would take. *Not revenge,* she corrected herself, *retribution. Justice.* Stian was right; Lord Roger's murderers needed to be punished. Not just for Roger's death, but the villeins and guards who had died deserved some justice as well. He was only wrong in thinking her a traitor.

Edythe said, "If we cannot be of service here, I'll take the women with me. We could make ourselves useful mending the hall tapestry."

"Thank you," Eleanor answered.

She would have preferred to have the thing burned. Every time she saw it from now on she would remember the inexplicable sword slashes that had torn it when the hall was invaded. She decided that frugal practicality should take precedence over personal distaste. Besides, the work would help keep Edythe occupied during this sad time.

"Get you to your chamber, sister. And I'll busy myself having the tapestry taken down and brought upstairs so you can mend it."

When she went down to the hall, the servants she'd left working there were buzzing with excitement as they headed for the door.

"What is happening?" she called as she rushed across the wide room, meeting Fiona by the hearth. "What?" she demanded.

"The sentry just sent word, my lady. I was coming up to tell you. The men are returning."

A jolt of fear went through Eleanor. "Returning?" A painful vision of Stian brought home as a corpse marched across her inner vision. "Holy Mother," she prayed. "What are they doing back so soon?" She hiked up her skirts and ran for the door.

"You didn't hit him in the head again, did you?"

She spoke the words as lightly as she could, trying to hide her fear as Malcolm and Ranald maneuvered Stian off his horse. Malcolm had already said, "Don't worry, he's breathing," as soon as they rode up.

Ranald had been riding behind Stian, holding him on the horse. "He was awake until a moment ago," he told her now. "He insisted on riding back to Harelby. Where do you want him?" the lad added pragmatically as he and Malcolm lowered the unconscious man onto the hall step.

Eleanor looked down at the still form at her feet, almost too frightened to find out how badly Stian was wounded. The pain he'd caused her bled away with her fear for him.

Lars distracted her from her fear for a moment by asking, "How is Lady Edythe faring?" as he jumped down from his horse.

Eleanor tried to take some consolation from the men's casual attitude toward the wounded man. If something were seriously wrong with him they would certainly show more concern. She dropped to her knees beside Stian. "Edythe is in mourning," she informed Lars. She looked up at Malcolm. "What happened? Is he hurt badly?"

"I think not," Malcolm answered. "He's lost some blood from the arm wound and caught a chill from sleeping on the damp ground last night, I think."

"He's feverish," Eleanor confirmed. She gestured the group of waiting servants forward. "Take him upstairs."

"A word with you first, Lady Eleanor?" Malcolm asked when she would have gone with Stian.

She chafed at the delay, but said to the servants, "Make him warm and comfortable, and I'll be up to tend him directly."

While she gave orders for her lord's care, Malcolm went back to his horse. Eleanor had barely noticed the thin youngster who'd ridden behind him. Now she took a closer look as Malcolm hauled the lad to the ground. She was surprised to see that he was bound. She was even more surprised a moment later, when Malcolm approached with the prisoner.

"You're a woman," Eleanor told the tall, thin stranger.

"So she is," Malcolm agreed. "Save your French, my lady; she wouldn't know a word of your civilized language if it bit her on the behind."

Eleanor had learned quite a bit of the Border dialect, but she understood it better than she could speak it. She was saved from trying to speak to the girl when Fiona came hurrying up.

"Katherine?" she asked the girl angrily. "Is that you, Long Kate? Were you with the raiding party?"

"She was," Malcolm answered. "Stian took her prisoner. She's to be ransomed back to the Muraghs. The girl's the Muragh heir," he added to Eleanor, "making her a very valuable commodity."

"I see," Eleanor said, though she did not see what a young woman had been doing traveling with the reivers, dressed like a man. She wanted to get to Stian, but she supposed she'd better deal with the presence of the prisoner first.

"I'll see to her, shall I, my lady?" Fiona volunteered before Eleanor could decide what was to be done with this Katherine Muragh. "We know each other."

Malcolm touched his sister's arm. "There's good reason Long Kate's bound," he told her. "She's grieving for her da and grandda, so she won't remember you were friends."

"I saw Lord Roger die," Fiona told her brother. "I won't forget who the enemy is." She looked the sneering Katherine over carefully. "I'll watch her close."

"Keep a guard with her at all times."

"I will. I'm not stupid, Mal."

Eleanor listened to the two of them disposing of the prisoner and wondered why Malcolm had asked her to stay. "Do what you think is best," she said to Fiona. She gave the prisoner one last cursory look. "Just find her some decent clothing. I must go to my husband."

She'd buried the pain of his words by the time she reached their room. Oh, she remembered all his unkind words and actions in the hours just after his father's death, but her rancor at all of it was nothing compared to her concern for his welfare. Well, if not completely forgotten, she began to hope that there was nothing that had happened that shouting and throwing a few things at him wouldn't settle. All she knew was that he was home, he was hurt, and he needed her.

"You have to get well," she whispered as she came into the room. "Get well, so I can break your head myself."

She went to the bed, where a serving woman was helping Ranald undress Stian. She waited until they were finished, then said, "Bring warm water and fresh bandages, Ranald. Wynnol, you fetch my herb box."

While Eleanor waited for her orders to be carried out, she gently began to remove the old bandage. She soon saw that it was encrusted with blood that would have to be soaked loose to prevent opening the wound again. The flesh around the bandage looked healthy enough, so perhaps it really wasn't such a bad cut.

"It'll need sewing," Ranald said when he came back with the water. "Not even Long Kate had a needle on her, or we would have sewn him up before bringing him home. He told me just to make the bandage tight, and that seems to have kept it from bleeding too much. Have you ever sewed up a wound before?" Ranald added with an anxious look between her and his master. "I can do it, if you want, my lady."

She patted the concerned squire's arm. "I can manage," she said. "Besides, my stitching is better than yours."

Ranald gave a faint laugh. "That's the truth, my lady. I'll just soak off the cloth, then, why don't I? And leave the rest to you."

Eleanor stepped back to give Ranald room. She was oddly cheered to hear Stian give out a low, grunting moan as the bandage came off. It gave her hope to think that he was not too deeply sunk in a fever. She just hoped he wasn't so close to waking that he would feel her sewing up the cut when Ranald was done. He did not wake, and she was soon finished. Afterward, she applied a poultice, then put on a fresh bandage with Ranald's and Wynnol's help.

When they were done, she propped pillows beneath Stian's head, so that he at least looked comfortable. His breathing was deep and regular; his color was a bit pale, but then he was a fair-skinned man. She supposed she might be exaggerating his pallor in her worry. Only time would tell if he was truly badly injured or not.

She turned to Ranald. "Tell the cook to keep broth and spiced wine warm for when I want them, then get some rest."

"Yes, my lady. Thank you, my lady." He gave one last look at Stian before he left. She was willing to wager he'd get his rest sleeping out on the landing.

"I used up the last of the orrisroot," she said to Wynnol. "Is there more in the storeroom?"

"No, my lady, I already looked there. I noticed it was nearly gone when I checked the box."

Eleanor frowned in frustration, for the only mixture she knew to draw poison from wounds was made from a paste of orrisroot. She found herself wishing that when she was growing up she'd listened more to lessons about mixing different medicines than to Lady Constance's amorous adventures.

"I need orris."

"Do you, my lady?"

"I do. Someone with more knowledge of herbs and cures might not."

"There's a wisewoman lives near Stobs. She might be of help."

Eleanor looked worriedly toward the big man stretched out on the bed. He looked vulnerable, helpless, and she hated seeing him that way. "Yes. Send for her. How long before she could get here?"

"Four, five days at most."

Eleanor shook her head. Stian would be better or the wound too infected to treat by then. "Never mind."

"What will you do, then, my lady?"

Eleanor paced from one side of the bed to the other and back again while she thought. She didn't take her gaze off Stian. "I think I saw irises growing in the pool by the cave," she said. "Perhaps those roots will be an adequate substitute for the kind I know."

"I know the place," Wynnol said. "Do you want me to fetch them, my lady?"

Eleanor looked Stian over carefully once more, touching his arm, his forehead, the spot over his heart. He was lying quietly, unaware they were even there. She didn't want to leave him, but didn't think he'd want just anyone tromping around his favorite place. It wasn't such a long trip; she could be back within the hour.

"No. I'll go. Stay with him," she told the servant. "I'll fetch a basket and dig them up myself."

As she left the hall she saw Malcolm and his men riding toward the castle gate, heading home to his own lands, no doubt. He lifted his hand to her in farewell. She returned the gesture with regret, for this was one cousin of Stian's she had grown very fond of.

She did not regret the chance to be away from the hall for a while, even though she left a sick husband behind her. She thought having a few minutes alone might help her fortify herself for the effort of nursing him and running the hall. She hoped she could sort through her roiling thoughts and emotions at the turn her life had taken while she dug up a few iris bulbs in the peaceful quiet of Stian's private place. It had seemed like *their* private place not so long ago. Perhaps she could catch some of the happiness they'd shared there and hold it close in memory.

It was less than a mile to the cave tucked into the wooded hillside. She had thought the journey a long one that first night, rolled up in a stifling cape and held fast in a surly horseman's arms. On this fine summer day, it took her only a few minutes to make the trip.

The cave mouth was almost overgrown with creeping vines, and the pool was clogged with water flowers. Wildflowers and weeds covered the small meadow. The place was humming with busy honeybees, while a magpie strutted across her path, boldly calling out his annoyance at her presence.

Eleanor laughed at the insolent rascal, then stripped off her overdress, rolled up her chemise sleeves, tucked the hem up around her hips, and waded into the sun-warmed water. A few minutes of grubbing around in the mud produced the roots she needed. She washed them off, tossed them into her basket, then washed herself and put her clothes back on.

As she finished dressing, she heard a low growl from close behind her. The sound sent a thrill of fear through her, followed closely by annoyance. Whirling around to face the black-faced wolf, she demanded, "What do you want?"

At the sound of her voice the animal took a quick step backwards, then snarled menacingly.

Eleanor refused to be impressed. "You're only a wolf," she told it as she stared angrily into its eyes. "Just teeth and claws and muscles. Why should I be afraid of you, eh?" Slowly, without taking her eyes off the wolf's, she bent and picked up the basket. "I'm going home now," she told it. "Good day to you." She walked forward as boldly as the magpie that still croaked in a nearby tree. "You *will* step aside," she told the wolf as she approached it. "Make way for the Lady of Harelby," she added with a slightly wild laugh.

The wolf backed up slowly as she advanced. Then it dropped its head and whined at her. Within moments, Eleanor found herself scratching the more than half-tame thing behind the ears. The wolf looked up at her, no menace in its gold eyes this time. It looked more imploring than anything else.

"You miss him, don't you? You don't know whether you belong in the wild or lying by the hearth-fire with a bone, do you? Poor lamb." She chuckled. "I beg your pardon, for you are no lamb, but Stian's lady-wolf. I miss him, too," she added. "For the man who called me traitor was not the Stian I thought I knew."

At the mention of Stian's name, the animal's sharp ears pricked up.

"Stian," Eleanor repeated, and got the same reaction. Along with a curious tilt of the head. The effect was appealing. Eleanor gave the wolf's fur one more pat, then walked away. She wasn't surprised when the animal, after some hesitation, followed her.

No one at Harelby seemed surprised either when the wolf accompanied her through the gate. If she'd hoped for cries of amazement all she got were a few comments from people who said they'd wondered when Stian's pup would get tired of wandering the woods and settle down to being a proper dog.

"She's half wild," Eleanor pointed out to an old guardsman standing before the hall door.

"Everyone of us at Harelby's at least half wild, my lady," he answered with a jagged-tooth smile. "That's no reason for Lark here to go scavenge out in the woods, is it? I always thought it a fool thing for the lad to try to make a pup suckled in a warm hall into a wild creature."

"She's a wolf."

"All dogs were wolves once. Or so I've heard."

Eleanor had no answer to his comment as she went past him into the castle. The wolf trotted in after. Here, the animal at least caused a stir among the hounds in the hall as it bounded forward with a loud growl. Eleanor stood back and waited while a snarling, snapping, barking confrontation was briefly played out before her.

It didn't take Lark—Lark?—long to settle just who was going to be in charge of the hall now that she was home. The dogs slunked off behind the hearth to lick their wounds, while the wolf trotted up the stairs beside Eleanor.

When she entered the bedroom she saw that Stian was awake. Eleanor sighed with relief and hurried forward. The wolf was faster, jumping up on the bed to lick Stian's face. He pushed it away with his good hand and it settled down beside him, panting happily. He put his right hand on the wolf's head.

All Eleanor could think of to say when she came up to man and animal on the bed was, "Lark? You named her Lark?"

Stian's eyes were dull with pain; even his mustache seemed to droop with weariness. His voice was barely a whisper when he answered, "She used to make this squeaking, chirping sound when she was little. Reminded me of a bird."

Eleanor shook her head and decided not to press the sick man for more conversation. This was no time to beg him to take back his harsh words. Besides, she was too proud to beg even if the time were right. She looked across the room to where Wynnol sat beneath the window with a piece of embroidery in her lap.

"His fever's worse, my lady," Wynnol said as she got up. She came and took the basket from Eleanor. "I fed him a bit of broth. Shall I fetch up the spiced wine now?"

"Yes, please. Then hang these up to dry." The servant gave her a curtsey—the first Eleanor ever remembered anyone giving her—then left. Eleanor turned back to Stian. "Rest," she told him.

She felt his forehead to find that his fever had indeed grown during her absence. Then she touched his cheek just to be in contact with him. He leaned his head into her cupped palm, closed his eyes, and gave a deep sigh. She thought he was asleep a moment later. She was left shaken and confused by the tenderness of the gesture.

Eleanor spent most of the rest of the day by his

bedside while Stian fell into an ever-more-restless sleep. When Wynnol brought both her and Lark dinner, the servant stood back looking like she had something on her mind. Eleanor sopped up a few hurried bites of boiled pork and greens with a thick chunk of dark bread. The meal tasted so good she realized she hadn't had an appetite for days.

Once her stomach was full she handed back the bowl and stood. "What is it?" she asked the worried-looking servant.

Wynnol glanced toward the door. "I hate disturbing you, Lady Eleanor, but I think you should see to matters in the hall."

"What matters?"

"It's the prisoner. Fiona brought her into the hall to sit with the women."

"And so she should have," Eleanor said. "That wild child looks like she could use time in the company of women."

"Aye, my lady," Wynnol agreed. "But the problem is, the men who fought with her kin are being surly about her presence. You know what men are like. And Long Kate, well, she just keeps glaring daggers at all who look her way. Perhaps your presence would calm everyone down. You could talk to the girl, perhaps."

Eleanor considered the situation. "Yes," she said, "I suppose I should go downstairs."

Though she'd made the decision to go, she lingered a few moments longer at Stian's bedside. The candles by the bedside gave out a warm glow, but it didn't disguise the unhealthy look of Stian's sweat-sheathed skin. He was mumbling, the words no more than low rumbles with the occasional understandable word, usually in answer to her own efforts to comfort him.

Eleanor hated the thought of leaving with him being so uncomfortable.

"You're needed in the hall," Wynnol spoke her own thought aloud. "I'll mind the lad while you're gone."

Eleanor nodded and went reluctantly out the door. She returned a few minutes later, sent the servant away, and said angrily to the sick man, "She bit me!"

"Lark?" His good hand groped through the wolf's thick fur. "Lark?" The animal had growled protectively at the sound of her angry voice.

"No, the Scotswoman." Eleanor held her hand out to the candle to examine the red mark the girl's teeth had left. "Katherine. Your Long Kate bit me."

She didn't know why she was telling him, since he couldn't comprehend anything in his current state. He might not even care if he were well. Perhaps it was just because she longed to have a conversation with him.

She touched his cheek. "It seems like years since we've spoken kindly to each other. While you're not a great one with words, sweeting—"

"Long Kate," he said.

Eleanor leaned closer, hoping that he was waking up. "Yes, Katherine. Your prisoner. Fiona said all was going well enough; she'd even found her a dress that almost fit. Then after the evening meal Lars said something that set the hellcat off and she tried to escape."

"Lars?" He tossed his head from side to side.

She put her hand out to calm him. The salt from his sweat stung the bite mark when she touched him. "There was quite a fight, apparently," she went on. "Your Kate had been trussed up like a chicken by the time I got down to the hall. There was a great deal of shouting, and she bit me when I got involved. I had her taken up to the bower, though I doubt Edythe will appreciate the company."

"Taken," he repeated, his voice a raw whisper. "Take her."

"Take her where?" Eleanor wondered, trying to hide her concern in flippancy.

"Plant a bastard in her."

The words were a rushed mumble, but Eleanor had no trouble understanding them. They chilled her to the bone. "What?"

"Take her. Revenge. For Roger."

Her throat constricted with fresh pain and her hand clutched protectively over her abdomen, as though trying to protect her unborn child from Stian's ugly words.

"Holy Mother," she whispered, staring in horror at the man on the bed. What was he saying? What did he mean? She had to know, though she didn't want to. In the faintest of whispers she asked, "You didn't rape that child, did you?"

He said no more, just tossed his head and moaned while she stood and backed away. Eleanor found her back pressed against the door, her fingers reaching for the latch. How could he? Holy Mother, how could he?

The answer was easy and obvious—women were always raped in war. Even the civilized men of Poitiers brought back tales of the vanquished women they'd taken by right of conquest. Lust seemed to ride into battle. She knew the mood in which Stian had gone after the raiders. She knew that village women had been raped by the Scots even though they'd been in a hurry to rescue Conner Muragh and be gone. Stian might have considered raping Conner Muragh's grandchild not only his right, but his duty.

Revenge. Revenge was all that counted with Stian of Harelby. Nothing else was important to him but seeing the murderers of his father punished. Why should she expect a half-wild savage such as her husband to behave any differently? Somehow, though, stupidly, she did. She expected so much from him when he was, in truth, worse than most, not better. He could accuse her of betraying his trust, then easily turn around and betray their marriage vows with no thought. He would tear her apart with word and deed to extract revenge for Roger. And there was nothing she could do but endure it. Nothing. Except hate him.

She couldn't breathe from the tears that clogged her throat. She couldn't stay here, not in the same room with him, no matter how sick the man was. All she wanted to do was escape, but she couldn't stop her appalled thoughts from pouring out.

"Or didn't you have time to rape her before you were wounded? Is that why you brought her back to Harelby? To keep her handy so you could despoil her once you're feeling up to it?" She hated the words that came from her, hated the images they conjured.

Blinded by tears, she tore the door open and ran, not caring where.

19

"His fever's broken, my lady. He's asking for you."

At the same moment, Fiona said, "About Long Kate?"

And Edythe touched her on the shoulder. "We must speak, my dear."

Eleanor continued warming her hands at the hearthfire. She wished she hadn't come back into the hall, but in the end there was nowhere else for her to go. She'd spent much of the night pacing the inner bailey, since the guard on the gate wouldn't let her out into the night no matter how much she shouted at him. Eventually, Hubert had appeared at her side and guided her into the chapel. He assumed she was upset about Stian's health, as well as grieving for Roger and all the village dead. She didn't tell him any different. Besides, she supposed she was in mourning for all she'd lost. They spent many hours praying together.

At least the time spent in prayer had helped calm her down. Only now she feared she was almost too calm, for she felt nothing but mild irritation at the entreating faces of the women surrounding her. She certainly didn't want to deal with them right now.

"Lord Stian, my lady?" Wynnol asked.

"Long Kate?"

"Eleanor?"

She looked at Wynnol first. "I want a bowl of porridge." The woman gave her a concerned look but went to do her bidding.

Eleanor looked at Fiona next. "Keep the girl under close watch in the bower," she ordered. "Add another guard outside the door. No man is to be allowed near her. No man. Not even Lord Stian."

"But—"

"Do you understand?"

"Yes, my lady," Fiona answered.

"I hold you responsible if any ill befalls the girl."

Fiona responded to the threat in Eleanor's voice by nodding and hurrying for the stairs.

This left only Edythe standing by her side. She put her arm around Eleanor's shoulders. Eleanor stayed stiffly erect for a moment, then leaned gratefully on her sister's comforting support. "You look terrible," Edythe told her.

"I feel terrible."

"Don't worry so, he's going to be fine. We can thank the saints for that."

Eleanor couldn't help but give a faint, tired laugh. "I've spent the night on my knees as it is." Though she didn't remember what she'd prayed for.

"Then I think you should go to bed."

"Perhaps I will," Eleanor agreed tiredly.

Wynnol came up with her breakfast. Eleanor took the bowl and walked up the step to the high table. By way of experiment she went to the pair of chairs set at the center of the long table and sat in one of them. When she didn't go up in flames for her presumption, and no one even gasped in shock, she admitted to herself that this was now her place.

"Oh, my," she whispered. Then she set about eating her meal while Edythe stood nearby, smiling benignly. Eleanor wasn't really hungry, but she made herself eat for duty's sake. Looking up at her sister, she asked, "Have I told you I'm with child?"

"No." Edythe sat down on the bench next to her chair. "I suspected you might be, though. You have a . . . glow about you when you're not terrified or run ragged."

"I don't feel glowing."

"Well, you look it. Not now. You look half dead right now."

Eleanor was heartsore, deeply angry, and very, very tired, but Edythe's presence warmed and soothed her. "You are like bright sunlight and summer wine," she told her sister. "I do not know what I would do without you. What's wrong?" she asked as Edythe's sweet expression changed to one of deep distress. "What is the matter?"

Edythe looked away. "I am not with child," she said quietly.

"I'm so sorry," Eleanor tried to comfort her. "Lord Roger would have wanted—"

"Oh, no," Edythe cut her off. "I'm glad, in a way, that I'm not to have his child. He was very dear to me, very good to me, but carrying Roger's child would just complicate things too much."

Eleanor had the feeling that Edythe was obliquely edging toward a difficult subject. *Please,* she prayed to any listening saint, *no more crises, no more trouble.* She didn't want to ask.

She pushed her bowl away and made herself sit up straight. She made her voice stay calm when she said, "What do you mean? Complicate what?"

Edythe couldn't seem to look at her. She looked at her hands, fingers laced together in her lap. "Complicate . . . things," she said after Eleanor waited for some time. "Arrangements. Dower rights and such."

"What about your dower rights?"

Edythe finally looked at her, expression earnest. "Oh, they don't matter. Nothing material matters. Lands and position aren't important. Not with a lifetime of happiness at stake."

"What nonsense," Eleanor snapped. "Have you been reading my copy of Ovid?"

"Of course not," Edythe answered. "I don't need books to tell me the truth of my own heart."

Edythe sounded like some damned Poitevan poet. It took all of Eleanor's self-control not to tell her so. There were poetry and jongleurs' tales, and then there was the starkness of real life. Eleanor would have sworn that her sister knew the difference.

"I'm tired," Eleanor said as she looked into Edythe's anxious face. "Too tired to understand your allusions. Just tell me your meaning in plain words. What are you talking about?"

"Marrying Lars," was Edythe's prompt answer. "I am going to marry Lars."

Eleanor found herself wishing she hadn't asked for simple words after all. "That's not possible."

"Of course it is possible," Edythe said, her tone as cheerful and positive as ever. "It simply isn't particularly probable. I love him," she added. "When you are in love all things are possible."

Eleanor cringed at the sound of the word. "You've been a widow for less than a week," she reminded her sister angrily. "How can you speak of marriage, of love, when you're still in mourning?" *Still in mourning,* Eleanor thought in outrage. *By the Holy Mother, woman, you've barely begun to be in mourning! Lord Roger deserves better from you.*

"Women often marry soon after becoming widows," Edythe said defensively.

"Aye," Eleanor agreed, "but it's usually done at swordpoint, and to the man who killed their first husband."

"Or for political reasons."

"You have neither reason for marrying Lars."

Edythe's complacent smile returned. "I am marrying for love. I know you will be happy for me."

Eleanor wished she could be, but she had other concerns than her sister's state of mind. "You cannot marry Lars," she stated. "What will Stian say? Are your marriage rights in his gift or Father's? What of Father? What of Mother? What of alliances they might want to make with your next marriage? You can't just run off and do what you want."

"Father is far away, Mother is as much a prisoner as the Queen, and Lars is Stian's best friend." Edythe stood, as if she'd just settled everything.

"But—" Eleanor sputtered, following her sister toward the stairs.

She tried to think of other reasons for Edythe not to marry Lars as they climbed to the bower. But every

consideration she came up with was a practical one.
She didn't think her sister was about to listen to any
practical excuse right now. Edythe had entered the
dangerous state of thinking with her heart instead of
her head.

"Damn those poets," Eleanor muttered as she followed behind her sister.

Eleanor paused briefly at the landing to the second
floor, but she didn't go into her own room. She would
see Stian later, she decided, and only because it was
her duty to attend her lord. Much later. Once she was
sure she would not betray her disgust at her husband's fevered revelations. She did not know if that
would be in hours or days, but, however long it was,
she had Edythe to deal with first.

As the bower door closed behind them, she said,
"You cannot do this. Or at least not for a decent
time."

"We cannot wait," Edythe answered. "We will be
married when we reach Denmark."

"Denmark." Eleanor said the word, but compre-
hension didn't dawn on her. Denmark was a country,
someplace very far from England, very far from
Harelby. What did Denmark have to do with anything? "Stian's mother was from Denmark," she said.
"He told me so." It was the only connection she could
make. The only connection she would let herself
make.

Edythe touched her cheek. "My dear, I've never
seen you so pale. What ails you?"

"What ails . . . ? Nothing."

"Well, come and rest."

Eleanor glanced briefly toward the alcove where
Fiona sat with Long Kate. A guard stood by Kate's

chair. The girl gave her a fierce glare, then transferred the look back to the piece of embroidery she was being made to work on.

"What an odd child," Edythe said, reclaiming Eleanor's attention. She took Eleanor by the hand and led her to the bed. "Sit down, my dear."

They sat down side by side. Edythe put her arm around Eleanor's shoulders. Eleanor tried not to think for a few minutes. She just rested in the familiar comfort of her sister's presence. They had spent their lives in each other's company, shared everything, both good and ill. She could not, would not, deal with the idea of Edythe not being part of her life. She tried not to pay any attention to Morwina and Blanche, who were bustling about, rearranging the contents of Edythe's clothes chests.

It was Edythe who broke the spell when she said, "I shall miss you so much."

"No," Eleanor whispered. "No. I don't want to know."

She sat rigidly, with her fingers bunched tightly in the material of her skirt, too aware that Edythe had pulled away. She bit her lip and squeezed her eyes shut to fight off tears. She wanted to stop her ears, to turn time back, to make everything the same as it had been before Lord Roger sent them off to York.

"I have to go," Edythe said.

The words came to Eleanor as though from very far away. As though Edythe were already gone and all she was hearing was a distant echo of her voice. To reassure herself that this wasn't so, Eleanor made herself open her eyes.

"You can't leave me," she said. "We promised to always be together. I came here because—"

"Oh, my dear, those were children's promises. We're women now. We must go where love demands. We must listen to our hearts."

"Our hearts." Edythe wavered in front of her. Eleanor wiped tears from her eyes to clear her vision. "Not our hearts, your heart. You're leaving me to follow your heart."

Edythe nodded. "I must. Lars must return to his own land."

"Why?" Her question had nothing to do with Lars.

Edythe answered as though it did. "He says his father grows old and needs him. Since his fealty was pledged to Lord Roger, and Roger is dead, Lars now feels free to return to Denmark. Besides," she added, "I believe he and Stian have had a falling out of late. At least Lars seems to think Stian might not wish his presence at Harelby."

Edythe acted as if she had no idea why Stian might be annoyed with Lars. "Could it be because Lars is his stepmother's lover?" Eleanor asked.

"We are not lovers," Edythe answered, her voice taking on unaccustomed harshness. "I did not betray Roger while he lived. You know I would not have." She looked away. "Though I was tempted." She gave a sad little laugh. "To think I enticed Lars for your sake, and found my true love in doing so."

"For my sake," Eleanor repeated. "For my sake you're leaving?" Her voice rose with every word. She sprang up off the bed and stalked toward her sister. "You're betraying my trust for that—barbarian!"

As usual, Edythe showed no sign of anxiety. "But my dear, you don't need me anymore," was her reasonable response.

"Don't need you?" Eleanor screamed the words

while the servants gaped. "What will I do without you?"

Edythe said, "It is you who don't need me. You have Harelby and all the other manors in the honor of Harelby to manage. You'll soon have a babe, and then another and another. You have Stian."

"Stian!" *Then I have nothing!* She screamed the words in her mind but could not speak that horror aloud.

"Whom you obviously adore. You have blossomed like a spring violet since we came to Harelby. I've never seen you so happy as when you are with Stian."

"I am not happy with Stian," Eleanor insisted. Each word weighed like a stone on her tongue. How could Edythe say such a foolish thing? Perhaps she'd been content, at least until Roger's death. She'd made the most of a bad situation, but what else could she have done? She would continue on as the unwanted mouse. She could only pray that she would stop wanting him. "I'm his wife."

Edythe just laughed. "Fortunate child. You have so much, and so do I. I have Lars. Be happy for me. Give me your blessing when I go."

"When you go?" Eleanor looked around, at the chest the women had been packing. She realized it would do no good to argue with her sister. Edythe would do what she would do. Eleanor supposed she could lock her sister in the bower and send Lars off to the nearest port under guard. But would that change how Edythe felt? Would that bring back the serenity and security of their childhood? No, there was nothing she could do, nothing more she could say.

Except, "When do you leave?"

"Today."

So soon? She saw the look of determination in Edythe's eyes. All Eleanor could do was take Edythe in her arms for one last, long embrace, and wish her happiness and Godspeed.

"I miss my wife."

One could say any fool thing to a priest, as long as it was true. Stian made the confession because he and Hubert were alone but for the wolf curled up on the end of the bed. They were alone because Eleanor never bothered to come to his room. At least she came no more than once a day, spoke a few words, saw to his needs, but never stayed long. He'd been in bed seven days now, and he was even willing to concede to being a bit petulant from the pain and inactivity. The pain wasn't so bad now, the arm was healing cleanly. The inactivity was beginning to wear on him at last.

It was inactivity he'd imposed on himself, really. He could have been out of bed sooner, he admitted, but it had been easier to curl up like a bear and sleep than put on a sling and go downstairs. Hubert had been telling him so before Stian mentioned Eleanor to him.

"You are right about everything, friend. I need to visit my father's grave," he said as he sat up.

He remembered how he'd scoffed at the idea of his father's mortality when Roger had commissioned a sculptor to carve his effigy on top of a stone tomb at the back of the chapel the year before. Now he could picture the statue of a sleeping knight quite clearly in his mind. It was a good likeness, drawn from life. His father rested under that carved piece of stone.

"Damn the man for dying on me," he grumbled as the ache of loss shot through him. It was a constant ache, really, just worse at some times than others.

Hubert hit him hard on his good arm. "Never swear so about the dead. Lord Roger's not damned. Though he's surely finding purgatory a bit uncomfortable just now. I'm sure my and Lady Eleanor's prayers are doing him good."

"Prayers? Eleanor's praying for my father?"

So that was where she spent her time instead of being with him. Stian couldn't fault her for her devotion to his father's memory. In fact, he was very touched, even if he did wish she spent more time with him.

"She spends much of each day in the chapel," Hubert answered.

The young priest's voice held just enough hint of recrimination for Stian to say, "I've been sick."

Perhaps seven days had been too long to lie in bed after the fever broke, he told himself. He'd put the future off while the past had become like a dream to him. Horrible things had happened, but they had blurred in his mind. He'd made this room into his world and healing from the wound his only occupation. Perhaps he should have at least gone down to the hall. He certainly should have gone to the chapel to pray.

Instead, he'd been staying within the safety of his own room, where he kept the future at bay and hoped his wife would pay more attention to him. Of course, if she had found time for him, he admitted, he probably would have been a silent, sulking, despondent companion. It was just as well, and wise, that she had kept her distance. Eleanor, he thought, was wonderfully wise.

While he'd been lost in a fog of pain and grief, she had been going about the business of setting Harelby to rights and attending to the safety of his father's soul. He couldn't fault Eleanor for what she did, but he missed her. He didn't fault himself for his behavior, either. He had to get beyond the pain of his father's death in his own way. He didn't feel ready to face the world, but he knew it was time he did. If he waited until he was ready he might never leave.

"I'm not prepared to make this a hermit's cell just yet. Not while I've a beautiful wife to share it with," he said and laughed at Hubert's puzzled look. "Send somebody for bath water," he told the priest.

First he was going to get clean, then he was going to get dressed. Then he was going to go find Eleanor.

"Come here, woman."

Eleanor was taken by surprise at the sound of Stian's voice behind her. She was even more surprised when he grabbed her around the waist with his good arm and spun her into a kiss. In the hall, on the dais. In front of everyone. And everyone cheered. It wasn't as if he hadn't kissed her in public before. Once. She'd bitten him that time.

This time she found herself melting against him, her mouth hungrily pressed against his, eager and willing. Until she remembered Katherine and his accusations. Then all she could be was surprised at her wanton reaction to his touch after all her prayers to the Virgin to numb her body to any womanly need.

As she broke away from him and hurried to put the width of the table between them, she told herself she'd only responded in such a lecherous fashion because he'd taken her unawares. It had been a reaction born of astonishment, that was all it was. She certainly hadn't missed kissing the likes of Stian of Harelby.

He was a rough, crude barbarian, she reminded herself as she faced him across the table. His mind was as often bent on raping as it was on lovemaking. Any kind of sex, with any female that moved, was all the same to him.

"Men," she muttered.

"What's wrong?" Stian asked, taking a step toward her. He looked bewildered.

"Nothing," she answered quickly. "How are you feeling?"

Her courtesy had an almost hostile undertone that Stian did not understand. He touched his left arm, which was supported by a sling made from one of her embroidered headrails. Perhaps that was what annoyed her, that he'd used what was probably a piece of delicate silk in such a way. He promised himself to have an ell of silk fetched from the merchants in York for her.

"The arm's mending well," he told her.

She nodded and pointed toward the high-backed chair. Her expression remained closed, unhappy. "Please sit down, my lord," she said. "I have to see to serving breakfast."

Stian had promised himself before coming downstairs that he wasn't going to growl or show any ill temper this day. He had put Eleanor through enough of his bad behavior recently. He was determined to make up for it.

Frustration bubbled near the surface as he made himself sit in his father's chair, but he held it in check. He'd been left wanting to do far more than just kiss her when she moved away. Jesu, but it had felt good to have her in his embrace, to have her mouth on his. He wanted her badly, but he already regretted the public show he'd made of his lust. She'd been right to stop it. He let her go about her duties though he would much rather have had her seated beside him as he presided over his first meal as the Lord of Harelby.

"Lord of Harelby," he whispered to himself as he watched his wife leave the hall. He crossed himself. *Sweet Jesu, help me. I am indeed Lord of Harelby.* So thinking, he turned to Hubert. "Since the steward's dead you might as well fetch me his work. Can't trust you to read the rolls and talley sticks. So I'd best do it until we can send to St. Randolf's for someone to take the steward's post." He'd consult with Eleanor about the needs of the manor when she returned from the kitchen.

Eleanor went outside to the kitchen and stayed there as long as she could. First she inspected the double cooking fires, one on either end of the building. She tested the meat already slow roasting for the evening meal over one fire and complained about the cleanliness of the porridge pot bubbling on the other. She complained about the coarsely ground state of the flour, though the fault was more the miller's than that of the cook she berated. She picked through a pile of freshly pulled carrots and counted baskets of eggs. She did everything she could to linger and to keep her mind off Stian.

Much to the cook's and his helpers' annoyance, she ended up pacing around the small building long after she was done with the food. All was in order in the kitchen; her presence wasn't needed. The place was crowded enough, hot and smoky besides. She was just in the way. Finally, the cook got up the courage to point all these things out to her. He asked her to leave.

Stian was probably long gone from the hall by this time, she decided. He might have gone back to bed, or to the stables, or to oversee fighting practice. It would be easy enough to go up to the bower without his seeing her. She could spend the rest of her day with the women.

But what about the night? she asked herself as she returned to the hall. Where could she hide from his bed now that he was getting well? She didn't know why she even wanted to. It was her duty to sleep with her husband, but she didn't want to. Well, perhaps her treacherous body was missing the sins of the flesh, but in her mind Eleanor was repulsed by the idea of sharing Stian's bed.

She found herself dwelling on his threats to Katherine to keep from thinking about the accusation that hurt more. She didn't know why she was so hurt by the things he'd said about rape in his fever. She didn't know why she expected him to be any different from every other man. She didn't know why she expected some sort of heroic self-restraint from him, some sort of fidelity to her. She wished her contentment with her marriage had not disappeared. She just knew that she did expect better of him, and that her soul was in pain. She felt more betrayed by his lack of constancy than she did by Edythe's leaving.

She thought perhaps she would not go up to the bower as she entered the hall. Instead, she wanted to find somewhere she could be alone to cry. She knew that neither privacy nor an escape from Stian was to be had the moment she glanced at the high table. He was still there, surrounded by a pile of parchments. His head came up the moment she looked at him. He smiled and waved her forward. There was nothing she could do but swallow her tears and join him, at his command.

As she took the chair beside him, he asked, "Where's Lars? Where's Long Kate?"

She answered the second question stiffly, "In the bower. Under guard. Two guards. And all the household women I can spare."

Stian chuckled. "That should keep her safe enough. Pity the poor gentlewomen, especially Lady Edythe. Now, where's my cousin? I've an errand for him to St. Randolf's."

"Errand?" Eleanor stood. "I'll fetch Ranald for you."

"I don't want my squire. Lars could use some time away from Harelby. I'll send him."

Stian didn't know why Eleanor was so nervous at the mention of Lars. Had the man tried to ravish Long Kate when he'd been told not to? If he had, he was a dead man. Surely Eleanor would never allow any impropriety under her roof.

Her roof. He smiled, liking the thought. His roof as well. He knew he would never stop missing his father, just as he would never stop missing his mother, but he was a man now. Harelby was his, his and Eleanor's. They'd make the blessed spirits of the last lord and lady proud of the heirs they'd left behind.

He turned to Hubert, who stood at the end of the table trying to look helpful though he could read neither Latin nor French nor count very well. "Go find Lars for me," he told the priest.

"I can't," Hubert answered promptly.

Stian's brows lowered in annoyance. "What do you mean, you can't find him? Where is he?"

"At sea by now, I expect."

Stian stared blankly at Hubert, but the priest offered no more explanation. He turned to Eleanor. She was looking anywhere but at him, and she was blushing. His arm was aching, which didn't help his mood any.

"What," Stian asked, holding hard on to his patience, "is going on? Where's my cousin?"

"Returning to Denmark," Hubert answered.

That came as a surprise, and as another painful jolt. Even as annoying as Lars's behavior had been recently, he was going to miss him. Why hadn't he even come to say good-bye? Had he left because he was angry at Stian? Or were there other reasons? Stian could tell from the look on Eleanor's face that there were.

"What? Where's Edythe?" he asked, suddenly suspicious.

The answer was barely audible. "With Lars."

"What?"

She flinched at his angry roar. "My lord, I—"

He was on his feet. He grabbed her arm with his good hand and hauled her up as well. "Look at me, woman." When she did, it was from beneath her thick lashes. The look in her dark eyes reminded him of a frightened fawn. He dropped his hand from her arm. "What happened?"

"They left."

"They—left. Together. My father's widow and my cousin left for Denmark. As lovers. You let them leave."

"Yes," she answered to all his statements.

"Why? Why did you let them leave?"

Eleanor could do no more than spread her hands in a helpless gesture. "They wanted to," she told the furious man before her. The rightfully furious man before her. "She's my sister," she added. "I want her to be happy."

Stian couldn't find words to argue with Eleanor's simple reasons. He didn't even want to argue with her. It was the runaway lovers he was angry with, not his wife. She probably couldn't have stopped them if they were really determined to leave. He sat back down. Eleanor did not; she backed away from the table. Since he didn't want her to be afraid, he let her.

"May I go, my lord?" she asked, voice quavering.

The sound of her fear twisted painfully in his gut. It hurt worse than the throb in his upper arm. "Stian," he said. "My name is Stian." When she didn't respond, he sighed. "Yes, of course you may go," he told her. "I'll see you tonight," he called as she hurried toward the stairs. Tonight, he told himself as she disappeared into the tower. Tonight he'd make it all up to her.

20

"*I am here, and she's over there.*"

"That's true," Hubert answered. The priest stopped scratching an importunate hound long enough to say, "You sound as if there's something wrong with your places in the hall."

The distance from the hearth to the windows wasn't so far, Stian acknowledged with a look around the hall. If that was so, why did it feel as if the whole world was between him and his wife?

Perhaps it wasn't the whole world, Stian thought. Maybe it was just himself. Eleanor might not be hostile at all. She'd said or done nothing to show anger. She'd done nothing to show any emotion at all. Perhaps it was just grief, the weight of her new position, loneliness for her sister. Perhaps she needed comforting. But if she did, why did she hide among her women instead of turning to him?

Perhaps if his own body hadn't betrayed him the

night before he wouldn't feel so worried about his marriage. He was feeling less than a man today; that certainly added to his unhappy mood. He'd planned to hold his wife in his arms last night, to make love to her. He'd hoped to make himself feel whole by proving to them both that they were still alive.

Instead, he'd grown tired long before coverfire. His arm had pained him, so he'd gone up to bed while dinner was still being served. He'd sent a servant to fetch Eleanor from the bower, but he'd been asleep long before she'd arrived. He remembered her beside him in the bed during the night. He'd welcomed her soft warmth and held her close with his good arm. He hadn't quite woken up enough to tell her how he'd missed her and wanted her. In his dreams he'd thought he'd felt the wet warmth of her tears and heard faint sobs.

She'd already been gone when he'd woken before dawn. It had been hours before he'd seen her again. She was just across the hall now. He wanted to go to her, but he had the feeling that wasn't what she wanted at all.

"What is the matter with that woman?" he muttered.

"It's the babe," Hubert immediately answered.

Stian gave the priest a puzzled look. As ever, Hubert was completely unperturbed. "What?"

"The babe. Women have strange moods when they're with child." He put his hand on Stian's arm. "All a man can do is treat a pregnant woman kindly, dry her tears, and duck when she throws things during the temper fits. That's what I do."

"Temper fits? Tears? I think she was crying last night."

Hubert nodded. "It's the babe, then."

Stian barely heard the priest's words as a hideous memory rushed back to the surface of his mind. *Don't strike me*, she had said, *I'm with child*. He hadn't cared. His wife was carrying his first babe and he hadn't cared. He'd even forgotten it in his headlong rush against the Muraghs. He'd come to think the things that had happened the night his father died had been some sort of fever-created nightmare. He'd pushed the memories away. Just as he'd pushed Eleanor away.

"She was crying last night." He knew why now. Knew why she was hiding among her women instead of standing at his side. His vicious words and accusations had driven her away. "Sweet Jesu, it's my fault."

Hubert nodded. "You are the father. It's just the babe causing her moods." He patted Stian again. "Don't worry."

Worry? How could he not worry? He was a brutal fool. He had to make it up to her somehow.

"She's with child." He slapped Hubert on the back, almost knocking the thin man into the firepit as the joy of the event overtook him. "I'm going to be a father."

Eleanor made him very happy, far happier than he deserved. He needed to do something to celebrate, to show her his devotion. He wondered what one of the gentle, true knights of her stories would do to honor the mother of his child.

She could feel his gaze on her, as heavy and hot as the embrace he'd locked her in as he slept the night before. At least sometimes she thought he was looking at her, though she would not raise her gaze to meet his.

She'd had the women come down to work on

mending the tapestry, which had proved too cumbersome to be moved to the bower. They'd brought Kate down with them, so Eleanor sat down next to the young prisoner at a bench set under the hall windows. She sat, and she stayed, and she pretended Stian wasn't just across the room.

Stian and some of the men had come in from the bailey soon after the women got to work. He'd stayed near the hearth with the hounds and Hubert, but she knew he kept his attention on her. Or Kate.

Did he want the girl? Was he still plotting revenge? She was almost tempted to ask. Tempted, but thought it was best to let the matter be rather than remind Stian of his wicked plans. She prayed he'd just forget and ransom the girl back to her people, and that it would be soon.

Though she tried not to pay any attention to Stian, she eventually began to cast glances his way. She studied him surreptitiously but carefully. A part of her was pleased to see he was recovering so well and quickly. The part of her that was an obedient chattel was pleased to see her lord recovering, she told herself. Stian's strong arm was needed, after all, to keep the people of Harelby safe.

Liar, she chastised herself. *It wasn't his strong arms I longed for when I crawled into bed beside him last night. I was just doing my duty*, she countered her own accusation. *I thought it better for him to spend his lust lawfully. That was all it was. It was not lust I was feeling.*

She almost laughed at her own effort at self-deception. She'd enjoyed spending the night in his arms far more than she should have. It made no sense that she should take comfort from just touching the miserable lout. She already knew her body was a traitor, for it hungered for him. There'd been a craving deep inside her that was still there, stronger because he was so near. Even though he'd slept through the night while she lay in half-denied need beside him, his size had felt more like a haven than a threat. That her spirit could take comfort from his closeness left her feeling guilty and confused.

That she could look at him and long for him left her even more confused. He was a creature of wicked temper and base desires, she told herself. And, even as she thought these things, she was remembering how he had defended Bertran. And how well their bodies fit together after they'd leapt, laughing, through the May Day fire. She wanted to cry, to scream, to fling crockery at the man's head, then throw him down on the bed and have him. She didn't know what she wanted.

Better to attend to the work, she decided, than to try to understand her own confused mind. "Fiona," she said. "I'm going to add some gold thread to outline the tapestry's design. Please go look through the thread box Lady Edythe left. I think there's gold thread in it."

"Yes, my lady."

Fiona hurried off to do her bidding. Eleanor watched her go and was surprised when Stian called her to him as she passed near the hearth. He spoke a few words with the girl, then she bobbed him a curtsey and went on her way. Eleanor wondered what the exchange had been about, and intended to ask Fiona when she returned. She hoped it wasn't something to do with Long Kate. She'd find out soon enough, she supposed, and looked back to her work.

The torn tapestry had been taken down from the

wall, then taken outside, where the dust was beaten out. Now the circle of women sat beneath the tall windows in the morning light, with candles burning in tall stands for added illumination, and worked on mending and enhancing the cloth before it was hung up again.

"This is a fine piece of work," Eleanor said as she ran her fingers along a line of stitching. "As fine as any in—oh, the devil with Poitiers and all its finery," she finished angrily.

Why was she always thinking of some faraway land when life at Harelby was busy enough to fill her days?

"It was Dame Beatrice who designed this," Wynnol said. "She has a fine eye for needlework, does the dame."

"Aye," one of the others said. "I've seen the state of the hangings in the abbey church. She'll have them down and fine new ones made soon enough."

There was a murmuring of amused agreement about Dame Beatrice's talents and managing ways. The women of Harelby obviously missed the former chatelaine. Eleanor was given to understand that Beatrice was a fine woman, though she had no cause to share their affection for her. She nodded at their kind words for Beatrice and went on stitching.

She did ask, "Did someone send word to Honcourt Abbey? Does Dame Beatrice know about Lord Roger's death?" She should have sent the messenger, she knew, but had completely forgotten.

"Oh, aye, my lady," Wynnol answered. "I saw to it."

"Thank you," Eleanor said with relief.

"She took it hard. I'm told she spends most of her time in church praying for his soul."

"I should visit her and pray with her."

"I'm sure she'd appreciate that, my lady," Wynnol answered, but she didn't sound very convincing.

Eleanor sighed and turned the conversation to another topic. "I've had the masons begin work in the tower again. It's going well. The garderobe will be finished by the feast of St. John." She said the words cheerfully, and received hostile looks in response. "What?" she asked the suddenly sullen women.

"It's not safe, my lady," one of the women finally answered. "We could all have been murdered thanks to that great hole in the wall."

"It's not a great hole," Eleanor defended the modern convenience Lord Roger had ordered. "And it's safer to have it done, with a strong iron grate bolted across the bottom, than to leave it as it is. When it's done you'll be grateful for it, I promise you that."

There was a look of stubborn disapproval on every face in the circle, except for Long Kate, who had eyes only for the needlework. She stabbed the needle into the cloth with such fierce deliberation Eleanor thought the girl must be pretending it was an enemy she stabbed rather than a tapestry. Long Kate never spoke except to Fiona, and then never more than a few words in her own language. Except for doing her best to protect the prisoner's virtue, Eleanor paid little heed to the hostile girl.

She kept her attention on her own women. "The garderobe will be a wonderful thing to have. They're very comfortable to use." Her words fell into a dense, staring silence.

Finally, Brione spoke up, "As you say, my lady."

"Well, I'll be glad when the stonemasons go back where they came from," Wynnol added. "It'll be good to have it done and them gone back to Durham."

"Housing and feeding them sly southerners is not so bad," the steward's widow said. "It's trying to understand their foreign talk. Our peasant folk hate taking orders they can't hardly understand."

"Foreign talk?" Eleanor asked. "Durham's not so far from Harelby."

"It's more than twenty miles," Wynnol answered. "That's farther than I'd want to go in my life."

Eleanor just shook her head at the agreeing comments the other women made. It made her wonder what they thought of her and her foreign ways, if they were so disapproving of people from just a few miles south of Harelby.

Sly, the steward's widow had called them. While the steward had had more dealings with the masons than she had, she certainly hadn't found them sly. They kept to themselves and stayed within the confines of the castle walls while engaged in their work. That was part of their contract; it was to limit contact with the outside world for safety's sake. The fewer the people who knew about alterations to a castle wall the better.

Eleanor looked suddenly up at Kate. "The fewer the better." The words came out as a rough whisper. "How did you discover the garderobe?" she asked the girl. Kate didn't look up. Besides, Eleanor's shocked words were barely audible. "Did a scouting party come across it by accident? Or—?"

Stian was right. Someone did betray the castle to the Scots.

Someone who knew about the garderobe. Not some peasant or castle guard, she was sure of that. Someone who knew about it and was angry at Lord Roger. Eleanor had no doubt who the traitor was.

She put down her needlework and marched up to Stian, full of a sense of certainty and outrage.

He turned a welcoming smile on her as she approached and held out his hand to her. "My—"

"Dame Beatrice," she cut him off. "There's your traitor, my lord."

"What?" he asked as if he had no idea what she was talking about.

"Traitor," she answered. Speaking slowly, so even a lackwit would understand, she went on. "You accused Lars. Edythe. Me. You accused *me* of betraying Harelby to the enemy."

"I know. I'm sorry I—"

"You spoke words to hurt, but you never really sought the truth."

Stian stood in the center of the room. He felt rooted there by the anger in Eleanor's dark eyes, the pain in her voice. The room had grown silent. Everyone was gaping at the pair of them. For once in his life he didn't care that people were watching, that he was the center of attention. Eleanor mattered.

"I know we were betrayed," he answered her. He spoke with swift earnestness. "I tried not to think about it after I'd killed Conner. I thought to let it go after the old man was in hell for my father's death. But for your honor I swear I will seek whoever did it. For I know you never would have betrayed Harelby. Because I hurt so badly I struck out at you. I never meant to hurt you, in truth I did not," he told his wife. "I'm a fool—"

"Will you listen to me? Dame Beatrice is the traitor!"

"Dame Beatrice?" he repeated. Then, what she was saying finally began to sink in. A spark of anger kindled in him as he grabbed his wife's shoulder with his good hand. "What?"

Eleanor barely felt Stian's tight grasp. She had no fear of the big, fierce man before her. She was too intent on convincing him of the truth. "She's the only one who could have done it. Harelby was betrayed, and it was by your aunt."

He didn't argue. He said, "But why?"

"Men!" Eleanor spat out the word. "She was jealous of Edythe, of course. I just realized it myself. She was furious with your father for bringing us here. Mostly I think she was furious over Edythe."

"Why?"

Faced with Stian's blank confusion, Eleanor almost laughed. "Men," she repeated. "You're blind fools who never take our feelings into consideration."

"That's true," Hubert piped up from nearby.

"Beatrice loved your father," Eleanor told her husband.

"Of course she loved him. But not like—"

"Of course like that! They're of an age, he was handsome and powerful. She raised his son and managed his house. Do you think she did it just for duty's sake? She was a fine-looking woman with a sizable dower portion; she could have easily married again."

"She wouldn't," Stian said. "She refused every suitor."

"Of course. Because she loved Roger."

Stian took his hand away from her shoulder to run it through his hair. "Aye," he conceded. "Perhaps. But—"

"Dame Beatrice left Harelby in anger. She's a Scotswoman, is she not?"

"Aye."

"Perhaps she remembered her people's quarrel with Lord Roger. So she used them to seek revenge for his spurning her."

"My aunt loves Harelby. Loves it as much as I do."

"Loved it," Eleanor insisted, "when she thought it and Roger belonged to her. Edythe changed everything."

Stian let silence draw out between them while he thought about all Eleanor had said. Anger twisted in him, and fresh pain. Beatrice had been his only comfort in the years after his mother died. While his father spent time at court and at his other estates, Beatrice had always been there. When his father came back to Harelby it was Beatrice who took Stian's part when he and Roger argued. She was there when there was accord between him and his father as well, laughing and joking with them, taking care of them. He had thought she'd always be a part of his life. Instead, it would seem that Beatrice was responsible for destroying so much that he cared for.

He took a deep breath as he fought off the fury from his growing sense of betrayal. "It seems," he said, "that I must pay a visit to Honcourt Abbey."

Eleanor searched Stian's too-calm face. "What will you do?"

His right hand came to rest on the dagger at his belt. "If it's all true? Kill the bitch."

"You're not going to ride?"

"Of course I'm going to ride. It's not far. Even a one-armed man could ride five miles. Besides, my arm is nearly healed."

"I'm going with you."

Stian looked up. He was standing on the bottom of the hall steps while he waited for his horse to be brought up. Eleanor was on the top step, standing at the hall door. She looked determined.

"Very well," he said. "You can come with me." She looked as surprised as he thought she would at his easy agreement. He added, "You deserve to face my aunt with your accusation, if you want."

In fact, he wanted her company more than he wanted her support in confronting Beatrice. He wanted to be with her as much as he wanted to uphold her honor. Even though this mission was a grim one, it at least gave them a chance to be together.

Eleanor frowned at the man. She wasn't interested in facing Dame Beatrice. Then why did she want to go? she asked herself as she hurried down the steps before Stian changed his mind. To keep him from killing the woman, perhaps. Though she didn't know how she could stop him, or if she even should.

"Thank you," she told him as Ranald brought up the horses.

First the squire helped Stian up, then he lifted Eleanor up behind him. She settled with one hand on her husband's waist and the other on the high back of the saddle. She was glad that Ranald had not brought Stian's warhorse, but his big, gentle mare. She was comfortable on the animal's broad back and knew its easy gait wouldn't strain Stian's healing arm too much.

When the squire swung up onto the second horse, Stian gave him an annoyed look. "Where do you think you're going?"

Ranald looked significantly at the arm Stian wore in a sling. "With you," he said in a tone that brooked no argument.

Stian let it go. The lad was right. Though it wasn't far and he wanted some time alone with his wife, it was safer to travel beyond the bounds of Harelby with a companion. So he nodded and rode away with Ranald closely bringing up the rear.

Though there was a faint line of dark clouds in the distance, the sky above was clear blue, with only a few clouds. It was a warm day, and Eleanor, born in a much brighter land, reveled in the heat and light. She turned her face up toward the sky, closed her eyes, and enjoyed the freedom of being outside Harelby's walls instead of thinking about the grim meeting that awaited them.

She tried not to think at all, actually, but her mind kept coming back to one thing. He'd said he was sorry. At the time, she'd been too intent on proving her case against Dame Beatrice to heed his words. Now, as time and countryside passed by, she couldn't help but hear his words over and over again in her mind. "*I'm sorry,*" Stian had said. "*I never meant to hurt you,*" and "*I'm a fool.*"

He had actually apologized. She found that it meant a great deal to her, that his gentle, contrite words had done much to ease some of the pain in her heart. She wanted to sing with the joy that was melting her heart. She wanted to take him in her arms and talk of the future, of their future. She was his lady and he said her honor was important to him. If it hadn't been for his cruel threats toward poor Kate, she might have felt herself completely at peace with him.

As it was, she found that at some point both her hands had crept around the man's narrow waist and that her head rested on his broad back. He didn't seem to mind. Far from being repulsed, far from chastising the weakness of her flesh, Eleanor simply stayed where she was and let the miles pass silently by and gratefully breathed in his warmth and scent.

She must have dozed for a bit, for she didn't quite notice when they left the woods and started on a path that crossed well-tended fields.

Stian said, "We'll be there soon." He didn't sound as if he relished the thought of their arrival.

"Does your arm pain you?" she asked as the out-buildings of the abbey came into view.

"No. I'm fine."

He didn't sound fine. He sounded tired. Worse, he sounded like a man who'd grappled with disillusion-ment and come out of it weary in his very soul. Eleanor began to wish she'd never faced him with the possibility of his aunt's treachery.

But then, he might never have said he was sorry.

Was an apology worth Beatrice's life?

No, of course not. But if the woman was guilty, there were lives that needed to be paid for. Not just Lord Roger's life had been stolen, but also the lives of the steward, the guards that had died in the fighting, and the villagers who were dead because of one per-son's need for revenge. Even Conner Muragh would be alive now if his family hadn't had the information they needed to rescue him.

The horses came to a halt in the abbey courtyard, and Ranald hurried to help her down. The squire got a fierce look when he tried to assist Stian, who man-aged to get down from the mare easily enough. Eleanor looked around at the peaceful surroundings. The courtyard was surrounded by cloistered living quarters on three sides. A refectory and a church stood next to each other on the fourth side of the square. The warm summer air was scented by unseen rose and herb gardens.

"This is a place of peace," she said as a nun approached them from the refectory. Eleanor wasn't sure if she'd just made a simple statement or if the words had been a plea to Stian not to shatter the peace with his aunt's blood.

Stian heard the uncertainty in his wife's voice, but had no time to tell her how much he shared her confusion before the black-clad woman came up to them.

The nun was very old, her voice a reedy whisper when she said, "The Harelby boy, is it not? You've grown a bit since I used to chase you when you stole apples from the abbey orchard."

Stian didn't remember the woman at all. Nor had he ever stolen from the abbey orchard. "I'm told I look like my grandfather," he told the nun. "Perhaps that is who you recall. Tell me, good dame," he went on before the old woman could reply. "Do you know where I might find my aunt Beatrice? She's recently come from Harelby to lodge at the abbey."

The nun bobbed her head. "Oh, aye, the new lodger. The one who spends her days weeping before the altar." She pointed toward the church. "That's where she'll be, lad. It's gotten so a body can't get any sleep during prayers for all that woman's carryings on," he heard the old nun grumble as he and Eleanor walked toward the church door.

Inside it was cool and dark, scented with beeswax, full of the warm glow of many candles. Sunlight came through a round window of stained glass above the altar. A hunched, weeping figure knelt at the bottom of the altar steps.

All the anger he felt, all the betrayal, all the hurt,

disappeared the moment he recognized the woman below the altar. "Aunt Beatrice?"

The woman turned with a shriek. In a quick, scuttling movement she backed up the stairs until the carved wood of the altar stopped her flight. She stayed where she was, staring at him in white-eyed terror.

"Stian!"

As Stian walked slowly forward, Eleanor waited, her back pressed against one of the pillars that held up the church roof. She couldn't take her eyes off the scene, yet she was reluctant to join it. She'd brought this meeting about, but she didn't feel a part of it. This was between Stian and the woman who had raised him. The woman who appeared to share his deep grief at losing Roger. Eleanor was an outsider, a watcher; Stian and Beatrice's shared blood and history excluded anyone else from their confrontation. She waited, and crossed herself and prayed.

Stian slowly eased his left arm out of the sling as he drew closer to where his aunt cowered. He flexed his fingers, stretched his arm out, decided the pain wasn't so bad after all. Then he took his aunt in his arms and held her close while she cried and sobbed and begged him for forgiveness. She was small, fragile. He'd never thought of the formidable Dame Beatrice, the woman who boxed his ears though he was a belted knight, as fragile before. She was bone thin under her robes, light as a feather in his embrace though she leaned her whole weight against him. And she seemed so . . . old. So empty of everything but pain.

"Hush," he said after a long time of silently listening to her incoherent cries. He stepped back from her a little, though he still held her in the circle of his arms. "Hush. It doesn't matter. It's over. Peace, Aunt, all is well."

She shook her head. "No. I knew when I came here nothing would ever be well for me again. David keeps telling me to leave, to come with him, to start over. He won't leave me alone."

"Sometimes even Ayrfell can be right," Stian told her.

"I couldn't leave here." Tears continued to trickle down her face as she spoke. "The abbey's so close to Harelby. I thought it would be easier to return from here. I thought Roger would see that he needed me, that he would come for me."

There was a long silence, punctuated by a few hiccuping sobs as Beatrice tried to stay in control of her emotions. Stian waited for her. Never mind the accusations he'd come prepared to throw at her; all he wanted now was to hear what she had to say.

"He never sent for me."

"I'm sorry."

"He didn't need me." Stian had no answer for that. There was another long wait before she said, "He was killed before he realized he needed me." Beatrice sighed and looked away. "It's all my fault."

Stian swallowed hard, then made himself say the damning words. "You betrayed Harelby."

At first Beatrice gave a violent shake of her head. Then she nodded. "I didn't realize it at first. When the news came of the attack—of his death—I was surprised that anyone could possibly have gotten into the keep. When I was told how the attackers breached the defenses my first thought was that Roger should have known better than to try to build such a fool thing. He did it for his pretty wife, to impress a foolish girl. I half believed he deserved what happened to him." She squeezed her eyes shut, but that didn't stop the tears from rolling down her cheeks. "But then, Holy Mother, but then . . ."

Stian very nearly shook her to get the rest of the story from her. Instead, he said gently, "What?"

She made herself look at him. "Then I realized that I had told David about the garderobe."

"Ayrfell?"

She nodded.

"You told David of Ayrfell how to sneak into my castle?" His angry shout filled every corner of the church with his outraged voice.

The voice that answered from behind him was not as loud, but it was equally outraged. "She did," said David of Ayrfell. "It's through me that Conner Muragh was freed."

Stian spun to face his hated cousin. Ayrfell already had a sword in his hand. Stian didn't hesitate in drawing his. "Conner Muragh isn't free," Stian said as he stalked down the altar steps. "Conner Muragh is dead."

"Dead?" Ayrfell looked stunned.

"Aye," Stian said bitterly. "And my father with him."

"Muragh dead? Lord Roger is dead?" Ayrfell shook his head as though he didn't believe what he'd just heard. "How could Lord Roger be dead? He was supposed to be at York." He looked past Stian to where Beatrice was slumped by the altar. "Is this true, Aunt?"

"Aye," she answered. "Dead."

The word came out on such a keening note of sorrow Stian felt as if there was a ghost behind him instead of a woman. He couldn't bring himself to look back at his sorrowing aunt. Couldn't even if he wanted to, not with the danger of David of Ayrfell before him. He wished he had a shield. He wished his left arm was in better condition, but wishing did no good when a fight was in the offing.

The news of Roger's and Conner's deaths had wiped the habitual sneer off Ayrfell's face for the moment. "I thought you might die at Harelby," he told Stian. "I never intended for Roger to die instead."

"Was that an apology?" Stian asked, closing the distance between them by a pace.

Ayrfell gave a cold laugh. "Roger made his own fate when he sided against the Scots. I only wanted to see Conner Muragh freed."

"We were going to ransom him back soon enough. Couldn't you have waited?"

Ayrfell gave another laugh. "It wouldn't be very good for me if the Muragh treasure was in Harelby's coffers."

"What the devil do you care about the Muraghs' property?"

"I'm betrothed to Long Kate, you ass. You think I'd take her without a large dowry? Do you think the Muraghs could have managed the dowry after paying the ransom? It was better for me to help Conner escape. So I sent them word of where and how to attack Harelby. That's the only part I had in it. I've my own affairs to look to."

"You killed my father for money?" Stian roared.

"I didn't kill him. I never intended to kill him." Ayrfell raised his sword. "Though I'd be happy to kill you."

As the men moved closer to each other, Eleanor darted out of the relative safety of the shadows. She'd understood only part of their conversation, but their intentions were impossible to mistake.

"Put up!" she cried. Any fear she might have had at the sight of the men's weapons was offset by outrage. "Cry sanctuary, for God's sake!" she shouted, looking from one surprised face to the other. "This is a church." She spoke with grim, fierce certainty. "You can't shed blood in the house of God. You'll call His wrath down on us all if you do." She put her hand over her abdomen. "Don't do this, my lord, for the babe's sake. Not here. Don't bring a curse on our child."

"Enough men have died!" Beatrice called out. "The girl's right. Leave be. Please."

How could he leave be? Stian wondered. What did he care about shedding blood in a church as long as it was done to obtain justice? This man, this man whom he'd hated all his life, was responsible for his father's death. Never mind that he said he hadn't intended for Roger of Harelby to die; the fact was he had died.

"Remember Thomas Becket," Eleanor warned.

"Who?"

"There's been a curse on the King ever since he had Becket murdered in church," Eleanor told him, the words tumbling out in frantic haste. "Now his wife and sons all hate him. Don't bring a curse like that down on your head, I beg you."

Intent on David of Ayrfell, Stian ignored her words. But before Stian could move to join battle, Ayrfell's gaze moved speculatively to Eleanor. He edged closer to her.

"Touch my wife," Stian warned quietly, "and you

truly are a dead man. It won't be a quick death, either, that I promise."

"Aye," Ranald's voice chimed in from the church door. "My lord Stian will surely kill you. But if he doesn't, I will."

"Get out of the way, Eleanor," Stian ordered without looking at her. He kept his eyes on David of Ayrfell. He caught the man's gaze with his and held it. He poured all his anger and hatred and determination into the look he gave his cousin. Ayrfell glared back with equal ferocity.

Eleanor moved back until she was once more pressed up against the cold stone pillar. The men faced off with only a sword's length between them. The danger that crackled in the atmosphere between them drove out any sense of this being a holy place. Instead, it took on the aspect of a killing ground. Still, she prayed, prayed that her husband would prevail.

"If anything happens to him," she whispered, "I don't know what I will do." Suddenly, the prospect of living without him was worse than all the annoyance of living with him. "Sweet Savior," she prayed, "don't let anything happen to him."

The men stood with their gazes locked for a long time. No sound stirred in the church; no one moved, not she nor Beatrice nor Ranald. The swordsmen might have been carved from stone. Neither seemed able to move or to turn away. Time stopped. Eleanor forgot to pray. After a while she forgot to breathe, then took in air on a long, painful gasp. Neither man paid any attention to the sound.

She focused entirely on the struggle of wills between the men. There was something familiar about this silent, still combat. Eventually, she recognized what it was she witnessed. She knew where she'd seen this sort of struggle for dominance before.

Wolves, she thought. *They're like a pair of wolves.*

She knew whoever looked away first would lose. Despite her own fear, Eleanor couldn't stop a small, triumphant smile. She had no doubt which of this pair of wolves was the stronger.

She was proved right a few moments later, when David of Ayrfell broke eye contact with Stian. His sword dropped to his side. "Damn you, Harelby!"

Stian paced closer, his gaze still intent on Ayrfell. His lips were pulled back in a feral snarl beneath his copper-colored mustache. His weapon was still held at the ready. Ayrfell backed hastily toward the church door. Ranald graciously stepped aside to let him through when Ayrfell turned to run for the outside.

Stian would have gone after him, but Eleanor stepped into his path. "No," she pleaded. "Let's have a day with no murder in it. Please."

She put her hand on his arm, his left arm. He winced, and the pain brought him back from the red haze of fury that had been consuming him. "Eleanor?"

She smiled up at him. "Yes. Eleanor."

She was so little, but so strong. "No mouse," he said. "A lioness, perhaps, but no mouse."

She shook her head. "Not a lioness. A wolf bitch, perhaps, but there's nothing of the cat about me. Or you either, my lord. Let him go," she added when Stian looked toward the church door. The sound of a horse ridden hurriedly away came from outside while they stood together in another short battle of wills. "Let the coward go," she said. "His knowing he's a coward is punishment enough."

Stian gave a deep sigh, then nodded. "Enough for

now," he agreed. "Someday, though . . ." He sheathed his sword. "Today he lives." He looked back at Beatrice, whose ravaged face shone out of the shadows. "She's been punished enough as well." He put his good arm around his wife's shoulders. "Come, my lady. Let us go back to Harelby."

The perfect day was clouding over when they left the church. Eleanor looked up at the sky and appreciated the promise of cool rain in the fresh breeze. "I want to go home," she said as Ranald helped her up onto the horse. "I just want to go home."

21

"*What are you doing here?*"

Malcolm turned from speaking to his sister and lifted a winecup toward Stian. "Congratulate me," he called out. "I'm getting married."

Stian went into the hall. Eleanor followed close behind him. It had just begun to rain as they arrived in the bailey. He shook raindrops out of his hair as he walked up to his boisterous cousin. Eleanor did not go with him. Out of the corner of his eye he saw her pull off her damp headrail. She gave him a nod, then beckoned for Fiona to attend her as she headed for the tower stairs. He watched her go with a fond smile. The ride back to Harelby had been no more talkative than the ride to the abbey, but it had seemed as if there was a more contented mood to the silence between them. He rubbed his left arm. He'd left the sling off on the ride home, and it didn't seem any worse for it.

Tonight, Eleanor. We'll make sweet love tonight, he promised himself before addressing the smiling Malcolm. "Married? You?" He clapped the other man on the shoulder. "What woman would be fool enough to have you?"

"Why, Long Kate of the Muraghs, of course," Malcolm answered promptly.

"What?"

When Stian took a surprised step back, Malcolm gestured for a servant to bring the Lord of Harelby a cup of wine. "Drink my health while I explain."

"Long Kate's my prisoner," Stian pointed out after he'd swallowed some wine.

"I know that." Malcolm gestured around the room. "That's why I'm here. I've come to negotiate the marriage contract with you."

"Me?" *What about the Muragh kindred?* Stian thought. "What about David of Ayrfell? He claims to be betrothed to the girl." Even as he spoke the words a wicked pleasure bubbled up in Stian's thoughts. He laughed. "Ayrfell isn't getting his greedy hands on her dowry."

"Or on Kate's pretty hide, either," Malcolm added. "Even a Muragh deserves better than that."

"Kate? Pretty? Are we speaking of the same spitfire?"

"Fiona says she could be pretty," Malcolm defended the woman he would marry. "This is Fiona's idea, by the way," he added. "She thought it up, then sent word to me. I think the lass is right. Better one of us married into the Muragh kindred than adding a troublemaker like Ayrfell to their ranks. Since you're already taken—"

"Very taken," Stian agreed.

"Then it's up to me to marry the girl," Malcolm offered cheerfully. In a more serious tone he added, "I'll treat the girl kindly—as long as she doesn't try to stab me in the vitals more than once a month."

The fact that she was a trained fighter and a sworn enemy didn't seem to bother Malcolm. Stian supposed it didn't really matter. Kate, for all her fierceness, was only a woman. Someone was going to have to marry her, for her lands and dowry and connections. Malcolm was the best choice he could think of.

"Does the girl know about this yet?"

Malcolm shook his head. "Fiona says it might not be wise to give her time to think on it. No reason for her to give you more trouble than you need."

"That's true," Stian answered. He took Malcolm into a quick hug. "Very well, cousin, congratulations. Let's talk over the details. Then we'll send for Long Kate and the priest."

Eleanor noticed the thin line of water running down the wall to pool below on the step as she paused beneath the window. *Something must be done about that leak,* she thought. There was always so much to do at Harelby. Why had she thought her life here was going to be dull?

Turning back to Fiona, she asked, "Who is Malcolm marrying?"

"Katherine," Fiona answered. The girl looked very pleased. "He'll be good for her, and the Lady knows it is time Malcolm settled with one woman."

"Katherine," Eleanor repeated. "Our Kate? The prisoner?" Fiona nodded. "But—"

"Lord Stian will agree, of that I'm sure," Fiona told

her. "It is a very good arrangement for everyone involved. Kate will even thank Stian someday."

Eleanor cringed at the girl's words. Her heart had been mended a great deal by the events of the last hours. Now she was reminded of the worst pain of all. "Thank him?" she asked bitterly. "Thank him? The girl might have been raped."

"Oh, aye." Fiona nodded. "But for Lord Stian she might have been. Though Malcolm claims he would have stopped it if Stian hadn't."

"Malcolm claims—?" Eleanor could make no sense of the girl's words. "What are you saying? That Stian didn't—that he didn't want to—"

She put her hand on the damp stone of the wall to support herself. Her head was spinning, and she thought her knees were about to buckle. Fiona reached out to touch her cheek. Only then did Eleanor realize tears were spilling out of her eyes.

"Is that what's been troubling you, my lady?" Fiona asked.

Eleanor looked away. No one had any business knowing the troubles of the Lady of Harelby. She had to be strong and imperturbable, though she felt as weak and vulnerable as a babe.

"Nothing's troubling me," she lied. "No more than concern for having lost my sister and Lord Roger," she amended. "Nothing more than that."

"Is that why you've been glaring so at Lord Stian, then?" Fiona's tone was serious, but Eleanor could also detect a hint of teasing in it.

"I have not been—"

"I thought you were angry with Stian because you didn't know what to do to civilize Kate. I thought that was why you kept so close to her. Having her in the bower is like having a wildcat in a basket of kittens, isn't it?" Eleanor nodded at the comparison. Fiona went on. "But you were afraid he would rape her, weren't you?"

Eleanor looked away. She was beginning to suspect she'd acted like a fool. "I do not wish to speak about it."

"It was Lars who threatened Kate," Fiona relentlessly went on. "Kate told me how Stian stopped him. So did Malcolm."

"Lars?" Eleanor's voice came out as a whispered rasp as her painful suspicions were torn away. "It was Lars?"

"Oh, yes. He's a bad-tempered one when he's not near Lady Edythe. I think the reason he insisted they leave so hastily was that he didn't want her to find out about his threatening Long Kate."

It hadn't been Stian. Of course it hadn't been Stian, her heart sang. How could she have thought so for even a minute? Stian was wonderful! Eleanor laughed silently at her own sudden blindness to the dear man's faults.

Could her suspicion possibly have come from his having kidnapped and threatened her on their wedding night? Or because of the way he'd acted toward her the night his father died? Might it have had something to do with the things he'd said in his fever? How could she have given any credence to his words? How could she have forgotten how he had respected her wishes when she'd told him no?

They were only fevered ravings, she told herself. Perhaps he'd only been repeating threats he'd stopped Lars from carrying out.

"He said—"

"Said what, my lady?"

Eleanor shook her head. "Never mind. Whatever was said meant nothing."

It was true, she realized. It meant nothing. Not to Stian, who didn't remember it. It no longer meant anything to her. She'd misjudged him. She should have trusted her heart.

Her heart? What did her heart have to do with anything?

She shook her head but didn't try to suppress the foolish, wonderful, heady emotion that flooded through her. She couldn't stop the smile that felt as if it spread from the top of her head to the tips of her toes. She wanted to laugh. She wanted to run down to the hall and take her husband in her arms and kiss him until there wasn't a spot on him her lips hadn't claimed as her own. She wanted to lead him up to their bed and take his body into hers, make herself his completely. It seemed like such a very long time since they had made love. She wanted the frantic joy of their joining and the contented peace of being held in his strong arms when they were sated and content. She wanted the taste of his flesh and the heat of his kisses. She wanted him.

She had never stopped wanting him. That was why the last few days had been filled with such pain. Now the pain was at an end. She could start living again, thank the Holy Mother. She almost kissed Fiona for the news that freed her from the last of her heavy grievances against Stian. She did hug the laughing girl.

The only thing that stopped her from running down to the hall and throwing herself into his arms was Malcolm. Her shy husband would not take it well if he had to put up with Malcolm's ribald teasing. She didn't want to do anything to upset him in the least. Stian deserved to be treated kindly, gently, with deference and respect. She would wait, not with any great patience, it was true, but she would wait.

Tonight, she said to herself as she turned to go up to her room. Tonight she would show him just how solicitous a wife could be. *Solicitous, aye, and randy,* too, she added with a silent chuckle.

When she would have gone into the room at the top of the landing, Fiona put out her hand to stop her. "No, my lady, that's not your room." Eleanor gave her a puzzled look, and the pleased girl explained, "Lord Stian told me to see to moving your things to the bower. He said it was time you and he took your rightful places in this household. And, my lady," Fiona went on while Eleanor was absorbing this piece of news, "a messenger arrived while you were gone. He brought a letter for you. All the way from Salisbury."

It seemed to Eleanor that too much was happening all at once. "The bower?" she said. "Salisbury?" She blinked. "Did you say Salisbury? From my mother? Where is this letter?"

"In the bower," Fiona answered. "I thought you might want to read it—"

Eleanor didn't wait for the girl to finish before she hiked up her skirts and ran all the way up the next flight of stairs. At the bower door she hesitated for a moment. *This is our room now,* she thought. *He accepts it as our place. He accepts us.* Her heart was so full of joy she thought it was going to burst.

The feeling only deepened when she pushed open the door to find a room full of flowers. Everywhere there were flowers. On the tables, on the chests, the chairs, strewn on the bed covers, and in the rushes. She stepped on blossoms as she moved into the center of the chamber, stirring up a heady scent as she went. She turned slowly, trying to take all the color in. She saw the blossoms of common roadside weeds side by side with roses from the garden, wood lilies mixed with heartsease, bunches of late-blooming violets from deep in the woods tied together with sprigs of sage and lavender from the kitchen. The effect was riotous, colorful, almost barbaric. Just like Stian.

"Flowers," she whispered. "Where did they come from? What are they for?"

"I can answer that easily, my lady," the bright-cheeked Fiona said as she followed Eleanor into the room. She gestured at the flower-bedecked room. "This is my lord Stian's doing. Well, my and many of the servants' doing, but at his order."

"Stian sent you out to gather flowers?"

"Aye." Fiona grinned happily. "That he did."

"But—why?"

The girl laughed knowingly, and Eleanor felt her cheeks burn. "You know well why, lady. Isn't it wonderful?"

Eleanor nodded slowly. "Yes." She picked up a white rose and buried her face for a moment in its scented softness. "It is wonderful. He did it for me?" she asked the girl, hungry for reassurance that it was true.

She remembered how Lars had brought spring flowers to Edythe. She'd told herself at the time that she wasn't jealous. She'd told herself that she didn't need such attention from a man. She had never thought any man would care enough to do anything like this for her. Looking around, she could see that she'd been wrong on every count. She had been jealous, she had wanted the attention. There was a man who cared. She was very close to crying again.

Fiona nodded. "He said that it was the sort of thing gentle, true knights do for their ladies."

"Yes," Eleanor agreed with a delighted laugh. "Yes, it is." The gift of the flowers made it even harder to keep from running down to Stian. Tonight, she reminded herself again, and laughed aloud at her own eagerness. "Where is this letter from my mother?" She wanted to see it as much to keep from rushing to Stian's side as she did because she longed for news from her mother.

Fiona was almost in awe as she brought the folded square of parchment to Eleanor. "You really can read, my lady?"

Eleanor nodded and took the letter from her. Since she wanted to read the letter in privacy, she said, "I don't know where you're keeping Kate—"

"In your old room, my lady. The other women are with her."

"You may join them, then," Eleanor told her. "And, Fiona," she added as the girl turned to go, "thank you for helping my lord with all this."

Eleanor broke the seal on the letter as soon as Fiona was gone. The scent of the rose still clung to her fingers as she unfolded the stiff parchment. She read the message while she stood in the center of a bower of fragrant flowers.

Lady Jeanne FitzWalter's letter to her daughter was full of very little news about herself. Eleanor supposed that was wise, considering that her mother was serving as lady-in-waiting to the captive Queen. While she was not a prisoner herself, not exactly, everything she did was closely scrutinized by those loyal to the King. She was wise not to say anything of her own life to her daughter. Better not to be involved, Eleanor reluctantly agreed, than to come under suspicion herself. Lord Roger had been correct in that she shouldn't have written her mother in the first place. Still, she was glad of even this tenuous connection to the mother she cared for very deeply.

After giving her sparse news, her mother switched to the subject of Eleanor herself. "As to this marriage your father has agreed to," Eleanor read, "I have spoken to my lord, the Archbishop of Canterbury, on the subject. He says that you were very wise to proclaim your protest of the marriage before a priest and witnesses. This protest should be sufficient enough to procure an annulment for you from this barbaric nobody your father forced upon you. With God's help you will soon escape from imprisonment in this far-off northern stronghold. I pray you write me with sworn statements from the priest and others so that I may—"

Eleanor didn't finish reading the rest of it. She found herself holding the parchment before her and speaking to it as though it were her mother. "Annulment? Why would I want an annulment? Do you know how much needs to be done at Harelby? Do you think I can just pack my chests and run back to play at courtiers' games?" Her words grew more indignant by the moment. "Barbaric? Imprisonment? By the rood, woman, don't you know how happy I am? How much I love Stian of Harelby?"

After she spoke the words, Eleanor backed up to a chair and sat down very hard on it. For a while she just stared off into the distance, not seeing anything, while her mind reeled under the realization. "I love

Stian of Harelby." She tilted her head to one side as though studying the words from a different angle.

In Poitiers she'd been taught that one was dutiful toward a husband, but found emotional and physical satisfaction with another man. She'd always been told it wasn't possible for a woman to love her husband. It was always claimed to be so in the Courts of Love. Men took concubines and women took lovers and everyone wrote poetry about it. In Poitiers it was fashionable to believe that love could not be found inside the bounds of an arranged marriage. In Poitiers love was an illicit, sophisticated, adulterous game.

In Poitiers, they were wrong.

She smiled. "I love Stian of Harelby."

She didn't know why it hadn't occurred to her before. What had Edythe said? That she obviously adored him? Well, it hadn't been obvious to her. She hadn't so much thought about how she felt about Stian as she had instinctively gone along with the growing, unnamed attachment. Attachment? What a tame word. There was nothing tame about what she felt.

"Love," she said, liking the sound of it. "Love. That's not a gentle word. Love is a strong word, a strong feeling. A hard feeling. Love is hard work and trust and fierce loyalty. And I like it."

She stood up and went back to pick up the letter. She knew what she was going to do with it even without bothering to finish reading it. She walked over to where a thick hour candle burned on one of the flower-covered chests. She set the parchment to the flame without hesitation.

"I'm sorry, Mother," she said as the letter burned down to ashes that mingled with the pile of blossoms. "For my barbarian can read, you see. He would take your offer of an annulment amiss, very amiss. He would worry about my rejecting him, I think. I don't know if he loves me, but I don't want to hurt him."

What was it Edythe had said about having to follow her heart? Eleanor knew that her sister had been right. She fervently wished her sister happiness with Lars in far-off Denmark. For Eleanor, her happiness was right here, for her heart was at Harelby, with Stian.

Eleanor looked around her, feeling the emptiness of the room. The chamber was flower-decked, a place where Stian had surely meant to spend the night with her in celebration. She didn't see any reason why they should have to wait. How foolish it seemed to her to be here when what she wanted was to be by her husband's side.

"He's just going to have to get used to my embarrassing him in public," she said decisively. "He can learn to live with teasing. And to hell with Malcolm," she added as she turned to run from the room. "I want my husband, and I want him now!"

Her thin leather shoes barely touched the treads of the staircase as she hurried downwards with her heavy skirts bunched in her hands. She rushed headlong, without thought for anything but who waited in the hall. Her heart was feather light, her head full of plans and longing and joy. She forgot about everything, including caution on the rain-soaked treads, in her haste to get to Stian.

"What was that?"

Stian didn't answer Malcolm's question because he was already running toward the stairs. He'd heard a scream. It had been a high, sharp sound, quickly cut off, but piercing enough to cut through the noise of conversation of the men in the hall. It had been a woman's scream, and Stian was already terrified that he knew who had screamed.

"Sweet Jesu," he prayed as he took the stairs two at a time. "Don't let her be hurt."

He saw that his prayer was not answered when he reached the first landing and saw Eleanor sprawled across the bottom steps. As he knelt beside her, his knees were immediately soaked by rainwater that had leaked in from the window in the wall overhead.

"Damn you!" he swore as he eased Eleanor down onto the landing. He pounded a fist against the wall. "Damn you!" he repeated to the very stones of Harelby. "If she's dead I'll tear down these walls with my bare hands."

He heard people crowd up the stairs behind him, and the door to what had once been his room was opened. Questions were called out, offers for help given. Mostly, the gathering crowd just stood and stared. Lark came trotting up the stairs, pushing between people's legs to get to Stian. The wolf sniffed gingerly at Eleanor's bloodied face before Stian pushed the animal away.

Stian paid no attention to anyone else as he took Eleanor in his arms and got to his feet. He didn't know how badly she'd been hurt or if she was even breathing. All he knew was that it was as if his own life was draining out as he watched the trickle of blood spread across her face.

He ignored the pain in his left arm as he carried his wife into their old bedroom. Fiona was there even as he placed Eleanor's still form on the bed. He snarled at her to get away, but she put a wet cloth in his hand instead.

"Here. Wipe the blood off her while I check for broken bones."

"Get away!" the terrified Stian ordered. "Just get away from my wife."

The girl backed off, muttering, but Stian paid her no more heed as he knelt by Eleanor's head. He did clean Eleanor's face, and pressed the cloth to the gash he found on her forehead. She looked pale to his eyes. A shocking contrast to her normally healthy brown complexion.

"Eleanor?" he whispered, his lips close to her ear. "Eleanor, sweeting, please don't be dead." There had been too much death. This was one grief he knew he could not survive. "Sweet Eleanor," he told her, running his fingers through the loosened strands of her black hair. He felt big and clumsy and helpless faced with her small, still form. "Don't die. I can't live without you," he told her. "I love you so much. I couldn't bear it if you were to die."

He rested his face against her throat and shivered in fear as he breathed in the warm scent of her skin. "I love you," he repeated. "Jesu, how I love you."

Then he felt her sigh against his cheek, and her fingers combing through his hair. "You do?" her voice questioned, sounding dazed and sleepy. "You love me? You can love a wife? How unsophisticated." She sounded delighted.

He lifted his head just enough to look into her deep brown eyes. They were barely open, but he saw a glint of humor in them, mixed with pain.

"You're hurt," he said. "Where are you hurt?" He sat up all the way and ran his hands down her body. She wriggled with pleasure as he was trying to find broken bones. "Where does it hurt?" he demanded.

"What of the babe? You're not bleeding—down there—are you?" If he heard the faint echo of Fiona's laughter, he ignored it.

Eleanor propped herself up on her elbows. "I twisted my ankle," she told him. The damp cloth had fallen off when she sat up. She pressed it back to the throbbing spot on her forehead. It was a small cut, really, just messy, as head cuts often were. "Must have hit my head. I'm fine. The babe's fine, I'm sure. Nothing aches—down there."

"You're sure?"

"They're hard to dislodge for at least nine months, or so I'm told. No, it was not a great fall. I'm just sore."

He sat down beside her and took her in his arms. "You're going to live?" he asked anxiously. "You promise?"

"Aye. I think so."

He still seemed frantic. "How can I tend you? What do I do to take care of you? Should I bring you a wolf to sleep on your bed?"

Eleanor forgot the pain as she returned his embrace. From the circle of his arms she said, "I've got you, man. What do I need with another wolf in my bed?"

Stian laughed at her words and took them as a compliment. "I'll never leave your bed," he promised. He kissed her, deep and long, and she melted against him, as hungry for the contact as he was.

After a while, she broke away to look him in the face. "Do you truly love me, Stian of Harelby?"

"I do," he answered. "With all my heart."

"I love you," she told him for the first time, but knew it would not be the last. "With all my heart." He turned on her the brightest smile she had ever seen. "I love you," she repeated just to see if his smile could grow brighter, and it did.

They held each other close for a while, just reveling in each other's dear company. Sometimes they whispered promises and love words, but nothing that made much sense. All they were really doing was renewing the joy of simply being together.

"Let's go to the cave," Stian said eventually. "Let us be alone together."

"I'd like that," Eleanor agreed. "Just the two of us together."

"Right now? Tonight?"

"What?" she asked. "And waste all those lovely flowers upstairs?" She shook her head. "Oh, no, my love. Tomorrow night we can share the cold, hard ground. Tonight," she promised, "I will show you how I love you on a bed of roses."

After we lock the door against Lark, she added to herself. *For that animal has yet to learn that I'm the only female my great red wolf needs in his bed.*

Vows Made in Wine by Susan Wiggs

Mistress Lark had no need for passion. All her devotion went to a secret cause she embraced with her whole heart—until she met Oliver de Lacey, a pleasure seeker with no time for love. Has Oliver finally met the woman who will change his reckless ways?

Almost Paradise by Barbara Ankrum

Grace Turner never dreamed she would find herself in a real-life Wild West adventure as exciting and romantic as the dime novels she had read. Trying to rescue her brother from Mexican Imperialists, she enlists the help of rugged ex–Texas Ranger Reese Donovan, and along the way, the two find true love.

Chickadee by Deborah Bedford

Long ago, Sarah left Jim, her high school sweetheart, in search of a new life. Upon returning to Star Valley, she faces the heartwrenching choices she made and must find a way to recapture the love of the man she has never forgotten.

A Window in Time by Carolyn Lampman

A delightful romp through time when Brianna Daniels trades places with her great-grandmother, Anna, who arrived in Wyoming Territory in 1860 to become the mail-order bride that Lucas Daniels never ordered. In the meantime, Anna falls in love with the hot-air balloon pilot she encounters in 1995.

Danny Boy by Leigh Riker

For most of their thirteen-year marriage, Erin Sinclair has lived apart from her husband Danny, a professional rodeo rider. Now he's back, and after years of hardening her heart to the man whose dreams of being a champion made a life together impossible, does she even dare to dream again?

Nothing Else Matters by Susan Sizemore

In the splendor of Medieval Scotland, a gently bred maiden's courtship is interrupted when her bridegroom's quest for revenge nearly tears them apart. Then the young lovers realize that nothing else matters once you have found the love of a lifetime.

Winds of Glory by Susan Wiggs

Wealthy Bethany had loved her family's indentured servant Ashton since childhood, but when his life is threatened for his spying for the Colonial cause, she hatches a wild scheme that results in marriage. Surely such a marriage of convenience would be doomed—unless she can match his defiant bravery, and claim her place in his fiery heart forever.

GLORY IN THE SPLENDOR OF SUMMER WITH

HarperMonogram's
101 DAYS OF ROMANCE

BUY 3 BOOKS, GET 1 FREE!

Take a book to the beach, relax by the pool, or read in the most quiet and romantic spot in your home. You can live through love all summer long when you redeem this exciting offer from HarperMonogram. Buy any three HarperMonogram romances in June, July, or August, and get a fourth book sent to you for FREE. See next page for the list of top-selling novels and romances by your favorite authors that you can choose from for your premium!

101 $\mathcal{D}$AYS OF $\mathcal{R}$OMANCE
BUY 3 BOOKS, GET 1 FREE!

CHOOSE A FREE BOOK FROM THIS OUTSTANDING
LIST OF AUTHORS AND TITLES:

HARPERMONOGRAM

____LORD OF THE NIGHT Susan Wiggs 0-06-108052-7

____ORCHIDS IN MOONLIGHT Patricia Hagan 0-06-108038-1

____TEARS OF JADE Leigh Riker 0-06-108047-0

____DIAMOND IN THE ROUGH Millie Criswell 0-06-108093-4

____HIGHLAND LOVE SONG Constance O'Banyon 0-06-108121-3

____CHEYENNE AMBER Catherine Anderson 0-06-108061-6

____OUTRAGEOUS Christina Dodd 0-06-108151-5

____THE COURT OF THREE SISTERS Marianne Willman 0-06-108053-5

____DIAMOND Sharon Sala 0-06-108196-5

____MOMENTS Georgia Bockoven 0-06-108164-7

HARPERPAPERBACKS

____THE SECRET SISTERS Ann Maxwell 0-06-104236-6

____EVERYWHERE THAT MARY WENT Lisa Scottoline 0-06-104293-5

____NOTHING PERSONAL Eileen Dreyer 0-06-104275-7

____OTHER LOVERS Erin Pizzey 0-06-109032-8

____MAGIC HOUR Susan Isaacs 0-06-109948-1

____A WOMAN BETRAYED Barbara Delinsky 0-06-104034-7

____OUTER BANKS Anne Rivers Siddons 0-06-109973-2

____KEEPER OF THE LIGHT Diane Chamberlain 0-06-109040-9

____ALMONDS AND RAISINS Maisie Mosco 0-06-100142-2

____HERE I STAY Barbara Michaels 0-06-100726-9

$\mathcal{T}$o receive your free book, simply send in this coupon **and** your store
receipt with the purchase prices circled. You may take part in this exclusive
offer as many times as you wish, but all qualifying purchases must be made
by September 4, 1995, and all requests must be postmarked by October 4,
1995. Please allow 6-8 weeks for delivery.

MAIL TO: HarperPaperbacks, Dept. FC-101
10 East 53rd Street, New York, N.Y. 10022-5299

Name_____

Address_____

City_____State_____Zip_____

Offer is subject to availability. HarperPaperbacks may make substitutions for
requested titles.

H09511